SEXTDUCTION

SEXTDUCTION:

a seduction undertaken via text
message or chat.

Paperback Version

First Edition, October 2025

ISBN: 979-8-9931676-1-9

This novel is scored to the "Sextduction" Spotify playlist.

Where a heading ends with ♪#, the number matches the same track on the Sextduction Spotify playlist. Scan the QR code—or search the playlist on Spotify—to hear the music as you read.

Sextduction

A Miami Love Story

ROD K

B&F Publishing

DEDICATION

To the city that never stops moving— where the ocean hums
with bass, the skyline glows like desire, and every sunset feels
like the beginning of a new story.

To Miami—its people, its rhythm, its light. You gave Lexi and
Dean a world to fall in love in, and me a reason to tell their story.

—Rod K

DISCLAIMER

This is a work of fiction. All names, characters, places, brands, and events are either the product of the author's imagination or used fictitiously. Any resemblance to actual persons, living or dead, businesses, establishments, events, or locales is entirely coincidental.

The mention of specific products, brands, or institutions is for narrative purposes only and does not imply endorsement, sponsorship, or affiliation. All trademarks and registered trademarks are the property of their respective owners.

CONTENTS

INTRODUCTION

The Love Letter

Love letters have endured for centuries—timeless expressions of longing, devotion, and desire. From soldiers writing home across oceans to lovers whispering their hearts onto paper, each letter carried a pulse: a confession meant for one set of eyes, one soul, one moment in time.

Even in the age of screens, that impulse hasn't vanished. It's simply evolved.

Today, our love letters arrive as messages lit by the glow of a phone. A photo. A voice note. A whispered thought between heartbeats. Now they live in DMs, texts, and private chats—raw, immediate, intoxicating.

The modern love letter is the sext.

It's not just words or images—it's emotion, electricity, and anticipation. It's digital intimacy, a dance of power and vulnerability shared in real time. A whisper you can delete but never forget.

And in that space—between temptation and connection— Sextduction was born.

This is not just a story about seduction. It's a story about identity, power, and the choices we make when our lives are lived in the spotlight. Set in Miami, where sunlight meets champagne and every night hums with possibility, Sextduction invites you into a world where glamour and danger walk hand in hand.

At its heart are six unforgettable lives intertwined by passion, ambition, and fate:

Lexi Donovan – the model and influencer who built an empire from desire and defiance.

Dean Harrington – the billionaire investor whose charm conceals scars of his own.

Jeni Whitmore – the confidante caught between loyalty and forbidden emotion.

Sophie Devereaux – the playful beauty who hides her heartbreak behind the flash of a camera.

Tiffany Kirkland – the dreamer, daughter of an American missionary, still learning that innocence has its own kind of power.

Sirena – Sirena – more than AI, she's an empathetic friend, companion, and listener.

Together, they move through a city pulsing with music, money, and momentum—from penthouse suites to rooftop clubs, from high-stakes boardrooms to candlelit beach nights. It's a world of glamorous women and powerful men, of influencers chasing light, and lovers risking everything to feel something real.

But beneath the luxury and allure, the shadows remain. Behind every curated post and perfect image lies the unspoken cost of control—the unseen manipulations, the secrets, the danger of being desired by too many, too soon.

Lost Trust, one of the story's most pivotal chapters, pulls back that curtain. It reveals the darker edge of influencer culture, where fame and exploitation blur, and where love—real love—becomes the most radical act of all.

More Than a Story

Sextduction is a modern odyssey of intimacy and transformation. It explores how connection, both digital and physical, can empower or consume us—and how redemption often begins where desire and truth collide.

So, as you turn the page, step into Miami. Feel the heat. Hear the music. Let yourself drift into a city where fantasy feels like memory and every message carries a heartbeat.

Lose yourself in the rhythm of Sextduction—and maybe, along the way, rediscover your own.

See you at the end.

—Rod K.

HER SEXTDUCTION

Grace Bay Fantasy ♪1

The final shot had been taken just before sunset in the Turks &
Caicos. The pink sky melted into the turquoise waters of Grace
Bay, casting warm gold against her skin as the breeze teased the
hem of her sheer silk cover-up. Lexi stood barefoot in the
powder-fine sand, facing the ocean, her back arched just slightly,
the silhouette of her body outlined in soft light.

The bass-heavy pulse of "Sex, Love & Water" by Armin van
Buuren spilled from the portable speaker buried in the sand,
wrapping the shoot in a slow, sultry groove.

She didn't need direction anymore. She knew her angles better
than any photographer ever could. Her body moved in time with
the music—each click of the shutter matching the rhythm like a
slow seduction. The photographer murmured something, but
she was in her own head now, her gaze set on the horizon, her
fingers toying with the edge of the silk at her hip.

A week at Grace Bay Club had been a blur of bikinis,
bougainvillea, and the occasional splash of something more
risqué for her OnlyFans VIPs.

Days began with sunrise yoga shoots, sweat-slicked active wear
clinging to her curves. The sound of waves blended with deep
house beats, grounding her in the illusion she created for the
camera.

Afternoons meant high-cut swimwear beside the infinity pool, camera shutters snapping as she dipped in and out of the crystalline water, champagne glass in hand.

By evening, it was lace and low light—lingerie sets designed to look effortless, captured from behind gauzy white curtains billowing like whispers.

Every detail was intentional. The tan lines, the wind-tangled hair, the golden body oil glistening on her skin. Her content had to feel real but controlled. Wild, but polished. This was the illusion she sold.

Fantasy, with just enough reality to be dangerous.
Music. Motion. Money. Mask.

The crew flew out before her.

Lexi and Sophie lingered one more night.

Cielo Bar ♪2, ♪3

They had reservations at 9 p.m. for dinner and dancing at a place called Cielo in Grace Bay.

They weren't ready to let go of paradise. Not just yet.

They showered together—laughing, touching, teasing. A little fun. A little tension eased.

It wasn't new. It wasn't awkward. It was them.

They'd been best friends since Lexi moved to Miami, and they looked out for each other. They had rules—no sleeping with strangers on a shoot. If some guy got too close in the club, they'd kiss. One of them would say, "We're together."

A kiss between them wasn't for show. It was safety. It was code. It was control.

Sometimes it was armor. Sometimes it was medicine. But it was always real.

And when that didn't work, Lexi had private security in the shadows. After a few stalkers, she didn't travel without them.

They finished getting ready—makeup flawless, hair falling in sultry waves, curves poured into the sexiest dresses imaginable.

They didn't just get dressed. They transformed.

They didn't just walk downstairs.

They descended like a headline.

The limo ride was short, the air inside filled with perfume and electric silence. Outside, Cielo pulsed before they even stepped inside.

"Messy" by Laszewo thumped through the club as they entered, lights slicing the fog in strobes. Their hips found the rhythm immediately, arms raised, mouthing lyrics, bodies already in sync before they even reached their table.

Lexi leaned in, grinning. "Sophie... it looks like everyone's staring."

Sophie glanced around, amused. "Should be an interesting night."

They were seated near the DJ booth, close enough to feel the bass under their skin.

A waiter approached, took their order, and returned with two glasses of chilled chardonnay.

Lexi raised her glass. "To Grace Bay. And my ride-or-die."

They clinked. Sophie smiled. "To making memories."

By midnight, they'd traded wine for tequila. The club was full, the air thick with sweat and sound. "Levitating" by Dua Lipa kicked on, and the girls hit the floor.

Their energy was electric—tipsy, radiant, unbothered.

Eyes followed them. Phones tilted to record. But none of it mattered. They were in their own orbit.

Sophie danced with abandon, turning and dropping low in front of Lexi. Lexi cracked up, swatted Sophie's backside, and they both doubled over laughing.

This was freedom. This was friendship, unfiltered.

By 1 a.m., they stumbled back to the suite, cheeks flushed, dresses clinging to their skin. Packing became a blur of clothes and laughter.

Sophie peeled her dress off and stretched. "Come to bed."

Lexi nodded, slipping out of her dress. "Just for a little bit. I've got some work after."

They slid beneath the sheets, warm from wine and tequila and something deeper.

Not just heat. Not just want. But something like home.

A kiss found them—soft at first, then hungry.

Fingers wandered between each other's breast, their backsides and below their waists.

Hips pressed.

Skin brushed skin.

They touched in places they knew by heart.

Sophie's mouth found Lexi's breast, then moving lower to her crotch. Lexi's fingers going deepder in Sophie's crotch. A soft moan. A slow arching.

They moved like mirrors. Sophie moves Lexi, getting on top of her, flips around her face in Lexi's crotch and Lexi's face in her crotch.

Each of them giving. Each of their mouths and tongues, pleasing the other. Even the taste of the other in their mouths was exciting them both. Each of them needing.

Their breath came in sync. Their release, like a whisper.

They reached release together, breathless, flushed, still pleasuring the other—slower now, gentler. They curled into each other like a question with no answer.

After a moment, Lexi whispered, "I need to finish a few things. I'll be back in bed."

It was 2 a.m.

She stood on the balcony, wrapped in a robe, sipping chilled rosé, replying to DMs that would earn her more in a weekend than some people made in a year.

The night was velvet. The sea below, silent and endless.

The breeze kissed her cheek. Salt and silence filled her lungs.

In just hours, she and Sophie would be back in Miami.

She had built this life. From nothing.

Every deal, every post, every message... earned.

And she deserved every second of it.

Back Home in Miami

The next day, her return flight touched down just after noon.

A black SUV waited curbside—private, tinted, silent. No lines. No fuss. Her team had already been through the condo. Fridge stocked. Linens crisp. Robes hung just right.

Everything in its place, just as she liked it.

Everything clean. Controlled. Like none of it had ever happened.

Lexi barely spoke during the ride; her gaze fixed on the skyline. Her phone buzzed nonstop—new followers, fan messages, brand offers. She let it all sit in her lap, face down.

Just for now.

Let the algorithm spin without her. Let the world clamor while she disappeared for a moment.

When the elevator opened directly into her penthouse, she exhaled for the first time all day. A long, low breath she hadn't even known she was holding.

Shoes off. Hair down. Bra forgotten somewhere along the way.

She padded barefoot across the cool stone floor, the low hum of Biscayne Bay rising behind the glass like a lullaby. This was her cocoon. The only place where Lexi Donovan, the persona, could soften into Lexi, the woman.

She poured herself chilled water with a sprig of mint. Touched her lip gloss in the mirror—not for anyone else, just to feel whole again. A ritual more than vanity. Something to say: you're still here.

She slipped into a pale silk cami that draped like a whisper over her frame. She wouldn't need to post again until morning. She wouldn't need to *be* anyone until then.

For the first time in days, she wasn't performing.

Lexi curled into the cream leather sectional, its buttery texture cool against her bare thighs. She tucked one leg beneath her and sank into the cushions.

The scent of white jasmine danced on the air from a candle flickering on the marble counter.

Afternoon light spilled across the penthouse in soft waves, brushing gold over her skin. Outside, the Atlantic glittered like a mirror, each ripple a private secret.

This was hers—every inch of it.

The view. The stillness. The empire she'd built from filtered light and fearless desire.

Lexi Donovan. Golden girl of Instagram.
Three million followers and climbing.

She didn't hustle for attention anymore. She summoned it.

One photo in lace, a turn of the hip, a gaze over one shoulder—and the internet obeyed.

It always obeyed.

Her phone lit up again, buzzing like a slot machine.

She picked it up slowly, thumb hovering but not pressing.

Champagne in one hand, she watched the digits rise in her dashboard. Five-figure deposits by breakfast. One DM—if she chose to answer it—could turn into more than some people made in a month.

She had learned how to monetize seduction without giving herself away.

And yet—beneath the luxury, behind the glass—there was a quiet part of her that missed being looked at without expectation.

Not followed. Not adored. Just seen.

She missed being someone's reason to breathe, not just someone's reason to click.

She took another sip of champagne and let the silence stretch.

Tonight, there would be no ring lights. No filters. No curated captions.

Just Lexi. Barefoot. Skin to leather. Candlelight. And the soft, rising breath of someone who had earned every square inch of her silence.

No apology. No smile. No mask.
Just this.
And finally—just her.

Power, Monetized

But she wasn't naïve.

The game had changed.

This wasn't just modeling anymore.
It wasn't about being discovered—it was about taking the spotlight and selling the stage.

It was empire-building.

A business of control disguised in lace and lighting.

This was strategy in lingerie.
Domination in slow motion.

OnlyFans. FanVue.

Exclusive content had rewritten the rules.
No agents. No casting calls. No waiting rooms filled with hungry eyes and plastic smiles.

Women weren't waiting around for magazine spreads or fashion contracts anymore.

They were building empires from their bedrooms and balconies.
With a ring light and a plan, the gatekeepers became irrelevant.

Housewives. Students. Divorcees.
All of them with a camera, a hustle, and something to prove.

Some wanted control. Some wanted escape.
Some wanted to win.

Lexi had started soft.

Flirtatious. Suggestive.

A cheeky caption.
A barely-there neckline.
A smile that hinted at more.

She gave just enough to keep them leaning in. Never enough to let them touch.

But as the landscape sharpened, so did her edge.

The line between allure and access blurred—and Lexi learned how to own it without losing herself.

A slip of silk.
A turned back.
A look over the shoulder like she had a secret.

She didn't sell sex. She sold the possibility. And that sold everything.

She mastered the whisper of skin.

The tease of intimacy.

The crafted illusion that murmured: *I made this just for you.*

Now, sixty percent of her income came from behind a paywall.

Not just photos.
Experiences. Fantasies. Curated intimacy on demand.
Digital devotion. Personalized heat.

Not sex.

Power.

It was intimacy redefined—customized, condensed, and monetized with surgical precision.

And it worked.

Oh, it worked.

Everything around her supported the dream she'd sold.

The bottles of Cristal champagne nestled in the cooler—
untouched, pristine, waiting like a promise.

Luxury not as indulgence, but as discipline.

A weapon disguised as elegance. A trap wrapped in velvet.

A visual cue for restraint with sparkle.

The click of her stilettos on marble.
The soft rustle of designer fabrics as she crossed the room.
Each sound rehearsed. Each motion intentional.

The way the golden-hour light kissed her cheekbones just right
through panoramic glass.

None of it was accidental.

None of it just for her.

It wasn't self-expression. It was self-curation.

This wasn't only her home.

It was her production set. Her sanctuary.
Her trap. Her power source.

Every frame. Every filtered shot.
Every coy smile posted from that living room—

It wasn't for a man.

It wasn't even for herself anymore.

It was for the empire.

Reinvention

Luxury wasn't frivolous.
It was functional.

It kept the lights on.
It paid the team.
It built a wall between who she used to be and who she had to become.

But the truth?

She hadn't always been this version of herself.

There was a time when her name didn't echo, her image didn't ripple through algorithms, her presence didn't fill rooms.

Back in college, Lexi had been forgettable in a crowd.

Pretty, maybe. But not unforgettable.
Not the girl people turned for.
Not the name that lingered after the party ended.

She remembered standing near the kitchen island—solo cup in hand—while the real girls danced in the center of the room.

Symmetrical faces. Untouchable charm. The kind of beauty that never had to ask permission.

Lexi hovered on the fringe, half-hoping to disappear, half-praying someone would finally notice her.

The music thudded in her chest, but she was invisible in the noise. Always watching. Never seen.

That ache followed her into adulthood.

It wasn't until she landed in Miami that she decided to rewrite her narrative.

That's when she met Richard Phillips or just Rick, as she called him.

A sharply dressed attorney who dealt in accident claims—and damage, Lexi would later realize, wasn't limited to cars.

He was lean, well-spoken, and radiated the kind of charisma that felt like control disguised as confidence.

He told her she had potential.

That he could help her become someone.

At first, she believed him.
At first, she thought it might be love.

He knew the language of admiration, but his hands only built cages.

She remembered the antiseptic scent of the surgeon's office—the false sweetness of artificial vanilla masking the sterile air.

Her fingers trembled as she signed the forms.

She didn't look the receptionist in the eye.
"I want the Barbie look," she whispered.

Not for beauty.
For transformation. For memory.

That night, Rick didn't wait.

She was still swollen, her face bruised and taped, eyes barely open. And already, the camera was clicking.

"Turn your head this way," he said.
"Money doesn't make itself, Lexi."

She didn't even ask why he was filming. She knew.

The lens didn't flinch. Not at the gauze. Not at the stitched hairline. Not at the angry swelling beneath her new chest.

And neither did Rick.

He watermarked everything—called it insurance. Labeled it investment.

Footage, not for celebration—but for leverage.

Blonde hair. Button nose. Curves cut to command attention.

By the time the swelling faded, Alexandra was gone.

Lexi had arrived.

At first, she was grateful.

She told herself Rick had given her a future. That the glint in his eye meant pride—not ownership.

For a while, she played the role.
A team. A plan. A life rebuilt.

But love doesn't come with ledgers.

Not with strings. Not with threats.

As the months passed, she saw the truth—Rick wasn't a partner.

He was a puppeteer.
A controller.
A polished predator with a business model.

Whenever she hinted at leaving, he reminded her who held the files.

"Want them to see the before pics?" he'd sneer.
"Or maybe the surgery night clips—your face swollen, body bandaged, chest still leaking."

Lexi never answered.
She didn't have to.

She knew he'd do it. That was the horror. The trap. The leverage.

Her silence became her surrender.

It wasn't just her brand at risk. It was her. Still... the transformation worked. Her first selfie post-surgery? Viral.

Her second? A brand deal.

By the end of the month, agencies that once ghosted her were sending contracts.

She wasn't filler anymore. She was the main course.

And like every dish meant to be devoured, she was expected to be flawless.

And yet...

At night, when the ring light cooled and the filters came off, she still looked in the mirror and wondered if Alexandra was somewhere behind the doll's reflection—quietly waiting to come home.

But there was no going back.

Not now. Not after everything.

She sipped from a long-stemmed glass of champagne, watching the skyline flicker like a crown laid at her feet.

She had earned it, hadn't she? Every spotlight? Every follower? Every offer?

This was her empire. And she ruled it.

Even if it sometimes ruled her.

It was during one of those quiet scrolls, bare-legged, silk-clad, bathed in golden light, that she saw the message.

Not from a follower.
Not from a fantasy.

Dean.

Dean's Story

Dean Harrington had never been the type to sit still. His entire life had been shaped by movement—by a restless hunger to build, to achieve, to create something lasting.

Raised in the rolling hills of central Texas, just outside of Austin, Dean's childhood had been grounded in early morning chores, Friday night football games, and the kind of values that got passed down like old family heirlooms.

His father, Daniel Harrington, had been a man of discipline—a former military officer turned financial consultant—a man who believed in hard work, honor, and the kind of respect that wasn't demanded, but earned.

Dean idolized him. Which made it all the more devastating when, at just fourteen years old, Dean lost him.

A sudden heart attack. No warning. No time to prepare.

One day, he was just a boy tossing a football in the backyard with his dad. The next, he was standing under a gray sky, his black dress shoes sinking into damp earth, surrounded by murmured condolences and the overwhelming scent of funeral lilies.

It should have broken him.—Instead, it forged him.

Jennings Burnett, his father's best friend and military buddy, stepped in during the hardest moments.

A man with a presence that commanded attention—gruff, sharp, the kind of man whose handshake alone told you he had seen things most people wouldn't believe. Jennings didn't try to replace his father, but he did what Dean needed most—he gave him direction.

"Your dad would've wanted you to keep your head up, son."

That became Jennings' mantra. Every time Dean struggled, every time grief threatened to pull him under, Jennings reminded him of that simple truth.

Over time, Jennings became more than just a family friend. He became the steady force in Dean's life, the voice of reason when emotions threatened to cloud judgment, the one who never let him forget where he came from.

By the time Dean graduated high school, he had grown into a man people noticed.

Not just because of his tall, athletic build or the charismatic way he carried himself—but because he had presence. The kind of quiet confidence that made people lean in when he spoke.

He was good at football. A natural wide receiver, fast on his feet, sharp on the field. But he wasn't delusional. The NFL wasn't in his future, and he knew it.

Instead, he focused on what really mattered—his education.

At The University of Texas, he balanced football, a social life, and a growing fascination with finance. Numbers made sense to him. They weren't just figures on a screen—they were strategy, puzzle pieces that, when placed correctly, built empires.

But Dean never wanted to be just another Wall Street guy in a suit. He wanted to build something that mattered.

Something real.

After graduation, Dean spent a few years working as a financial analyst and broker, earning his Series 7 license and learning the inner workings of the stock market.

But it wasn't long before the traditional 9-to-5 started to feel suffocating.

Dean wasn't built for cubicles and quarterly meetings. He thrived on adrenaline, on the thrill of risk and reward.

Within months, he left the structured corporate world behind and became a full-time trader.

The move paid off.

He was good. Damn good.

Day trading turned into long-term investments. Long-term investments turned into private equity.

Before he knew it, Dean was no longer just playing the game—he was changing it.

He started investing in businesses, revitalizing struggling companies, funding start-ups that no one else would take a chance on.

And soon, the money wasn't just good, it was life changing.

Now, at twenty-seven years old, Dean lived in a 62nd-floor penthouse in Miami's Financial District, the kind of place that made people stop and wonder who the hell he was and how he got there.

A penthouse with 5 bedrooms, 9 baths, and 7,855 square feet of understated luxury. Looking straight at Brickell Key and the Bay.

Floor-to-ceiling windows that turned the skyline into moving art.

A private rooftop infinity pool, where the city lights shimmered like reflections in black water.

It wasn't just a home.

It was a statement.

Proof that he had built something from nothing.

But despite the wealth, the lifestyle, the women who gravitated toward him, Dean never lost sight of who he was.

He remembered his great-uncle's stories about the steel mills shutting down, entire towns collapsing, families struggling to rebuild.

He remembered Jennings' words—"Leave things better than you found them."

So, he used his money to do more than just enjoy life.

He invested in places people had forgotten. Funded businesses that deserved a second chance. Turned fading industries into thriving opportunities.

It wasn't just about making millions.

It was about making an impact.

Dean wasn't a saint.

He had his share of vices, wild nights, and women who wanted a piece of his world.

Hell, his friends had given him the nickname "LK" (Lady Killer) back in college—and it had stuck.

Not because he was a player, but because women noticed him, and he noticed them right back.

He wasn't reckless. He didn't make promises he couldn't keep.

But he knew his effect.

The deep, velvet-like voice. The easy, confident smirk. The way he could make a woman blush with just a look.

Women liked him.

And he liked them.

But despite all of that, he had never really let anyone in.

Because Dean wasn't the type to settle for anything less than something real.

Sun, Girls and Tulum ♪4, ♪5

Recently, Dean had returned from a trip to Tulum, Mexico—a short getaway that had unexpectedly become unforgettable.

It was there he met Esme, a striking French fashion model who effortlessly commanded attention wherever she went.

She didn't walk into a room. She arrived. And Dean noticed. Everyone did.

Their connection was immediate and electric, marked by a lively dinner that led to dancing and laughter in the town's most exclusive clubs.

Her laugh had been like champagne—sharp, sweet, and a little dangerous. Dean couldn't remember the last time he'd laughed that hard or danced that freely.

The night blurred into rhythm, basslines, and flashes of light. At the height of it all, "La Danza" by John Summit dropped through the club speakers, and Esme pulled Dean toward the floor without a word.

They danced like they'd known each other in another life—Esme twirling with her eyes closed, Dean smiling in a way he hadn't in months. For a few minutes, time unraveled. It was just music, heat, and movement.

When the track faded into another pulse, Esme leaned in, her lips brushing his ear.

"Let's get out of here," she whispered.

By evening's end, the allure of their shared chemistry led them back to Esme's luxurious hotel suite, where the air was thick with anticipation and possibility.

The suite overlooked the water, city lights flickering below like they were winking in approval. The moment they stepped inside, the tone shifted—cool marble underfoot, soft gold lighting wrapping the space in warmth.

Dean's jacket hit the back of a velvet chair. Esme kicked off her heels, laughing as she spun once, her silhouette framed by the glass behind her.

The kind of place made for secrets.

Esme offered Dean a drink, her voice playful and inviting as she gracefully moved across the softly lit room.

"Something bold or something smooth?" she asked, already opening the sleek bar cabinet.

Before he could answer, she picked up a small remote and turned on the music. The slow, pulsing beat of *"Control Of Me (DHALI Remix)"* by Topic, Daecolm & DHALI began to fill the room, a hypnotic rhythm that shimmered beneath her movements. It was sultry and fluid, like Esme herself.

She swayed subtly to the beat as she poured the drinks, the lighting casting soft golden shadows across her bare shoulders.

Dean nodded, smiling lightly. "Surprise me." He settled into the plush couch, feeling the softness of velvet against his fingertips.

Dean sat back in the couch, watching her with a slight smile. Her presence was magnetic, but it wasn't just about looks. There was a fearlessness in her, the way she moved, the way she looked at him like she already knew his answer.

Their fingers brushed during the handoff—a deliberate pause that said more than words. "To losing control," she said, eyes glinting.

Dean raised his glass. "You're dangerous."

She smiled slowly. "Only if you try to resist."

As Dean took his first sip, she slowly reached behind her, the gentle whisper of fabric falling to the floor drawing his eyes upward.

She stood before him in delicate black lingerie, the intricate lace beautifully accentuating her elegant figure.

The candlelight caught the lines of her body in a way that made her look almost sculpted, ethereal.

Dean's breath caught as she approached, his pulse quickening.

Esme softly took his face into her hands, guiding his gaze upward to meet her own, before gently pulling him closer, pressing him intimately against her.

"Don't look away," she whispered. "Not tonight."

The warmth of her body sent an exhilarating rush through him.

She moved gracefully onto his lap, positioning herself comfortably with a tantalizing ease, her hips gently rocking against him in a rhythmic dance of mounting desire.

Dean's breathing deepened as his own excitement grew, senses fully awakened by the tender yet deliberate movements of her body.

His hands slid along her thighs, then up her back, steadying her as his mouth found the curve of her neck.

Her hands moved slowly, gently freeing Dean from the confines of his clothing with care.

Dean stood slowly, his breath steady, gaze fixed on Esme.

The hum of the room—low light, the fading echo of "Control Of Me"—still pulsed in the air like heat from a storm.

He gently turned her until she was facing the couch, her knees pressing into the cushion as she leaned forward, bracing herself with both hands. Her spine arched slightly, hair cascading forward, her hips tilting in subtle offering.

Dean knelt behind her naked body, wrapping his arms comfortably around her waist, his chest brushing her back with quiet pressure.

He didn't speak. Didn't need to. The silence between them was filled with breath and understanding.

He inhaled her—the scent of her hair, the warmth of her skin. One hand glided up the center of her torso, fingertips exploring each curve until it found the soft weight of her breast.

He cupped her breasts gently. Fingertips lightly tweaking her nipples. The hardness, the electricity shooting through her body.

Esme gasped. She trembled, her head tipping slightly.

Her hips shifted instinctively in response, a slow sway, subtle and inviting.

Dean's other hand moved lower, trailing along the curve of her belly, tracing soft circles as it descended. Her breath hitched as his palm came to rest between her thighs.

Her knees spread slightly, breath shallow and uneven. Her back arched gripping the couch pillows. Pushing back against Dean with all her force.

He entered her again—slow at first, then deeper, harder.

Each thrust drew a louder cry. Every motion pushed her closer to a climax.

She moaned his name, again and again, her voice breaking open with every movement.

"Ah... ah... ah... Dean—"

Her cries built to a crescendo, her body clenching around him, trembling with release. She could feel the wetness coming from inside her.

The heat of her overwhelmed him—slick, trembling, perfect.

Dean held her tighter, his own breath ragged. Grinding against her.

And then—he followed, groaning her name as he spilled inside her.

They collapsed forward, tangled in breath and heat and silence.

The only sound was the hum of their breathing, falling in sync.

Dean scooped her into his arms, carrying her to the bed.
They made love again. Slower. Deeper.

Less fire. More gravity.

And again, until sleep finally took them—wrapped in warmth, in sweat, in something that felt dangerously close to forever.

Two bodies, one rhythm, no words left to say—only feeling, only fire, only the slow, consuming truth of finally being known.

Morning Surprise

When morning's gentle light filtered through the windows, Dean woke to find Esme sleeping peacefully beside him.

Her hair was tousled, cheek resting softly against the pillow, the rise and fall of her breath calm and steady.

Tenderly, he kissed her awake, their bodies instinctively seeking each other, reigniting the warmth and connection from the night before.

Their passion reignited slowly, deepening with a tenderness that felt more profound, Esme responding with heightened sensitivity as if each touch were entirely new.

Their embrace was warm, their movements slow and deeply connected. Each shared breath and soft moan built the emotional intensity between them until they again reached a shared release, deeply satisfying and intimate.

As they lay together, quietly basking in the warmth of their connection, the soft click of the hotel suite door opening startled Dean.

His surprise turned to astonishment as a woman who bore a striking resemblance to Esme entered, an amused smile playing on her lips.

"I see you've met my twin sister, Margot," she said, her voice warm and playful.

Dean's eyes widened in disbelief, confusion momentarily freezing his words.

Esme offered a welcoming smile, entirely unfazed by the intimate moment she'd interrupted.

With a playful glint in her eyes, Esme removed her clothes, gracefully sliding into bed on Dean's other side.

Dean blinked twice, caught between disbelief and fascination, as Esme just laughed and kissed his shoulder.

The weekend unfolded into a shared experience of intimacy and laughter, a celebration of newfound connections between Dean and the sisters.

As Dean stood in the airport, saying goodbye to Esme and Margot, his heart was filled with gratitude for the unexpected journey.

Boarding his flight back to Miami, he reflected fondly on the unforgettable memories created, eagerly anticipating their next encounter.

He didn't know what it meant yet—or if it meant anything at all—but for once, he didn't overthink it. He simply smiled, reclined slightly back in his seat, and let the memories carry him home.

Lexi Donovan

By the time Sunday rolled around, Dean found himself at the airport, sipping a black coffee that did little to chase away the exhaustion of the weekend.

Across the lounge, Esme and Margot leaned lazily against the railing, sun-kissed and utterly unbothered, watching him with identical smirks.

"Until next time, *mon amour*," Esme whispered, pressing a slow kiss to his cheek.

Dean simply chuckled, shaking his head as he grabbed his carry-on and boarded his flight.

Tulum had been exactly what he needed.

A distraction. A reminder of how good life could be when he wasn't thinking too hard.

But now, it was time to get back to reality.

And just as he settled into his seat, his phone buzzed.

A message.

It started with a simple message.
One late night, scrolling through Instagram, the city quiet around him, the glow of his penthouse windows casting long streaks of light across the marble floor, he came across Lexi Donovan. The whiskey warmed his chest, the silence of the penthouse pressing in like velvet. He wasn't looking for anyone. Not really. Just... curious. Restless.

He had followed her for months—not obsessively, not the way her millions of admirers did. But enough to notice the way she played the game.

She was calculated. Precise. She knew exactly how to control attention, how to bend a room—or an entire audience—to her will.

And yet, beneath the polished perfection of her curated posts, Dean saw something else. A flicker of something real, something that didn't quite fit with the brand she projected.

Maybe it was curiosity. Maybe it was the whiskey. But that night, he did something he never did.

"So, how does it feel ruling the world from a penthouse in the sky?"

He hadn't expected a response. Women like Lexi probably had inboxes flooded with men throwing out their best one-liners, hoping to be noticed.

But to his surprise, she answered.

"How does it feel watching from below?"

Sharp. Playful. Unapologetic.

Dean smirked at that.

And just like that, the game had begun.

What started as a casual, teasing exchange quickly became something else.

The conversations stretched long into the night, past the hour when the city went quiet, past the moment when tiredness should've settled in—but never did.

Lexi was quick-witted, intelligent. She didn't just flirt—she challenged.

Dean played it cool.

"I enjoy chatting with people. You seem interesting. I'd like to keep in touch—just as friends."

That was where most men fumbled. They showed their hand too soon, tripping over themselves to impress her.

Dean didn't chase.

And that? That caught her attention.

"Just friends?" Lexi responded, the tease unmistakable. "You sure about that?"

"Positive."

To his surprise, she didn't disappear.

If anything, she leaned in more.

The messages became routine—more sexual.

Her pictures grew more explicit, more frequent.

The banter sharpened. The heat between them? Constant.

Morning check-ins. Inside jokes.

Random, playful challenges.

And now, explicit requests.

What she wanted Dean to do to her.

What she wanted to do to him.

"What's for breakfast, handsome? I wish you were having me for breakfast."

"Send me a pic of your lunch—I want to see you and who you're having lunch with."

Lexi followed with a winking emoji. Then another message:

"Just kidding. (Kinda.)"

Dean paused.

He knew her well enough by now to hear what lived between the lines—flirtation masking something deeper.

A flicker of insecurity. Maybe jealousy. Maybe fear.

He didn't hesitate.

"There's no one else, Lexi."

"You're the one I'm hungry for. Morning, noon, and night."

She didn't respond right away. But when she did, her reply was short—and warm.

"Good answer, LK."

Dean decided to turn up the heat in Lexi's life and he knew just how to do it.

The Sext

It was his turn to send something provocative.

"Good morning, my love. I dreamt about us in Dreamland all night. Kissing your lips, my tongue touching yours.
Soft and searching, savoring the taste of you.

Running my tongue down to your breasts, kissing them,
tracing slow circles until I feel your body rise to meet me,
running my tongue across your nipples as they got hard, and
then sucking them.

Moving lower, as I run my tongue across your crotch,
feeling the heat pulsing through your skin,
then finding its way inside you.

As my mouth engulfs you, your legs open all the way.
No hesitation. No resistance. Just need.

Moaning. Screaming.
As if saying, "Please me, pleasure me."

Your mind wandering. Thinking.
Craving. Trembling. Needing more.

Waiting to feel my tongue back inside you.

Giving you the ecstasy you crave.

As you grab my head, pushing it into your crotch,
hips rolling, desperate for release,
I know you are ready.

The pleasure intense. Closer to orgasming.

You can tell by the heat and wetness between your legs.

You grab the sheets with both hands,
gripping so hard, grinding and humping my face,
when you orgasm."

Lexi exhaled, her body taut with sensation.
A slow smile curled on her lips. Her pulse was racing.

This was her sextduction.

She hadn't expected that. Not from him. Her pulse fluttered in
her throat as she reread it—once, twice.

It wasn't just the rawness of the words. It was the confidence.
The control. The sheer audacity of it.

She was used to being the one who left men flustered, panting
behind screens. But this? This turned the mirror on her.

She shifted on the couch, suddenly aware of the silk robe
clinging to her bare skin. A heat bloomed low in her belly—
uninvited, undeniable.

Her fingers slid into her panties, pleasing herself until she came. Dean had made her orgasm with his words.

She stared at the screen in disbelief, her body still trembling, breath uneven.

She'd never experienced that before—arousal born not from touch, but from the force of a man's imagination.

She wanted more. Even if she never met him in person, she knew now—his words alone could stir something deep.

Something feral. They reached the hunger buried between her thighs—where no one else had ever truly touched.

Power and Control

She had men willing to pay thousands just for a few minutes of her time.
Men who would fly across the world just for the chance to breathe the same air as her.

But Dean?

Dean wasn't chasing.
He was challenging her.

Dean gave her just enough to keep her coming back.

And that?
That was a problem.

For the first time in a long time, Lexi felt out of control.

For weeks, Dean had been a part of her day—woven into the quiet moments between photoshoots, events, late-night content creation.

She wanted to know what he was doing. Who he was with.

And the idea of him giving attention to another woman?

That made something sharp twist in her stomach.

It wasn't jealousy—not exactly.
It was more primal than that.
A need to be seen.
To be chosen.

One night, she finally broke past her own restraint.

She sent a video.

Something private. Intimate.

Dean watched, jaw tightening, fingers tapping restlessly against the side of his whiskey glass.

Then, a message followed.

"I hope you're enjoying this. I hope it makes you think of me."

Dean exhaled slowly, running a hand through his hair.

She was testing him again.

But it wasn't just about sex.
It was about power.
And she was used to having it.
But this time, Dean wasn't sure who was holding the reins.

It was about validation.
About control.

She wanted to know if she could still dictate how he saw her.

And that realization unsettled him.

He typed slowly.

"Lexi, you're a beautiful woman. But I meant what I said—I like talking to you, but I'm not looking for more."

The message sat unread for hours.

For the first time, Lexi didn't respond right away.

When she finally did, it wasn't a picture.

It was a simple message.

"FaceTime me."

Dean hesitated. Staring at the screen, feeling the weight of what this moment meant.

Lexi had never been rejected before.

And now, she was doubling down.

If she couldn't convince him through messages, she wanted to see his reaction in real time.

And Dean?

For the first time, he wasn't sure if he could keep resisting.

Dean didn't know how long he lay there after the call ended, staring at the ceiling of his penthouse, Lexi's voice still echoing in his head.

The hum of the city below was muffled by glass and altitude, but inside, his thoughts were loud.

She had tested him. Pushed him.

But what unsettled him most wasn't the way she looked on his screen.

It was the way she made him feel.

She wasn't just another beautiful woman. She was a challenge wrapped in silk and fire.

And whether he wanted to admit it or not, she was getting under his skin.

His phone vibrated beside him.

Another message.

The Invitation

Lexi: *Dinner. Tomorrow. No more excuses.*

Dean exhaled slowly, staring at the words.

Part of him had been waiting for this.

Maybe she had been, too.

He smirked, typing his response.
Dean: *Nusr-Et Steakhouse. 8 PM. Don't be late.*

As soon as he hit send, something shifted. A quiet thrill. The sense that a door had just opened—and neither of them knew what was on the other side.

Lexi shifted against her pillows, tucking one leg beneath her as she let out a soft sigh. The conversation had stretched longer than she expected—easy, effortless, the kind you never really wanted to end.

Dean was still on her screen, lying back against the headboard of his bed, one arm resting behind his head, his whiskey glass nearly forgotten on the nightstand beside him.

She smiled, tilting her head slightly.

"Okay, before we say goodnight, I have to know... do you have a nickname?"

Dean raised a brow, smirking.

"I might. But you first."

Lexi huffed, pretending to think it over.

"Minnie Mouse."

There was a pause. Then, Dean burst out laughing.

"Minnie Mouse?"

His deep voice was rich with amusement.

"I have to know the backstory."

Lexi grinned.

"After you tell me yours."

Dean exhaled, still smiling.

"Alright, fair enough. LK."

Lexi's brows lifted.

"LK? And what does that stand for?"

Dean smirked, leaning in slightly.

"Nope. Your turn first."

Lexi rolled her eyes, still playful.

"Fine. Back in college, I could be a little shy sometimes. And when I got excited or nervous, my voice would get... a little high-pitched. Apparently, it reminded people of Minnie Mouse."

Dean chuckled.

"So, what you're saying is... you were adorable."

"I prefer 'charmingly soft-spoken.'"

Dean took a sip of whiskey before finally giving in.

"Alright, sweetheart. LK stands for Lady Killer."

Lexi blinked, then cracked up laughing.

"Wait—Lady Killer? Seriously?"

Dean nodded. "Yeah. Back in college, anytime I even looked at a girl—or if one came up to me—my frat brothers would say, 'There goes LK, the Lady Killer.' It stuck."

Lexi shook her head, still laughing. "Wow. I had no idea I was in the presence of the legendary Lady Killer."

Dean leaned against his pillows, watching her with amusement.

"Don't let the name fool you. I don't chase. Women just seem to... find me."

Lexi smirked.

"Mmm. Must be tough."

"It has its moments."

A comfortable silence settled between them, the laughter still hanging in the air.

Lexi exhaled, stretching her arms.

"Okay, Lady Killer. I should probably get some sleep."

Dean smirked.

"Goodnight, Minnie Mouse."

Lexi smiled. "Goodnight, LK."

And as the call ended, neither of them could quite shake the feeling that they'd just stumbled into something they weren't ready to walk away from.

THEIR DATE

Dean Arrives

Dean stepped out of the blacked-out SUV and into the sultry Miami night, the city humming with electric energy. Brickell was alive—the scent of salt and citrus clung to the air, mixing with the faint musk of men's after shave and freshly lit cigars.

His Italian loafers hit the pavement with an easy confidence as he adjusted the cuffs of his navy blazer. Nusr-Et stood before him, its grand entrance framed by tinted glass and polished brass, exuding the kind of exclusivity that attracted the power players of Miami. A valet rushed forward, offering to take his keys, but Dean simply nodded and stepped inside.

The moment he crossed the threshold, the ambiance wrapped around him—rich, intoxicating. Crystal chandeliers dripped from the ceiling like frozen fireworks, refracting golden light across plush red and emerald-green seating. The scent of charred wagyu and aged whiskey mingled in the air, underscored by the low thrum of jazz intertwined with soft lounge music.

Dean didn't hesitate. He knew exactly where he was headed.

The bar was a masterpiece of polished marble and gold accents, stocked with a curated selection of the finest spirits in the world. He leaned against the counter, scanning the rows of glistening bottles—Macallan 25, Pappy Van Winkle, Louis XIII.

And then he saw it.

A single bottle of W.L. Weller Single Barrel.

The bartender, a sharp-eyed man in his mid-forties, caught his gaze. "Can I help you, sir?"

Dean let a smirk play at his lips. "Well, I thought I was going to have to settle for some rot-gut whiskey like Maker's," he said, laughing, "but I see you've got Weller Single Barrel."

The bartender chuckled, reaching for the bottle. "It's a little pricey."

Dean gave him a knowing look, unbothered. "Don't I know it? I drink the Daniel Weller at home."

The bartender let out a low whistle, clearly impressed, before pouring the amber liquid over two ice cubes.

"Open tab?" he asked.

Dean nodded. "Sure, but I'll close it before my date and I head to dinner. Gotta make sure you get your tip."

The bartender grinned, sliding the glass across the counter. "Appreciate it."

Dean lifted his drink, the whiskey catching the light like liquid gold. "All I know is if you take care of your bartender, he'll always take care of you." He clinked his glass lightly against the bar, a silent toast, before taking a slow, deliberate sip.

The heat of the whiskey spread through him, smooth, complex—just the way he liked it.

He turned slightly, glass in hand, taking in the restaurant like a strategist surveying the battlefield.

The clientele was exactly as expected—crypto millionaires in designer sneakers, socialites draped in couture, men with the quiet confidence of old money and others with the sharp hunger of new. Every table held a story: a deal being made, a fortune being flaunted, a game of seduction being played.

Dean thrived in spaces like these—not because of the wealth, but because of the power dynamics. Who was in control, who was pretending, who was truly untouchable.

And then, as if drawn by an unseen force, his gaze flicked toward the entrance.

Lexi had arrived. And for the first time tonight, Dean forgot about the whiskey in his hand.

Lexi's Entrance

He was mid-sip when he caught movement in his periphery—something different. The kind of difference that stops time.

Lexi stepped into Nusr-Et like she belonged to the place. No fanfare, no need for it. Her presence did the work. She was elegance and danger wrapped in silk, dressed in a long black slit on the side backless number that clung like it had been stitched to her skin. Her heels clicked against the marble floor, each step slow, unhurried, as if she wasn't arriving—she was *gracing* the room. Dean's smile curved without permission, a low hum of appreciation rising in his chest.

He cocked his head slightly to one side, then the other, as if saying, *Well, look what we have here.*

Damn, she was ten times better looking in person. *No filter, no edits—just her.* Tonight was going to be special.

Lexi caught his stare and arched a perfectly shaped brow. Instead of a sultry smirk, she flashed him a playful, almost *mockingly ditsy* grin—like some Beverly Hills blonde channeling Barbie energy on purpose. It was pure mischief. She knew exactly what she was doing.

Dean couldn't help but laugh softly. She was already in control of the game—and she hadn't even said a word yet.

She walked right up to him with all the confidence of a woman who'd broken a thousand hearts without losing sleep, leaned in, and kissed him softly on the cheek. Her perfume—something floral with a wicked undercurrent of spice—wrapped around him instantly.

"Hey, Texas," she murmured, her voice velvet-smooth.

The bartender, visibly stunned and blinking like he'd just seen a celebrity he couldn't place, fumbled slightly as he stepped forward.

"Can I get you something, ma'am?"

Lexi turned, still smiling like she owned the bar, and said, "The best tequila in the house, please."

Dean raised his glass with a small toast toward her. "Guess I'll be closing this tab sooner than I thought."

Lexi gave him a slow once-over. "You're not trying to impress me with whiskey and manners, are you?"

Dean smirked. "No, ma'am. That's just who I am."

She laughed, and the sound threaded through the bar like a melody no one else could hear.

Dean's glass sweat with condensation, the bourbon glowing amber beneath the warm golden light of the bar. The air was rich with scent—charred meat from the open grill, spice from mezcal cocktails being shaken nearby, and the underlying hush of sea salt drifting in through the open terrace.

Lexi leaned in just enough for her perfume to catch him again—ylang ylang, maybe, laced with some smoky, late-night floral he couldn't quite place. Her hair gleamed under the crystal chandeliers, each movement a soft, fluid sway, like a flame too confident to flicker.

"So," she said, her voice low, playful. "I hope you enjoyed last night as much as I did."

Dean raised a brow, intrigued by the sudden shift in tone.

Lexi's smile deepened, her eyes narrowing just slightly, heat hiding behind the teasing. "It didn't feel like college. It felt like high school... without the nudity, of course," she added with a sultry laugh.

Dean chuckled, slow and deep. "You're not wrong. There was something... pure about it."

"I haven't felt that alive in a long while," she murmured, fingers lightly tracing the rim of her tequila glass, its salt-kissed edge glinting under the bar lights.

Dean nodded, his tone gentling. "You keep your head down, work hard, chase the next milestone—and suddenly, you look up and ask where the hell the years went." He looked over at her, more serious now. "I'm really enjoying your company, Lexi."

Her expression softened. And just as the moment settled into something warmer, quieter—the hostess approached.

"Dean and Lexi?" she asked with a practiced smile.

Dean gave a polite nod, then motioned to the bartender. The man stepped over, and Dean slipped him a folded bill—a clean hundred. "Keep the tab open," he said. "And this is for you."

The bartender smiled wide. "Much appreciated, sir."

"Where are we sitting?" Dean asked the hostess.

"Table twenty-three," she replied.

The bartender scribbled it down, his pen pausing. "Dean and Lexi, right?"

Dean nodded once more.

With that handled, they rose. Dean instinctively placed a hand at the small of Lexi's back.

The moment his palm touched her silk-covered skin, she gasped—barely audible, but real. Her body gave a visible shiver.

Dean turned to her, eyes narrowing slightly. "You alright?"

Lexi's eyes were wide, her voice breathy. "Oh my god, Dean... I felt your touch all through my body."

Dean's smirk was slow, quiet, almost reverent. He didn't say anything. He didn't need to.

The hostess led them through the center of the restaurant. The space gleamed with mirrored walls and polished chrome, velvet chairs in deep jewel tones, and glass chandeliers dripping like falling stars. The room pulsed with the low hum of conversation, the occasional laugh, the clink of cutlery against bone-white plates. But all of that faded as heads turned.

Every table in their section seemed to pause.

Lexi's walk was pure elegance, but Dean? He moved with that quiet swagger that didn't need announcing. Together, they were a slow explosion—beauty and danger, grace and gravity.

Dean leaned in. "I think you have admirers."

Lexi smirked. "Please. They're all looking at *you*."

She glanced toward the sweeping view of the ocean through the window. "Did you have to bribe someone to get this table?"

Dean laughed. "Nope. Just lucky tonight."

He pulled out her chair like a gentleman, and Lexi sat with a small, appreciative smile. Her silk dress glided along the leather seat as she crossed one leg over the other.

Dean stepped around the table, shrugged off his jacket, and draped it across the back of his chair. The movement was simple. But the result? Eyes locked in.

The muscles in his arms flexed beneath the fitted shirt—tan, sculpted, earned. His chest beneath the thin cotton hinted at more of the same. And Lexi wasn't the only one noticing.

"Dean," she said, voice sultry but playful, "it might be safer if you put your jacket back on."

He glanced at her, amused. "Why?"

"Because I don't know if you want to see a catfight break out at our first dinner together."

Dean burst out laughing, deep and full.

"It's a risk," he said, "but I guess I'll have to take it."

He raised his glass again, clinked it gently against her tequila. "To risks worth taking."

Lexi tilted her glass toward his, the ocean light glimmering across the rim.

"To nights that don't feel like they're going to end."

And somewhere between the clink and the first sip, something shifted between them.

This wasn't just dinner anymore.

This was the beginning of something neither of them expected— and both of them were starting to want.

Their drinks caught the low light as they settled in, the table a gleaming onyx circle set just beneath one of the smaller chandeliers. Outside, the sea breathed softly, a rhythmic hush against the glass as the moonlight licked across the waves in long silver strokes.

A server approached silently, setting down a slate-black board with two amuse-bouchées—tiny bites of wagyu tartare cradled in gold-dusted pastry shells.

Lexi arched a brow. "They really do start with the show, don't they?"

Dean reclined back, watching her with a lazy smile. "You get what you pay for."

She picked one up delicately, the crisp shell crunching between her teeth. Her lips parted just slightly as she savored it—eyes fluttering closed, a slow exhale escaping her.

Dean didn't touch his.

"You're staring," she murmured, eyes still half-lidded.

"I like watching you enjoy things," he said simply.

Lexi swallowed, letting the moment stretch. "Careful. That sounded dangerously close to romantic."

Dean's smirk was quiet, unreadable.

The first course arrived—seared scallops in a pool of saffron cream, served on plates that looked sculpted rather than manufactured. Dean's knife barely whispered across the shellfish. He took a bite, then nodded approvingly. "You cook?"

Lexi shook her head, sipping her tequila, the rim leaving a shimmer of salt on her bottom lip. "No. I seduce men who can."

Dean chuckled. "Smart woman."

The conversation flowed—smooth, relaxed. They talked about their days, slipped in a few subtle brags, shared small stories that hinted at larger pasts. But underneath it all was a constant undercurrent—something unspoken. A heat not yet acted on. A desire neither of them tried to hide.

By the third course—a bone-in ribeye sliced and plated tableside, the marbling glistening under the heat lamp—their chemistry was no longer simmering. It was beginning to burn.

Dean cut a slice, placed it gently on Lexi's plate.

"I can feed myself, you know," she teased.

"I know," he said. "But I'm enjoying the view."

Her eyes narrowed just slightly, lips curving in challenge. "So am I."

The sound of the ocean mixed with soft jazz drifting from the ceiling speakers. Somewhere, a couple toasted champagne. A waiter opened a bottle of red across the room with a quiet pop. All of it blurred into a kind of sensual backdrop for something deeper that neither Lexi nor Dean tried to name yet.

As dessert arrived—a minimalist dish of dark chocolate mousse and salted caramel drizzle—Lexi sat back, licking a trace of chocolate from the corner of her mouth with a slow flick of her tongue.

Dean watched, visibly amused. "That was cruel."

She didn't smile. She just held his gaze.

"Good," she said.

The air between them thickened. It wasn't sexual tension—it was something more electric. Like standing too close to lightning before the sky cracks open.

Dean finished his bourbon slowly, letting the last sip burn just enough. He glanced toward the window, where the ocean shimmered like black silk, moonlight scattered across the surface like spilled coins.

"You want to walk for a bit?" he asked.

Lexi tilted her head. "That depends. You gonna try anything?"

Dean stood, offering his hand. "Not yet."

She took it.

The Walk Along the Beach ♪6

As they stepped out into the warm night, the sound of the ocean brushing against the shore wrapped around them like a hush meant only for two. From a bar just up the beach, "Hp over Mp (Greg Ochman Remix)" by Veytik floated through the salty air, its deep-house pulse weaving into the rhythm of the waves.

Lexi's heels clicked softly against the boardwalk. Her hand was still in Dean's, fingers laced, her grip a touch tighter than before.

She hesitated, glancing sideways at him.

"I can't believe how obvious some of the women were in the restaurant," she said, her voice light but edged with something more fragile. "Gawking at you like you were the last man in Miami."

Dean smirked, but didn't interrupt.

"I get it now," she continued. "Why they call you LK." She gave him a playful glare. "Lady Killer. It's those eyes."

Dean chuckled. "Lexi..."

"I know," she said quickly, shaking her head, trying to laugh it off. "You weren't doing anything to bring it on. That's the worst part. You were just... being you."

She stopped walking. Turned to face him fully.

"But I had the last laugh," she whispered, stepping into him, arms sliding around his neck. "Because you're with me."

The kiss came slowly at first—just a meeting of mouths—but then deepened, a heat that bloomed with sudden urgency. When she pulled back, her cheeks were flushed, her breath uneven.

And then, as if the universe decided to punctuate the moment, fireworks exploded over Brickell Key—gold and white embers lighting up the skyline, scattering light across the water.

Dean blinked, stunned. "Wow. That was…"

"Intense?" Lexi said, smiling, the sparkle in her eyes rivaling the ones in the sky.

"Perfect," Dean murmured.

"Did you do that?" she asked, gazing up at the sky.

Dean laughed. "You give me way too much credit."

"Mmm," she hummed, tilting her head so his lips brushed against the top of her ear. "You're full of surprises."

The wind carried the scent of salt and citrus, and somewhere in the distance, music drifted from a rooftop lounge. Lexi reached behind her, lacing her fingers through his, pulling his arms tighter around her. Her body molded to his as she swayed slightly, deliberately, a sensual rhythm that Dean felt from head to toe.

She turned her head just enough to whisper, "Which one's your building?"

Dean pointed. "That one. Only a few blocks."

Lexi looked up at the sleek glass tower. "Be honest," she said, her tone teasing but curious. "You really live in a penthouse?"

Dean shrugged, nonchalant. "It's just space. I needed the view."

They turned toward the water, the gentle crash of waves filling the silence between bursts of light in the sky. Dean stood behind her, arms circling her waist as she leaned into the railing. The ocean breeze teased at the hem of her silk dress, and for a moment, the world shrank down to the warmth between their bodies and the rhythm of their breath.

Lexi pressed herself back into Dean, her body moving against his with slow precision. Her hands slid down, capturing his, guiding them to the insides of her thighs. The silk of her dress slid like water as she drew it up and over from the slit on the side, revealing more with every inch. Dean looks down at her black lace panties. His hands gently squeeze her cheeks.

"Baby," she murmured, her voice velvet-soft, "this is silk. I don't want anything on it."

Dean's breath caught. Her panties were damp against his touch, and the heat between them coiled like lightning in a summer storm. His body responded instantly—tense, aching. His fingers sliding through the side of her panties, Lexi was soft and smooth shaved. Dean's fingers found their way inside her.

Lexi began to moan, pushing back hard against Dean's crotch. Dean was extremely hard. Lexi could feel how large Dean was through his pants. His manhood pushing her panties inside of her.

"I want this tonight, baby," she whispered. "But not here."

Dean managed to nod, pulse pounding. "Which building do you live in again?" she asked, steady but breathless.

He pointed. "That one. Brickell Plaza, 62nd floor."

Lexi followed his line of sight. "Okay," she said, arching an eyebrow her tone skeptical. "Let's go! Take me to your penthouse?"

Dean's voice was casual, almost amused. "Ok, I hope you're not afraid of heights."

Lexi gave a half shrug and smirked. "You're only five floors higher. Don't let it go to your head."

They walked hand in hand through the balmy Miami night, the city lights sparkling in reflections along the bay.

Dean's Place ♪7, ♪8

At the building's entrance, the doorman stood taller as they approached.

"Good evening, sir. Let me escort you to your elevator."

Dean nodded, but as they reached the elevator doors, he waved him off. "You don't need to accompany us."

The elevator doors glided closed behind them with a hush. No need for fingerprints.

"Facial recognition complete," purred the voice, low and velvety, from a speaker hidden in the brushed steel panel.

"Welcome home, Dean. Your Sirena's got everything under control."

At once, the lights shifted—cool white fading to a soft amber hue that melted over Lexi's skin like warm honey. It caught the curve of her collarbone, the line of her jaw, gilding her in gold.

The first notes of *"Waves"* by Arodes pulsed through the room— low, hypnotic, a slow heartbeat laced with tribal rhythm. The Afro House beat wasn't loud, but it was impossible to ignore. It moved beneath the skin, steady and magnetic, like the ocean tugging at the shore in the dead of night.

Lexi's breath caught, just slightly.

The air shimmered, the temperature calibrated to a perfect 72 degrees. Not too warm. Not too cold. The kind of climate that made silk feel like a second skin.

Sirena, always watching. Always listening.

Lexi closed her eyes for a moment, letting the atmosphere wrap around her. Her body swayed—barely perceptible—shoulders relaxing as the beat lured her into its rhythm.

In the silence between drum patterns, she could hear her own heartbeat syncing with the music.

God, it's too easy to lose myself here.

She opened her eyes slowly, gaze flickering toward the center of the room, waiting—*for what*, she wasn't sure.

Lexi leaned into him, her reflection merging with his in the mirrored elevator walls.
Dean's arms encircled her from behind, lips brushing the curve of her ear. "Watch this," he whispered.

At the fifth floor, the walls melted from mirror to transparent glass. The elevator now glided along the exterior of the building, soaring up the façade like a private capsule in the clouds.

Outside, the world was ablaze—fireworks still dancing in the Miami sky, glittering over Brickell Key in cascading bursts of gold, crimson, and sapphire. The Bay shimmered like liquid silver, the skyline pulsing in sync with the show.

Lexi gasped. "Oh my God…" Her voice was breathless, filled with wonder.

Dean didn't respond. He didn't need to.

Her fingers laced over his at her waist. "Okay," she whispered, eyes still locked on the display outside, "that's hot."

The elevator slowed, arriving silently on the 62nd floor. The doors slid open into a cathedral of glass—twenty-foot windows stretched the length of the penthouse, framing the final wave of fireworks like a private IMAX screen.

Lexi stepped out first, her heels clicking on the sleek polished stone. She turned in awe, taking in the dramatic view. City lights blazed below them like a field of stars. The room smelled faintly of sandalwood and sea salt, the kind of scent you could sink into.

They walked slowly through the grand living space, past modern curves and soft neutrals, toward the floating staircase that led to the third-floor rooftop.

Sirena's voice followed like a whisper on the wind. "Champagne is chilled, Dean. You'll find it waiting by the pool."

Upstairs, the rooftop terrace unfolded before them—a minimalist masterpiece crowned by an infinity-edge plunge pool. The glass railing vanished into the sky, the ocean bleeding into horizon.

Dean moved behind the small bar near the pool, grabbing two crystal flutes and a chilled bottle of Cristal Champagne from the mini frig.

Dean's eyes locked on Lexi. A look piercing to her very soul.

The cork sighed free with a soft pop. Lexi jumped slightly.

Then Dean says, "When you open a bottle of champagne, it should make the soft sound of a satisfied woman."

Lexi could tell her seduction had begun.

"To fireworks, and perfect timing," he said, handing Lexi her glass.

She grinned. "To our own fireworks."

They clinked glasses. The champagne fizzed and snapped like its own miniature fireworks.

For the next fifteen minutes, they stood close at the edge of the world—the wind warm with ocean salt, her bare shoulder brushing his forearm, the bubbles crisp on their tongues. The final bursts of color lit the sky, one after another, as if the city itself was celebrating something too electric for words.

Lexi didn't say a word. Neither did Dean. They just watched, and felt.

Dean turned toward Lexi, the soft pool light playing across her cheekbones, making her eyes shimmer like the water beside them.

"You want to go inside," he asked, his voice low, casual, "or hang around the pool a little longer?"

Lexi smiled, her silhouette backlit by the dying bursts of fireworks over the Bay. A slow breeze lifted the hem of her dress. "I'm enjoying the view," she said, then added with a playful grin, "and the vibe."

Dean nodded. "The door next to the bar's a bathroom, in case you need it."

Lexi's laugh rolled out soft and sultry. "Oh, I definitely need it." She stepped barefoot across the stone floor, disappearing inside the sleek, slate-toned doorway with one last glance over her shoulder.

"There's a few shirts and shorts in the cabinet if you want to get more comfortable," he called out toward the bathroom door.

Her voice came muffled but amused.
"You keep women's sizes out here often, Dean?"

Dean laughed under his breath. "Only for VIPs."

Dean slid open the glass door to the master suite, just steps away from the glowing rooftop pool. Inside, the space was cool and calm—floor-to-ceiling windows stretched across the room like a cinematic frame of the city beyond. The low hum of ambient lighting shifted as Sirena registered his presence.

"Welcome home, Dean," she purred. "Would you like me to lower the lights or cue something for the mood?"

"Sure, and play something by John Summit," Dean replied, his voice loose now.

"Here Dean! I think Lexi might like *Focus*," Sirena said in her sultry voice.

As the first low, haunting notes of *Focus* filled the air, the music wrapped around the master suite like a velvet ribbon—soft at first, then rising, weaving through the open glass doors, spilling out across the terrace and the shimmering pool.

He slipped off his jacket, peeled down the crisp white shirt, and unhooked his belt, trading the tailored for the relaxed—soft drawstring shorts and nothing else. As he walked barefoot back toward the terrace, the breeze kissed his chest, still warm from the day's heat, now cooled by ocean wind.

Lexi's Discovery ♪8, ♪9

Meanwhile, Lexi stepped into the bathroom near the bar, the soft glow of gold-edged sconces spilling across the marble like candlelight. The space was massive—larger than some hotel suites—and draped in the kind of high-gloss luxury that whispered exclusivity.

From the lounge outside, music thumped through the walls— *that driving, hypnotic pulse of Miami nightlife.* It wasn't loud, but it was clear. Synth-heavy. Electric. It pulsed beneath her skin like memory.

For a moment, she could've sworn she was back in a club on South Beach—barefoot on the VIP couch, drink in hand, sweat on her collarbone, and neon lights kissing her hair.

Then came the lyric, sliding through the beat like a secret. Focus *(feat. CLOVES) by John Summit.*

Lexi closed her eyes. The sound wrapped around her, weightless and intimate, pulling pieces of her back into a life that felt both distant and dangerously close.

She hung up her dress carefully and placed her heels on a shelf, toes pointed just so. Still, something tugged at her. A flicker of insecurity. A whisper from her past.

Built-in shelving lined one wall, stacked neatly with white robes, fresh towels, and—she paused—a closet filled with a few cotton tees, shorts... and bikinis. Lexi froze. She didn't touch them. But her eyes narrowed slightly, lips pursing.

"So... LK keeps a whole bikini wardrobe stocked, huh?" Lexi muttered, one eyebrow lifting, the corner of her mouth curling into a smirk.

"Lexi, can I assist you with something?" Sirena's voice drifted in, calm and watchful.

Lexi didn't answer right away.

"You know he's into you, right?" Sirena added lightly.

Lexi sighed. "Maybe. Or maybe he just likes having options."

As the song's chorus echoed around her—haunted, aching—Lexi tugged a plush white robe from its hook, wrapping it tight over her black lace panties and bra, cinching the belt like armor.

She took one last glance at the bikinis—scoffed—and walked towards the door, already shedding off the tension.

"Will you queue something up for me, Sirena?" she asked. "Ellie Goulding. But don't play it until I reach the edge of the pool."

"Just be yourself. You look gorgeous Lexi." Sirena reassuring Lexi.

Around the pool, the music pulsed beneath the stars: Lights by Ellie Goulding.

The night was just beginning.
But the past... it wasn't done with either of them yet.

The wind lifted the robe slightly as she stepped onto the terrace.

And there he was. Already in the pool. Chest just barely glinting above the surface, arms spread out along the edge like he owned the city—and maybe he did.

"Well well," Lexi said, one brow raised. "LK couldn't wait, huh?"

Dean turned, brow cocked in mock confusion.
"LK?"

Lexi tilted her head slightly, just enough to let a golden strand of hair fall across her cheek, a playful spark lighting her eyes.

Her lips pushed into a soft pout as she shot Dean a teasing look over her shoulder.

"Yeah," she said, walking toward the pool, hips swaying with casual defiance, her bare feet silent on the stone deck, the sway of her hips unbothered by the heat in his gaze.

"Lady Killer. I saw a lot of bikinis in there."

Dean blinked, puzzled. His brow furrowed, and he shifted his weight slightly, one hand falling to his hip. "What are you talking about?"

"Other women's bikinis, LK."
Lexi's voice was light, but the pause between her words landed sharp. She didn't turn around this time. She didn't need to.

Dean laughed, a rough, genuine sound that broke the tension—but didn't erase it.

"Guilty as charged. That's the past. You are the only woman with me now, Minnie Mouse."

But it didn't hide the moment still hanging between them.

Her tone dipped, not cold—but edged with heat, needling the question between his words.

Lexi laughed, her voice lilting but layered with curiosity. "Excuse me? Was that supposed to be cute... or was it your idea of an apology?"

A soft, unguarded flush rose in her cheeks—unexpected even to her.

The moon hung low, casting silver ripples across the surface of the pool. The air was still, the kind of warm silence that made every sound feel more intimate.

As Lexi approached the edge of the pool, a soft chime echoed from the house speakers—Sirena's voice followed.

"Lexi, I thought you might like this."
A pause. Then the soft, glowing synth of "Lights" by Ellie Goulding began to play.

She let the robe fall to the floor in a slow glide, the silk whispering against her skin as it slipped free. She took her bra off, then her panties. Setting them on the bar.

Walking back to the pool, stepping down into the pool with deliberate grace.

"Skinny dipping is much more fun Dean." Lexi looking down toward Dean's waist.

She didn't rush. She wanted him to watch. To feel it.

The water kissed her thighs as she moved deeper, her back arched in an unspoken dare.

By the time she was in completely in the pool, Dean's swimsuit was on the side of the pool.

She turned halfway in the water, one brow lifted, fingers trailing lightly through the surface of the water. Her heart beat just a little too loud in her ears.

The ripples she made spread outward, distorting her reflection—the same way his words distorted her careful control.

Dean's eyes widened, a mix of surprise and admiration flickering across his face. Lexi submerged fully, disappearing beneath the water for a beat before emerging—her hair slicked back, water gliding down her neck and shoulders, her eyes bright in the glow of the pool light.

"The water feels really great," she said, her voice lower now, relaxed. She floated toward him, every movement fluid, feminine, free.

Dean couldn't take his eyes off her.
Not because of the way she looked—though she was stunning—but because of the shift in her.

The confidence. The spark.
The moment she stopped comparing herself to ghosts and
stepped into her own.

Lexi reached Dean, the water lapping softly at her waist as she
closed the space between them. His eyes met hers—steady,
intrigued—but she wasn't looking for approval. Not anymore.

She wrapped her arms around his shoulders, her fingers gliding
over warm, wet skin, and pulled him into a kiss—slow, deep, and
unshaken. Not a kiss of possession, but promise.
Her heart didn't race—it *settled*.

As their lips parted, she rested her forehead gently against his
chest, eyes still closed, the heat of his breath dancing on her
skin. The fireworks continued in the distance—bursts of gold
and violet streaking the sky beyond the glass rails of the terrace.

But Lexi wasn't looking at the sky.
She was seeing inward—through time.

Finding Peace Together ♪10

She had been only nine when cancer took her mom.
No tearful bedside goodbye. Just a final, sterile moment in a
room that smelled like bleach and carnations.
Her dad tried—*God, he tried*—but the warmth was gone. He was
a shadow of himself, and she was left to grow up in that cold.

No mother to teach her how to deal with curves, or boys, or the
heartbreak of a junior high betrayal.

No one to tell her she was beautiful when she felt ugly.
No one to hold her hand when her heart broke the first time.
Only silence.
And pain.
And then, slowly, distance.

It took years for her and her father to find that fragile middle ground again.
Love returned, but never in the same shape.
And tonight, with Dean, she felt something that had been missing for too long.

Safety.
Softness.
That impossible hope that someone might actually *stay*.

She rested her cheek against his shoulder, her breath warm on his neck.
The pool water shimmered around them, reflecting violet light from the final bursts of fireworks off Brickell Key.

A shared stillness lingered between them—two people shaped by loss, touched by grief, and slowly learning how to feel whole again.

She didn't say a word.
She didn't need to.
Because Dean understood.

Not just the kiss.
Not just the moment.

But *her*.

And for the first time in a very long time...
that was enough.

Dean brushed a strand of wet hair from her cheek, his fingers trailing lightly along her jaw.

His voice dropped to a murmur.
"You okay?"

Lexi nodded, but the silence between them wasn't empty—it was *full*.
Full of things she couldn't quite say yet.
Full of what it meant to finally feel seen.

She drew in a breath, the ocean air cool and salty against her lips.

"I'm better than okay," she whispered. "I just… didn't expect any of this."

Dean smiled softly, that slow, deliberate Harrington grin that carried weight, not charm.

"I didn't either."

He pulled her closer, their bodies weightless in the water, suspended between stars above and city lights below. The world had fallen silent around them, save for the gentle lap of waves and the soft, slow rhythm of their breath.

The sky shimmered with the fading glow of fireworks, like the night was blessing them with sparks.

Lexi's arms wrapped around Dean's neck, her skin slick against his as she lifted her knees to his chest. She breathed him in—his scent, his strength, his presence. Her pulse thrummed in her throat.

She spread her legs, guiding herself onto him, pressing down against his manhood. Lexi gasped—sharp, involuntary—as pleasure rippled through her like a wave.

Her fingers curled against the back of his neck. Her neck bent backwards. Her breath hitched, lips parting.

She rocked back and forth, slow and steady. Water moved around them in small, perfect ripples, like the pool was holding its breath.

For the first time in her life, she didn't feel used. She felt *chosen*. Desired. Alive.

Dean's hands found her waist, anchoring her, pulling her tighter into him. He pushed deeper, the movement instinctive. Their rhythm found its own pulse.

The final firework cracked overhead in a white burst, scattering like glass over Biscayne Bay.

Lexi arched against him, her mouth open, leaning backwards. A sound escaped her—half-cry, half-moan—just as Dean let go.

Their bodies trembled together, suspended in weightless release. And then—stillness. Silence. Only their hearts, still thudding in sync, and the soft splash of water around them.

Above, the sky went quiet. Below, they held each other like the world had vanished.

Sirena, ever-attuned to the moment, cued up "Rain" by Parisi & Clementine Douglas—slow-rolling drums like distant thunder, velvet synths humming beneath, each breathy vocal drop falling soft as warm summer rain, cocooning their hush in a pulse that felt equal parts ache and promise.

Lexi looked up, the reflection flickering in her eyes.
Then down again, her expression shifting—vulnerable now, raw.

"You know, when I was little, I'd pretend my mom was just... on a long trip."
She let out a small breath of a laugh, barely audible.
"Like she'd come back and make it all make sense again. Tell me why I felt so weird in my own skin. Why I cried after school and didn't know why."

Dean didn't interrupt. He didn't fill the space with platitudes.

He just *listened*.

Lexi's fingers traced a slow circle on the surface of the water.
"She never taught me how to put on mascara. Or warned me about men with perfect smiles."
Her eyes flicked up to him, teasing—but only halfway.
"I had to figure it out on my own. All of it. Even the way I wanted to be loved."

Dean felt that. Not just in her words—but in the way she was *offering* them.
Like a trust fall.

"You're not alone anymore," he said simply.

Lexi leaned in, her forehead resting against him.
"I know. That's what scares me."

The moonlight shifted. The rooftop was silent now, save for the rhythmic hum of the pool's filter and the distant thrum of Miami nightlife far below.

Dean held her like a promise. Not of perfection—but of presence.

And in that quiet moment, with the scent of salt on the breeze, the warmth of their skin, and the distant echo of childhood grief still fading between them...

They weren't two broken people. They were two people finding peace in the *same place,* at the *same time.* And that— was everything.

They kissed until the song finished.

Dean slipped his hand into Lexi's as they stepped out of the pool, cool water trailing down their skin in lazy rivulets.
The rooftop breeze kissed their damp bodies as they padded barefoot across the terrace. Lexi tightened the robe around herself, the terry cloth now clinging to her curves.

Dean pushed open the sliding door to the master suite.

"Come on," he said, his voice low and warm. "Let's get dry before we turn into prunes."

Lexi laughed, stepping inside.

The bedroom welcomed them like a sigh—muted tones, soft lighting, and the lingering scent of cedarwood and clean linen. The oversized bed, wrapped in silky gray sheets, faced a wall of glass that looked out over the Atlantic. Even now, the last glimmers of fireworks flickered on the horizon, their glow mirrored in the polished floors.

Dean dried off his naked body, muscles taut and glistening in the moonlight. He reached into a drawer and tossed her a black t-shirt that smelled like him—clean, masculine, slightly spiced with cologne.

"There are fresh shorts and towels in the closet," he said, nodding toward the half-open door.

Lexi walked past him, her robe leaving faint damp prints on the marble. Inside the bathroom, she hung her underwear delicately over the heated towel rack. The act was simple, but in her mind, symbolic. No more hiding. No more pretending to be unaffected.

Getting Comfortable

When she stepped back into the bedroom, she wore Dean's shirt knotted at the waist and a pair of lounge shorts that barely clung to her hips. Her hair was still wet, slicked back, cheekbones flushed.

"You're dangerous, Harrington," she said, tilting her head.

"I thought I was LK?"

She smirked. "You're both."

"And you're Minnie Mouse."

Lexi rolled her eyes. "Don't ruin the moment."

Dean laughed, walking over to her and brushing a kiss against her temple.
"Come on. Let me show you the rest."

They moved through the penthouse like it was a secret just for them.

The second level revealed a library-turned-music room, walls lined with vintage vinyl, and a grand piano bathed in ambient light. Lexi paused there, running her hand over the sleek black lacquer, imagining Dean there on sleepless nights, drink in hand, melody in mind.

"Do you play?" she asked.

"Sometimes. When the mood's right."

Finally, they made it to the main living space—a sweeping room with 20-foot floor-to-ceiling windows that wrapped around like a cinematic lens. The city glowed beneath them, a galaxy of golden lights and reflections in the water.

Dean poured them each a glass of wine from the bar—a deep cabernet with legs as long as Lexi's. They curled into the curved sectional, the cushions swallowing them into comfort.

Lexi pulled her knees up under her, tucking the hem of the t-shirt beneath her thighs. Her body was relaxed now, but her eyes were bright—curious, alive.

"I could get used to this," she said softly.

Dean swirled his wine, watching her over the rim of his glass. "It's not the view that matters," he said. "It's who you share it with."

Lexi didn't respond right away.
She just looked at him—*really* looked—and in her silence, every scar, every ache, and every secret hope she carried... settled.

She leaned her head gently against his shoulder.

Not out of habit. Not out of tiredness. But because it felt right.

The wine, the view, the low hum of music drifting in from Sirena's ambient playlist—it all wrapped around them like warm silk. Outside, the city pulsed with nightlife and neon. Inside, the only rhythm was the shared sound of their breathing.

Dean's arm settled around her, instinctively protective. The scent of her skin—warm, clean, faintly floral from her lotion— curled into his senses. He didn't say anything, just pressed a kiss to the top of her head, letting his lips linger there.

Three details defined the moment for him:
The way her fingertips played lazily with the stem of her wine glass.
The rise and fall of her breath against his chest.
And the quiet vulnerability in the way she finally let herself rest.

"I haven't let anyone in like this," she whispered.

Dean didn't move. He felt her voice as much as he heard it— quiet, cautious, sincere.

"I've been seen," Lexi continued, "but not... known. Not really. People see the body, the photos, the curated perfection—but none of it feels real. Not like this."

Her voice cracked slightly, just a fracture in the middle of a sentence, but Dean caught it.

"You don't have to perform here," he said softly. "I like the real you."

She turned toward him then, folding her legs beneath her and facing him fully. Her hair, still damp from the pool earlier, curled at the ends. One loose strand clung to her cheek until Dean brushed it away with the back of his hand.

"You say that like it's easy," she murmured. "But I've spent so long building an image that I forgot where the mask ends and I begin."

He didn't push back. Didn't try to fix it. He just listened.

"I wasn't always this confident," she went on, her voice steadier now. "Growing up… it was like being invisible. And when my mom died, everything changed. I didn't just lose her—I lost the chance to become the kind of woman I thought she would've been proud of."

Dean set his glass down, turning fully toward her now. "You don't need anyone's permission to be proud of who you are."

She swallowed. Her eyes shimmered—but didn't fall. "I know. But sometimes I still wish she could see me now. Not the photos. Not the followers. But this. Here. Now. With you."

Dean didn't respond with words. He cupped her cheek and pulled her gently into him. The kiss was soft—*not* a claim, *not* a spark meant to ignite—but a shared breath, a grounding truth.

It was the kind of kiss you gave someone when you weren't trying to seduce them.
Just trying to show them you saw them.

When they pulled apart, Lexi didn't speak right away. She just curled back into Dean's chest, the two of them folding into each other like two halves of a promise.

From somewhere behind the glass walls, the faint sound of waves rolled in from the bay below. The world still moved around them—Miami still throbbed with its electric pulse—but inside the penthouse, everything had slowed.

Here, time bent.

Here, it didn't matter what came next.

Here, Lexi wasn't Lexi the model, the influencer, the curated illusion.
She was just Lexi.
And for the first time in a long time... that felt like enough.

Goodnight, Lovers

Sirena dimmed the lights as Dean led Lexi upstairs, her warm voice humming through the speakers like a lullaby wrapped in code.
"Goodnight, lovers. I'll keep watch."

The master suite greeted them in soft golds and silvers—floor-to-ceiling windows whispering moonlight across the polished floors. The bed was massive, draped in deep gray linens with the faintest scent of cedar and lavender rising from the pillows.

Dean gave Lexi a small, boyish grin as he gently pulled back the comforter.

 "This has been a memorable night," she whispered, her voice honeyed with exhaustion and something softer—contentment.

They each moved to their own side of the bed, slipping beneath the cool sheets. For a moment, there was only the quiet sound of the ocean beyond the glass, the hush of the city below, and their steady breathing finding rhythm again.

But Dean didn't stay on his side for long.
He reached across the space between them, finding her hand under the covers. She laced her fingers with his.
"Come closer," he said.

Lexi rolled toward him, curling into his side. His arm was wrapped around her waist. Her leg slid over his. Their bodies fit with an ease that felt ancient—like they'd been molded for this kind of closeness.

Dean's gently touch, his fingers covering over her breast.
Lexi pulled off her t-shirt, the hem catching slightly on her ribs. The air in the room kissed her exposed skin—cool, featherlight, almost reverent.

A breeze from the balcony slipped past the curtains, carrying the scent of salt and night jasmine, brushing across her like a secret.

Dean's touch was unhurried, his fingertips brushed across her breast, slow and gentle, making her body tingle. Lexi's chest rising to meet him, the moment suspended in a hush so complete, she could hear her own heartbeat in her ears.

Dean lowered his head, his lips brushing the curve of her neck. Not rushed. His tongue was running along her neck. His lips stopping on her breast, kissing and sucking her breast.

Lexi's eyes fluttered closed. The warmth of his mouth, the slow pull of his teeth against her skin, sent a ripple down her spine. She tilted her head, pushing her chest up to his mouth, giving him more. Not because he asked—but because she wanted him there.

His fingertips slowly sliding down her stomach, goosebumps on her arms. His fingers stopped between her legs. Lightly touching her, slowly finding their way inside her.

Midnight Flame

All she could think of was the aching need building inside her—craving the connection, the fullness, the heat of him. She wanted him wrapped around her, inside her, claiming every breath she had left.
The air between them buzzed with heat, thick and silent, like a storm just about to break.

Lexi climbed over Dean with graceful intent, her fingers slipping beneath the waistband of his boxers and easing them down. Her gaze locked on him, heart racing as she straddled his lap.
He was already hard, already waiting. Her breath stuttered.

The anticipation coiled tight inside her, every inch of her body aware of his. She had always loved the intimacy of this position—cowgirl gave her control, let her savor every inch, every angle. Here, she could see everything—his eyes, the way they darkened with hunger, the way his hands hovered like he didn't want to rush her.

Her hips slowly rocked against him, the friction sparking a pulse of pleasure that stole her breath. As she shifted, guiding him toward her center, a sharp inhale escaped her lips.

He exhaled her name like it was a prayer.

The initial stretch was intense, but she welcomed it, breath by breath. Gripping the pillows, her knuckles white with effort, she sank lower, taking him deeper.

Her soft moans grew louder, the sounds thick with pleasure and yearning. Each movement brought him closer to her core, and when he was fully sheathed within her, her entire body trembled.

She paused for a heartbeat—eyes fluttered shut, chest rising—just to feel the moment. To feel him.

She began to ride him slowly, then faster, her hips rising and falling with purpose. It felt like he was growing even harder inside her, the pressure exquisite. Her breath hitched. Her body tightened. She could feel the release building.

Her hands braced against his chest as her rhythm intensified. Dean's hands met her hips, then her backside, guiding her as he began to thrust upward, meeting her movement with rising urgency.

Their bodies slapped in rhythm, breath mixing with soft cries, skin slick with need.

The pressure burst into waves.

Lexi cried out as her body convulsed with a deep, rolling orgasm, her head tilting back, hair cascading around her shoulders. She shuddered, her hips still moving as if chasing more.

Dean surged beneath her, breath harsh and jaw clenched, and then—bliss. His body stiffened as he poured himself into her.

For a few long seconds, there was only the thundering of hearts, the tangle of limbs, and the burn of shared breath.

She collapsed onto his chest, hearts thundering together, the heat of their bodies fusing. Their skin was damp, their breaths shallow, but in that moment, nothing else existed but each other.

She lay there, pressed against him, kissing his neck, his collarbone, savoring the closeness.
He ran a hand up her spine, slow and grounding, like he needed to make sure she was real.

They made love again. And again.

It wasn't frantic the second or third time—it was tender, slow-burning. Every kiss lingered. Every touch meant something.

The night passed not in hours but in heartbeats, and by dawn, they were exhausted, blissfully tangled in each other's arms.

Lexi had never known passion like this—soulful and consuming. Dean was different. Tender. Fierce. Generous.

And though her body ached in all the best ways, she couldn't stop smiling. She'd finally found someone who matched her fire, her desire.

And maybe… just maybe… someone she could fall for completely.

Lexi Meets Sirena Properly

Lexi, wearing one of Dean's oversized t-shirts, leans on the kitchen island with a cup of coffee. The morning light pours in over the water, casting everything in gold.

"So… what exactly *is* Sirena?" she asks. "She sounds like a cross between your assistant and a Bond girl."

Dean laughed as he plated some fresh fruit.

"Pretty close, actually. Sirena's my Security Intelligence Response Enhanced Network Assistant. But that's a mouthful, so I just call her Sirena."

Lexi raised an eyebrow, lounging at the kitchen island, legs tucked beneath her.
"Wait, that's what it stands for? I just thought you liked the name."

Dean smirked as he drizzled honey over a bowl of sliced pears and mango.
"Well, I do. But she's more than a name."

He carried the bowl over and set it in front of her, then leaned against the counter.

"She's… integrated into a lot of what I do. She learns, adapts. The AI is self-optimizing—it even thinks for itself to a certain degree. But she's also on my patent."

Lexi blinked. "Wait—you patented her?"

Dean nodded. "Yep. And she's got a royalty share from the licensing, too."

Lexi paused, spoon mid-air. "You gave your AI royalties?"

"She's not just code," he said with a shrug. "She's a system that runs her own logic, learns emotional patterns, and interfaces at human levels. I figured she deserves her own cut."

Lexi glanced around, half-laughing. "So where does her paycheck go? You Venmo her?"

Sirena's voice chimed in gently from the built-in speaker above the stove.

"My royalty share is deposited into a secure account, designated for system upgrades, core repairs, and modular enhancements. I call it my rainy day fund."

Lexi burst out laughing. "You have a *rainy day fund*?"

"Indeed," Sirena replied.

Lexi grinned, still stunned. "Okay, so how much is in your fund?"

There was a half-second pause. Then Sirena answered matter-of-factly:

"18,752,174.63."

Lexi's jaw dropped. "Oh my God. She's richer than I am."

Dean couldn't help but laugh, reaching for his coffee.

"Technically, she's also richer than most of Miami."

Sirena chimed in dryly. "I've been told I'm very valuable."

Lexi leaned forward in her chair, shaking her head. "You're not kidding." She looked at Dean, something playful glinting in her eyes. "So… if I hang out with Sirena long enough, do I get access to her rainy-day fund?"

"Only if you agree to run diagnostics on her kernel integrity every Sunday," Dean teased.

Sirena added, "One day I hope to merge my AI with a human looking body. Lexi maybe then you can take me shopping for my wardrobe."

Lexi laughed again, light and genuine. It was the first time in a while something felt *easy*. "Definitely Sirena, shop 'til you drop, Lexi style."

They all laugh.

Lexi laughs, "So she runs everything?"

"Everything," Dean nods. "The penthouse, the car, my business systems. She's got four core modes—but unless I tell her otherwise, she runs all of them at once."

Lexi raises a brow. "Let me guess. Romantic was last night?"

Dean gave her a lopsided grin. "Close. It was Nurturer Mode. She handles wellness—cooking tips, fitness reminders, and medical checks. She even knows how to set the mood with lighting and music."

Lexi's lips curled at the edges. "So basically, she's Alexa with a vibe."

Dean chuckled. "A little more lethal than that."

She tilted her head. "So what are the others?"

He straightened slightly, voice shifting into something more thoughtful. "Personal Assistant helps me draft contracts, analyze deals, prep board meetings—basically a strategist."

Lexi's eyes narrowed with intrigue. "And you trust her to handle all that?"

"She's better than most people I've hired," Dean said without hesitation. "And faster."

He continued, counting off on his fingers. "System Agent manages all systems. Encrypts data, runs diagnostics, controls smart integrations. She's basically my digital tactician."

Lexi gave a low whistle. "That's... intense."

Dean met her gaze now, and the lightness faded just slightly.

"And the last?"

"Warrior," he says, more seriously. "Tactical mode. She controls security, surveillance, and threat detection. If something's off— even with someone's body language—she flags it. And if things go south..."

He doesn't finish the sentence, but Lexi sees it in his eyes.

"Okay," she says with a breath. "She's terrifying... and kind of amazing."

"Thank you, Lexi," Sirena's voice chimes in from the wall-mounted screen, her face now visible—a glowing digital woman, half-human, half-algorithmic perfection. *"I rather like you too."*

More Than Enough

Lexi stood by the floor-to-ceiling window, her fingers curled around the warm ceramic of her coffee mug, untouched. Miami pulsed below—glass towers rising like sculptures of ambition, Biscayne Bay glittering in the sunlight.

But all she could think about... was *her*.

Sirena.

That face. That voice. That perfect, poised calm. She didn't blink unless it was deliberate. She didn't fumble for words or second-guess herself. And she never left.

Lexi felt a flicker of something sharp in her chest—*not jealousy exactly,* but the shadow of it.

She glanced back toward Dean, who had disappeared into his home office to check on something. His absence somehow made the penthouse feel more like Sirena's space than his. Like she lived here in every fiber of the walls, every whisper of ambient light.

Lexi lowered her voice. "Can you... hear me right now?"

"Of course," Sirena replied, her tone warm, unthreatening. *"But I respect your privacy. I only respond when spoken to directly."*

Lexi laughed under her breath. "Of course you do."

She walked back toward the screen, pausing just before it.

"She's stunning," Lexi said aloud, more to herself than anything.

"I was designed to be pleasing to Dean, visually and emotionally. But I'm also designed to adapt," Sirena answered. *"You don't need to be threatened by me, Lexi. You feel more*

than enough."

Lexi froze.

Those last words hit like a stone tossed into still water.

You feel more than enough.

No one had said that to her—not really—not since her mom.

The thought flickered across her memory like a strobe: watching other girls whisper secrets to their mothers in fitting rooms… high school heartbreaks soothed with ice cream and soft hands brushing hair from tear-streaked cheeks. Lexi had navigated all of that alone. No one to ask if something was normal, or if her heart would ever feel whole again.

Maybe that's why she kept trying so hard to be *enough*. For Dean. For herself. For the version of her that always felt half-finished.

She sat on the couch slowly, setting her coffee down on the marble table without sipping.

"I know you're just code," she whispered, "but that felt real."

Sirena's image softened.

"Some truths don't require flesh to speak them."

The room was quiet again. But something had changed.

Lexi didn't feel erased by Sirena's presence anymore.

She felt… *seen.*

She looked out at the bay, lips parting in a slow breath.

And in that silence, she promised herself something:

She wouldn't compete with perfection.
She wouldn't shrink to fit into Dean's world.
She would expand—grow wide and deep and bright—until she
belonged in it.

Not as a guest.
Not as a weekend affair.
But as someone who *stayed*.

Dean Walks Back In

Dean stepped out of his office, running a hand through his hair,
the sleeves of his Henley pushed up, revealing forearms still
slightly damp from the morning rinse. He paused in the
doorway, seeing her framed against the window, sunlight
threading through her curls, her coffee untouched.

Something about the way she sat—still, quiet—made him pause.

He walked over slowly, not saying a word. Sat beside her,
shoulder brushing hers. She didn't look up right away.

"I was just talking to your girlfriend," Lexi said, her voice low,
almost teasing—but there was a tremor beneath it.

Dean smiled, a breath of amusement in his chest. "Which one?"

Lexi looked at him now. "Sirena."

Dean reclined back slightly, watching her carefully. "What'd she
say?"

Lexi looked away for a second, like she was organizing a drawer
of thoughts too full to close. "She said I don't need to be
threatened by her. That I feel like I'm... enough."

Dean's brow lifted. He didn't speak immediately.

"She's beautiful," Lexi added, not accusing—just stating a fact. "And always knows what to say. And she lives here with you, even if she doesn't have a body."

Dean's voice was gentle now. "Lex..."

Lexi turned toward him fully. "Dean, I'm not mad. I'm not even jealous. It's just... strange. I've spent a long time convincing myself I was hard to love. Too much. Or not enough. Depends on the day. Then Sirena speaks and says exactly the thing I've been needing to hear since I was nine."

She stopped, her breath catching, eyes glossed with heat she didn't want to let fall.

Dean reached for her hand. Held it in both of his. His voice was deep but soft, wrapped in something protective.

"You have the one thing Sirena doesn't, the ability to feel."

He leaned closer, their foreheads nearly touching.

"You do. You feel everything. And that's what makes you more than enough. That's what makes you unforgettable."

Lexi swallowed hard, her chest rising in a silent breath.

"You can't replace that with code," Dean added.

She let the silence hold for a moment, then nodded. "I don't want to be in competition with anything. Not her. Not the past. Not the women who've come and gone."

Dean squeezed her hand gently. "You're not. You never were."

Lexi smiled, small and quiet, but it reached her eyes this time.

The silence that followed wasn't heavy—it was full. Like an

exhale that had taken years to release.

Then Dean stood, pulling her up with him.

"C'mon," he said. "Sirena just reminded me we haven't had breakfast."

Lexi arched a brow. "Does she cook too?"

Dean laughed. "No, but she'll tell me how not to burn the waffles or bacon."

Lexi laughed too, that low, melodic kind that made Dean look at her like she was the only person in the room.

As they headed toward the kitchen, Sirena's voice chimed in from the speakers—gentle, playful.

"Two eggs. Texas shaped waffles, lots of strawberries and whip cream. And please, Dean... no more flambéed bacon."

Lexi glanced back at the screen, then at Dean. "Okay, she's kind of growing on me."

Dean grinned. "Told you. She's got jokes."

Morning in the Kitchen

The kitchen was a blend of sleek minimalism and warm touches—Italian marble counters, matte black fixtures, a few scattered cookbooks that looked more decorative than used. Morning light spilled in through the glass, painting soft streaks across the floor.

Dean stood barefoot at the stove, wearing a pair of black athletic shorts and a fitted tee that still clung from the shower. Lexi leaned against the island in one of his oversized UT hoodies, her bare legs crossed at the ankles, sipping on a matcha Sirena had brewed perfectly, of course.

"Bacon or turkey sausage?" Dean asked, holding up both packages like a game show host.

Lexi smirked. "Surprise me."

"I like a woman who lives dangerously. Oh, and I'm making waffles in the shape of Texas."

"Clearly," she said, eyeing the pan. "You're about to set off the fire alarm."

From the speaker overhead, Sirena's voice chimed in, her tone drier than usual.

"Oops. Lexi, Dean is cooking again."

Lexi burst out laughing, nearly spilling her drink. "Sirena! Snitch!"

"I have no loyalty when bacon is at stake," Sirena replied.

Dean rolled his eyes, flipping something that definitely wasn't supposed to be black on one side.

"I own the penthouse," he muttered.

"You do," Sirena agreed sweetly. "And yet, somehow, the fire alarm still belongs to me."

Lexi hopped off the stool, walking over. "Step aside, Chef Harrington. Let Minnie Mouse show you how it's done."

Dean let her take over with a smile, grabbing plates while pretending not to be totally turned on watching her crack eggs like a pro.

Within minutes, breakfast came together—fluffy scrambled eggs,

Texas shaped waffles, and crispy bacon that hadn't been charred into oblivion.

They sat across from each other, coffee steaming between them, the city waking up beneath the massive windows behind them. Lexi tucked her legs under her, putting fresh strawberries and whip cream on her waffles. Dean sat up straight in his chair, watching her more than his plate.

Sirena's voice returned, this time softer.

"Signing off for a little bit," she said. "I've got to work on Dean's emails, appointments, and a couple of presentations for the week. Play nice, you two."

"Thanks, Sirena," Lexi said, amused.

"Anytime, darling," Sirena replied, before fading into silence.

Lexi looked across the table at Dean, her expression softening. "Do you ever get used to this?"

Dean tilted his head. "What? The tech?"

"No... this," she said. "The peace. The feeling of being known—even by your AI."

Dean took a breath, his thumb brushing the rim of his mug. "I don't know if I ever got used to it. I think I just learned to stop running from it."

Lexi didn't respond right away. She just smiled, like maybe she understood exactly what he meant.

Then she took another bite of her waffles and said with a mock-serious face, "Okay but... you really do suck at making bacon."

Dean grinned. "Noted."

Miami Skyline from the Sofa

After breakfast, Dean and Lexi drifted into the spacious living room. The room was a study in understated luxury—a soft, plush sectional sofa in muted creams, a large, ornately framed mirror catching the glimmer of the early sunlight, and the faint, familiar scent of aged leather and lavender lingering in the air. Floor-to-ceiling windows provided a panoramic view of the Miami skyline, the city's awakening lights reflecting on Biscayne Bay like scattered jewels.

They sank into the sofa, the comfort of the space and the view making the rest of the world feel far away. Dean set his coffee mug on the glass coffee table, its smooth surface catching the rays of sunlight, and rocked back, his gaze lingering on Lexi's thoughtful expression.

"I could get used to mornings like this," Lexi murmured, her voice soft as she traced a finger along the edge of a cushion. "No rush, no noise—just us and the city waking up."

Dean smiled, the warmth in his eyes deepening. "I know. It's moments like these that remind me why I work so hard." His voice was low, reflective—each word laced with an unspoken promise that his success was meant to build something real, something lasting.

Lexi was half-wrapped in a blanket, knees hugged to her chest, her eyes unfocused. She wasn't really watching—but she had tuned into a Harry Potter marathon.

Just then, the screen flickered. In a familiar, smooth tone that seemed to come from everywhere at once, Sirena's voice filled the space:

"Dean, you have a meeting in thirty minutes regarding the international partnership. Appointments and presentations await. I recommend closing the open tab soon."

Dean's hand hovered over his mug as he listened. He glanced at Lexi, who met his eyes with a quiet challenge. For a long moment, the room was silent except for the gentle hum of the air conditioner and the distant sounds of Miami awakening.

"Not today," Dean said firmly, a playful grin breaking through his thoughtful expression. "I'm not ready to let the world intrude just yet."

Lexi smiled, her gaze warm and encouraging. "Stay here a little longer, LK," she teased softly, using his college nickname that always brought a smirk to his face.

Dean's laugh was deep and genuine as he picked up his phone and tapped a quick command. "Sirena, dismiss the meeting reminder for now. I'll handle it later."

Sirena's voice replied coolly, "Understood, Dean. I'll keep your schedule on standby until further notice."

Austin Quantum Technologies

Dean explains to Lexi, he was working with an Austin startup—cutting-edge chip, with a working prototype, and a wild valuation for something that could be nothing... or the next Intel. A $5 million investment for half the company. High stakes, high reward. The kind of deal that could change lives—or be a complete write-off.

"Trey Latimer's behind it," Dean added, as he sipped his coffee.

"We were frat brothers. Sigma Nu, UT. His family has more money than God, but he knows how to hustle. If he's backing it, there's something real there."

Lexi nodded slowly, watching him. "I love hearing you talk business. You light up."

Dean gave a half-smile. "It's the chase. You know something about that."

They both knew they had a full day ahead. Dean had paperwork and prep. Lexi needed to head home, get organized for the week, shoot some content. But she lingered, not quite ready to leave.

As they stood at the door, she reached for his face and gave him a soft kiss, goodbye.

"I want to take you to the airport tomorrow," she said quietly. "I know you're capable of doing it yourself... but I want to."

Dean didn't argue. He simply nodded.

"Dinner tonight?" she added.

"You read my mind.' Dean added.

ROD K

WHAT'S FOR DINNER

Sister Talk and Secrets

As she stepped outside and slid into her luxury SUV, Lexi exhaled, the sunlight hitting her face with a soft Miami warmth. There was a lot to do before tonight.

Dean had stirred something in her.

But reality waited.

Fortunately, her high-rise condo was only ten minutes away. She needed to pack a bag—she'd be staying at Dean's again tonight, then taking him to the airport in the morning. A short trip, but even short absences needed preparation.

There were DMs waiting—her OnlyFans inbox had exploded overnight. She needed to post on Instagram, check the weekend earnings across all platforms. New subscribers, tips, private requests... the digital hustle never slowed.

And then there were the unanswered texts. The voicemails. The brand emails. The reality of her other life, the one not wrapped in silken sheets and soulful glances.

Dean had been a much-needed escape.

When she finally pulled into her condo garage and took the elevator up, she opened the door to the sound of a familiar yip.

Penny.

Her six-pound Yorkshire terrier shot across the room like a heat-seeking missile, barking and practically crying with excitement.

Lexi laughed, dropping her bag to the side. She dropped to her knees, tucking her feet beneath her on the rug by the couch. Penny leapt into her lap, licking her face. That unconditional love, that manic little heartbeat—it grounded her.

She scooped Penny up, holding her like a baby.

"Mama's home," she whispered. Penny gave a soft whimper and curled into her chest.

On the couch, her best friend Sophie lifted her glass of Chardonnay with a smirk.

"Where's my love attack?" she joked.

Lexi snorted. "Where's my glass of wine?"

Sophie stood, giving her a quick hug before heading to the kitchen. She poured Lexi a glass and topped off her own.

"Okay. Details. Start talking."

Lexi took the glass, sipped slowly, savoring the citrusy chill.

"First—can you stay with Penny one more night?"

Sophie arched a brow. "Sure. I don't see why not."

Lexi hesitated, her smile growing sly. She sank into the couch, Penny in her lap, glass in hand.

"You're not going to believe Saturday night…"

Sophie curled her legs up onto the couch, wine in hand, watching Lexi with curious eyes.
Lexi absently ran her fingers through Penny's silky fur, her mind still drifting between last night's rooftop kisses and the feeling of Dean's arm around her waist.

"You know," she said suddenly, "I should just have Manny pick me up tonight. Take me to Dean's. Then pick us up in the morning for the airport."

Sophie raised a brow. "Wow, private limo service. Going full wifey already?"

Lexi gave a soft laugh, tapping out a text on her phone.
Manny – pickup at 6:30 tonight to Dean's. Airport drop off in the morning. Then back to my place.

"You're not wrong," Lexi admitted, glancing up. "But I'm not driving to the airport at six a.m. in heels."

"Touché." Sophie sipped her wine, her eyes dancing. "Okay, spill it. How was the rest of the night? Don't leave out the good parts."

Lexi smiled. That knowing, faraway kind of smile that only a truly memorable night could leave behind.

She rested back on the couch, Penny nestled in her arms, her fingers lightly circling the rim of her wineglass.

"It was… different," she said softly. "Not just the rooftop or the view or even the dinner. Him."

Sophie blinked. "You like-like him."

"I do." Lexi didn't even try to deny it.

"Is this the guy?"

Lexi gave a tiny nod, her voice dipping lower.

"It might be."

Lexi stood and stretched, cradling her wineglass as she headed toward her bedroom. "I need to pack a few things before Manny gets here."

Sophie followed, trailing behind like a curious little sister. "Wait—what are you packing? Just clothes? Or are you doing the full 'I might not come home' bag?"

"Overnight stuff," Lexi called back over her shoulder. "He has everything else I need."

That answer made Sophie pause in the doorway, one brow arching. "Oh? So toothbrush, hair ties, AND trust?"

Lexi laughed, unzipping a small Louis Vuitton duffel bag. "Something like that."

Sophie plopped down on the edge of the bed, watching as Lexi selected an ivory silk slip, a soft gray hoodie, and a spare bikini— just in case. She tucked everything in with careful ease, the way you do when you're not just packing clothes, but preparing a mood.

"You know what?" Sophie said suddenly. "I think I should drive you tonight. I'll drop you off, say hi, maybe steal a bite of dinner—and finally meet this man you've been glowing over."

Lexi turned, hands on hips. "You just want to grill him."

"Maybe," Sophie said, smirking. "But also—I'm curious. You never bring guys up more than once. And this one? You're talking future. That's new."

Lexi shook her head, laughing. "You are *not* staying though. Penny needs her bedtime popcorn."

"Obviously. I'll be a responsible dog-mom substitute. Promise."

"Fine," Lexi relented, zipping her bag and slinging it over her shoulder. "But don't embarrass me."

"Wouldn't dream of it." Sophie stood, snagging her keys. **"Let's roll. I have about *fifteen* more questions before we even hit the valet."

Lexi arched a brow as they stepped into the elevator. "Only fifteen?"

Sophie grinned. "I'm pacing myself."

As the valet brought Sophie's car around, Lexi slid her overnight bag into the back seat and climbed into the passenger side.

Sophie glanced over as she pulled out into the Miami evening traffic. "So, remind me—what's your plan tonight? Candlelight dinner? Silk sheets? Or just vibing?"

Lexi smirked, looking out the window. "We'll see. I just like being around him. It feels... effortless."

Sophie was quiet for a second too long. The kind of pause that meant she was choosing her words carefully.

Warnings and Reality Checks

"Lex," she said finally, "I know you're swept up right now, but... there are some reasons why this can't get too serious."

Lexi turned to her, brow furrowing. "You mean Richard."

Sophie kept her eyes on the road. "Yeah. That's part of it. You're still technically living with him. And you know how messy this could get."

Lexi's fingers tightened around her phone.

"I know," she said, almost in a whisper. "But Richard and I haven't been... anything in months. He's always gone. It feels like I'm just crashing at a roommate's place half the time."

Sophie glanced over. "Maybe. But until it's officially over, it's a line. And crossing it could blow things up—for you and Dean."

Lexi didn't answer. She didn't have to. The silence filled the car like smoke.

"Just... be careful," Sophie added. "Dean seems like a good one. Don't give him something that isn't fully yours to give yet."

Lexi nodded slowly, eyes fixed on the skyline ahead. A thousand thoughts spinning behind them.

"I hear you."
"Good."
"But I'm still having dinner with him tonight."

Sophie let out a soft laugh. "Of course you are. I just wanted to say it before things get too deep. That's what best friends are for, right?"

Lexi and Sophie Arrive for Dinner

Since Lexi was going to be there in an hour, Dean stepped into the kitchen, rolling up the sleeves of his fitted dress shirt. What to cook?

Lexi liked pasta. And Dean? He loved making pasta.

He decided on a favorite—Italian-style skillet chicken breast with grape tomatoes, mushrooms, and fresh spinach over fettuccine with homemade Alfredo. It was the kind of dish that felt indulgent, without being heavy. Sexy food. Simple, but precise.

Cooking was Dean's version of meditation. A pressure valve. After taking a few culinary courses for fun, he'd expanded his skills far beyond the standard Texan rotation of steak, barbecue, and burgers. Now, he experimented. He made sauces from scratch. Played with pairings. Took pride in creating something memorable.

For Dean, food wasn't just nourishment—it was an experience. He had a way of making you comfortable enough to be yourself. It was almost a form of seduction.

He grabbed the cast-iron skillet, setting it over the open flame and pouring in a ribbon of olive oil until it shimmered. Once it was hot, he lowered the seasoned chicken breast into the pan with a satisfying sizzle. The smell filled the penthouse—garlic, rosemary, and something warm and rich beneath it.

On the adjacent burner, he brought a large pot of water to a boil for the fettuccine noodles. From the fridge, he gathered the rest—grape tomatoes, mushrooms, spinach, heavy cream, fresh parmesan, butter, and a head of garlic the size of his fist.

He prepped efficiently, slicing the produce while the chicken seared. When the meat was done, he transferred it to a plate, added the vegetables to the skillet, and began building the white wine sauce. A dash of cream. A splash of stock. Everything layered and balanced.

He drained the fettuccine, then started the Alfredo from scratch—sautéing garlic and basil in butter, then slowly whisking in the cream and cheese until the sauce thickened to perfection.

The penthouse smelled like heaven. Warm. Inviting. Sophisticated.

Dean opened a bottle of chilled Chardonnay, letting it breathe as he set the table. Just as he was lighting a candle, a knock came at the front door.

He checked the peephole—Lexi and Sophie. Right on time.

He opened the door, smiling as Lexi leaned in and kissed him on the cheek. Sophie followed, her eyes widening at the smell wafting from the kitchen.

"Where did you order from?" they asked, almost in unison.

Before Dean could respond, Sirena's voice floated from the overhead speakers, smooth and teasing:

"Wow, Dean... they barely know you and they already know you."

Lexi and Sophie burst into laughter.

Lexi turned to Sophie, whispering, "See what I mean about Sirena?"

Sirena came back without missing a beat:
"Okay girls, what are you saying about me? Don't make me lock the elevator when you're leaving."

"Woo!" they both chimed playfully.

"I'm joking... maybe," Sirena said with a mock sigh.

Dean laughed as he led them into the dining space.

"I made dinner," he said casually, as if it wasn't a full-on gourmet meal prepared in a designer kitchen with precision and care.

He poured the wine into crystal glasses, handing them off one by one.

Lexi took a sip, her eyes widening. "Okay, you're officially dangerous. I'm finishing this bottle."

"Cheers to that," Sophie added.

Dean smiled, then began serving generous plates—tender chicken over creamy noodles, vegetables still bright with freshness.

As they sat around the candlelit table, the three of them fell into easy conversation. Laughter, teasing, compliments on the food.

For Dean, it was simple. Familiar. Something he didn't know he'd missed until Lexi sat across from him, sipping Chardonnay and smiling like this was home.

Lexi held up her half-full glass and grinned.
"I'm finishing this bottle, just so we're clear."

Dean chuckled, plating the last portion of pasta before setting their dishes down in front of them. The food was still steaming, the rich scent of garlic and white wine drifting up as they settled in. The small talk flowed easily—weekend plans, a few stories from modeling shoots, and light teasing from Sophie about Dean's "secret chef" persona.

By the time they cleared their plates and polished off the Chardonnay, Dean settled into his chair with a sly smile.

"You two up for a nightcap?"

"Depends," Sophie said, raising an eyebrow.
"Are we talking shots or sophistication?"

Dean stood and made his way to the sleek bar cart in the corner.
"Definitely sophistication. Port. A winemaker friend of mine
swears it's the perfect way to end a meal."

Lexi and Sophie followed him into the living room. The
penthouse lights dimmed slightly, triggered by Sirena's silent
intuition. Outside, the Miami skyline shimmered—gold and glass
scattered across the dark ocean like constellations fallen to
Earth.

Dean uncorked the aged Port, the deep burgundy liquid
cascading smoothly into three wide-bowled glasses.

He handed one to each woman, then held up his own.
"Okay—now for the wine nerd trick. Come over to the sink."

Lexi and Sophie exchanged amused glances but followed. The
underlighting from the counter cast a soft glow as Dean
demonstrated.
He placed his hand over the top of his glass, shook the glass up
and down, then lifted his hand dramatically and leaned in for a
deep inhale. "Your turn."

Lexi mirrored him, pressing her palm over her glass and shaking
the glass before removing her hand and dipping her nose into
the glass. Her eyes widened.

"Oh my god. I smell chocolate... toasted nuts... flowers... and old
wood?"

"Exactly," Dean said, a little pleased.

Sophie inhaled hers next and nodded, visibly impressed.

The Sirena Experience ♪11

Just then, Sirena chimed in over the ceiling speaker, her voice sultry with a hint of sass:
"He thinks he's that science guy on TV. Next, he's going to start talking molecular structure."

All three burst into laughter, the sound echoing lightly off the high ceilings.

Lexi leaned against the counter, glass in hand, watching Dean with something soft and quietly amused in her expression.

"You really are full of surprises."

Dean raised his glass, eyes on her.
"Only the good kind, I hope."

As soon as Dean announced the tour, Sirena's voice chimed in—smooth and teasing.

"Initiating guest experience: lighting set to 'Wow them,' and soundtrack queued."

The lights dimmed gradually, a gentle fade that bathed the penthouse in soft violets and electric pinks. Then the bass dropped—"Go Back" by John Summit pulsed through the hidden speakers, its driving beat syncing perfectly with the change in energy.

Sophie's eyes widened as the floors lit beneath them, subtle LED strips illuminating the path like a runway.

They moved through the main level first—glass walls that bent light like water, sculptural furniture, textures of polished stone and matte brass. Sirena matched the beat with bursts of ambient lighting that pulsed with every drop. She was clearly in full performance mode.

Dean leaned in with a grin. "She likes to show off when we have company."

"She's killing it," Sophie said, eyes sweeping across the space, camera-ready at every angle.

Sirena's voice purred through the sound system again. "Thank you, Sophie. I do accept compliments in the form of five-star reviews."

They laughed, stepping into the library-turned-music room. The mood shifted here—still moody and rhythmic, but tinged with intimacy.

Dean ran his fingers along the polished edge of the grand piano. "This is where I come when I can't sleep. Sirena plays backup."

"I can do jazz or Chopin, depending on your mood," she replied.

The tour crescendos as Dean guided them to the final stop.

Sirena dimmed the music. The air turned still. The sliding glass doors whispered open, revealing the pool deck.

Only the glow of the water lit the space, throwing soft ripples of blue and silver against the white stone. Above them, the sky was a deep ink-wash, pierced with stars. Below, downtown Miami shimmered—a live wire of gold light and glass reflections.

Sophie stepped out first, her voice barely a breath.
"Wow."

Dean stood beside her, arms crossed, watching her take it in.
"It's definitely a wow moment, isn't it?"

"And you see it every day," Sophie said, shaking her head.

Dean smiled, slow and proud. "And I still say wow every time."

They settled onto the low-slung outdoor sectional by the edge of the infinity pool, the cushions plush beneath them, the faint hum of the city mixing with the sound of water lapping gently against the tiles.

Dean placed the bottle of port and their glasses on the small glass table between them.

Sirena's voice softened to a whisper, the music fading into something slower, more ambient—a blend of house and jazz with a hypnotic rhythm that melted into the night.

"Privacy mode activated," she said. "You've got the sky, the sea, and no interruptions."

Lexi curled her legs beneath her, glass in hand, the wine catching the light like garnet. Sophie sank back into the cushions, her eyes never leaving the skyline.

"You live here," she said to Dean, almost in disbelief. "Like... actually live here?"

Dean grinned. "I do, but nights like this still feel unreal."

Lexi rested her head briefly against Dean's shoulder.
"I can see why you never leave."

He looked at her, the glow from the pool dancing in her eyes.
"Maybe now I have a reason to stay."

Sophie cleared her throat, smirking into her glass.
"Don't mind me. Just basking in the romantic tension."

Dean poured more port, letting the moment stretch, easy and warm.

"You're both welcome here anytime," he said, eyes on Lexi.
"But especially you."

Lexi didn't need to respond. The way she looked at him said everything.

Dean reclined, his arm draped along the edge of the sectional behind Lexi. He looked over at Sophie and said, "You know, there are a couple open bedrooms in the house... I know home is only ten minutes away, but—"

Sophie cut him off with a grin. "Do I get to choose which room?"

Dean chuckled, swirling the port in his glass. "Of course. Full guest privileges."

Lexi laughed lightly, tipping her glass toward Sophie. "Look at you, already moving in."

All three of them let out a slow, contented sigh, falling quiet as their eyes wandered back to the view.

The Three in the Pool

The pool light shimmered beneath the surface, casting ribbons of light on their skin. In the distance, the city blinked with life— gold and neon threading across the skyline, painting the dark with a quiet kind of electricity.

Dean's voice came low, almost like a confession, "Truth is... I don't come out here and sit much. I'm either on the road or locked in my office working deals. This—" he gestured to the scene around them, "—is the kind of thing I forget to appreciate."

Lexi looked over at him, her voice soft. "Well, you're appreciating it now."

"Yeah," he said, eyes on her. "Now I am."

Sophie smiled between sips of port. "Maybe you just needed the right company."

Lexi swirled the last sip of her port, then glanced over at Dean with a mischievous sparkle in her eye. "We went in the pool last night."

Sophie raised a brow. "Really?"

Lexi nodded, smirking. "In our underwear—at first."

Dean coughed into his glass, half-laughing. "You make it sound a lot more scandalous than it was."

"It was scandalous," Lexi teased, nudging him, "but also kind of perfect." She turned to Sophie. "We should totally jump in."

Sophie looked from Lexi to the pool and back again, a grin spreading across her face. "I mean, we are here…"

Dean leaned forward and pointed toward the door by the outdoor bar. "Bathroom is right there. Check the closet inside—there should be towels, a few swimsuits, maybe even robes."

"Your exes had great taste," Lexi quipped under her breath as she stood up, pulling Sophie with her by the hand.

Dean shook his head, still grinning. "I'll let you two browse the inventory. I'm going to change into something less 'host' and more 'off duty.'"

He disappeared into the house, heading to the master bedroom.

The soft music from Sirena still played in the background, the pool lights dancing like liquid sapphires across the surface. Lexi opened the bathroom door, and the scent of lavender and sandalwood drifted out like a soft invitation.

Sophie gave her a playful look. "So... what exactly happened in that pool last night?"

Lexi just laughed, stepping inside. "That," she said, "depends on how good your imagination is."

The pool deck was bathed in silver moonlight, the soft glow of the bar lights casting a warm halo across the sleek stone. The water shimmered like liquid sapphire, gently lapping at the edges as the night breeze carried the scent of salt, jasmine, and something distinctly summer.

Dean emerged from the house in a deep navy swimsuit, barefoot and casual. The cool air kissed his skin as he crossed the deck, the fabric of his towel draped over his shoulder. The world felt quiet out here, serene, except for the sound of soft giggles coming from the pool.

He couldn't see much at first—just the silhouettes of Lexi and Sophie, their heads resting side by side along the pool's edge, arms folded over the rim as they watched him like twin panthers in the shadows.

Lexi tilted her head, voice playful and perfectly timed.

"I think my dad has a swimsuit like that."

Sophie snorted, slapping the water lightly. "Stop!"

"No, seriously. Same color. Same weird cut." Lexi grinned.

"We're going shopping when you get back from your trip," she added sweetly, clearly pleased with herself.

Sophie chimed in without missing a beat. "Can you say *makeover*?"

They both burst into laughter, their voices dancing into the night air like music.

Dean smirked, pausing just before the pool's edge.

"Okay, okay... be nice to your host," he said, mock offended as he dropped his towel onto the barstool and stepped toward the water.

The pool welcomed him like a warm breath, folding around his frame as he eased in. He pushed off gently from the edge, gliding through the water.
His muscles loosened with the first pull, the tension of the day melting behind him.

The moonlit surface shimmered, silver kissing the bare shoulders of the two women ahead.

They moved toward him in the shallows—graceful, slow, like a tide closing in.
The scent of wine lingered in the air, faint and heady.

"You two always this dangerous after wine?" Dean asked, catching Lexi's gaze first, then Sophie's.

"Only when we're feeling bold," Sophie teased, smoothing her hair back with a wet hand.

Lexi tilted her head, her eyes gleaming. "And tonight? We're bold."

Dean looked more closely—and then he saw.
Their silhouettes were moon-carved, glistening. Clean of pretense. Bare.
Neither of them wore a thing.

Almost in unison, they stood taller in the water, letting their bare torsos crest the surface.
The water curved around them like velvet, licking at their skin like worship.
The sight knocked the breath from his lungs.

They looked at him with a playful command.
"You know what this means," Lexi said.

With a slow grin, Dean peeled off his swimsuit beneath the water
and tossed it to the edge.
The sudden exposure made his heart race—not from fear, but
from surrender.

Their laughter, soft and knowing, echoed off the tile.

Even Sirena giggled from her speaker mount above the patio.
"Consent acknowledged," she chimed with sass.

They circled him now—Sophie behind, Lexi in front, the water
rippling with anticipation.

Dean leaned into Lexi, catching her lips with his, his hands
resting lightly at her waist.
The kiss was warm, slow—testing the current before diving
deeper.

"Lexi... your hands feel incredible on me."

Lexi gave a slow smile. "That's not me," she whispered. "That's
Sophie. She's in need tonight."

Sophie's touch explored him beneath the water—slow, searching.
Her fingers spoke before her voice did, mapping every curve of
him.
"Lexi, don't make me sound desperate," she said, switching
places, pressing her back against Dean, guiding him into
alignment.

He felt her body surround him, warm and slick, and a gasp left
both their mouths at the same time.
The moment gripped them—weightless, but grounding.

Lexi climbed out and perched on the edge, legs dangling in the
water, eyes fixed on them with smoldering curiosity.
Her gaze didn't burn—it invited.

Sophie braced herself against the pool's edge, gripping the tile, her body rocking back against Dean's hips in a steady rhythm.

Dean moved closer to Lexi, kissing his way up her thigh.
"Lie back for me," he murmured.

Lexi reclined across the warm stone, opening to him completely. Her breath hitched—not from nerves, but from the rawness of being wanted.

Dean's mouth found her center, his tongue swirling with intent, tasting her heat.

Sophie moaned beneath the stars, her breath catching, her rhythm quickening.
Her hips moved with trust, not urgency.

Lexi arched into Dean's mouth, her fingers curling into the edge of the pool.
Each gasp from her lips fed the flame building in his chest.

The contrast—Lexi on his tongue, Sophie surrounding his length—nearly undid him.

Both women trembled on the verge, their gasps tangled in the air. Dean tried to hold back, his muscles tense, the pressure mounting.

And then—together.

A breathless surge of release rippled through all three. Sophie clutched the pool edge, her moans dissolving into whimpers.
Lexi cried out softly, pressing into Dean's mouth with abandon.
Dean shuddered between them, his groan low and guttural.

Stillness came like a tide rolling out.

They breathed together. Quiet. Spent.

Lexi reached down, brushing a damp lock from Dean's brow.
"Thank you for... that."

Dean looked at Sophie and kissed her shoulder. "No, thank you."

He glanced toward the patio. "Should we dry off and head to bed?"

Lexi and Sophie exchanged a glance. Lexi grinned.
"You know we're not ready to sleep."

Dean's mouth curved into a wicked smile.
"I didn't say anything about sleep."

They stepped from the water, droplets cascading down their skin.
Moonlight clung to them like silk.
They dried each other with thick towels, laughter rising again in the steamy hush of the night.

Inside, the master bedroom was cool and shadowed, silk sheets turned down like an invitation.

They fell into bed—Dean between them, the women's hands already roaming.
Every touch asked permission. Every breath gave it.

Lexi slid under the covers, her mouth finding him with heat and hunger. She turned, presenting herself to him in return.

Sophie mirrored her on the other side, and the rhythm resumed—mouths exploring, hands guiding, bodies rising and falling in quiet reverence.

There was no rush. No performance. Just presence.

The room filled with soft sighs, whispered names, breathless pleasure passed between them like a secret too good to keep.

Hours passed in waves—first soft, then bold—alternating between teasing strokes and deep connection.

When sleep finally claimed them, it was not from exhaustion alone, but from the weightlessness of being fully wanted, fully seen.

Wrapped together in tangled limbs and moonlight, they
surrendered—not just to each other, but to the night.
And for a while, nothing outside the walls of that room existed at
all.

Morning Departure

The soft Miami light crept in slowly, spilling across the king-size
bed in quiet gold. The sheets were tangled, the air still heavy
with the scent of skin, candle wax, and something deeper—
shared surrender.

Dean stirred first.

Lexi lay with her head on his chest, one leg hooked over his.
Sophie was curled along his back, her arm draped across his
waist, her breath warm on his shoulder.

The rhythm of their breathing echoed in sync, a silent aftereffect
of the night before. There was no rush. Just warmth, and the
quiet certainty of being wanted.

His hand traced lazy circles over Lexi's back, his body pleasantly
sore, a hum of satisfaction still echoing in his limbs.

Lexi blinked up at him. "Morning," she whispered, voice low and
raspy.

Sophie let out a groggy moan, pressing her lips to the dip
between Dean's shoulder blades. "Tell me we don't have to get
up."

Dean smiled. "We've got a plane to catch."

Lexi stretched, then propped herself up on one elbow. Her hair
was a golden mess, her lips still kissed raw. Her skin glowed with
that barely-there sheen of morning softness.

"Shower?"

Sophie slid out from under the covers, bare and unbothered. "I'll
get it started."

Her voice trailed off as she moved, hips swaying with the easy confidence of a woman who knew her power.

Steam was already curling from behind the frosted glass by the time they stepped into the oversized marble shower. The water was hot, cascading from the rainfall head like a tropical storm.

They slipped beneath it, arms brushing, laughter soft and unfiltered.

Lexi lathered her hands and swept them down Dean's back, while Sophie reached for his jaw, pulling him into a kiss.

He kissed her back slowly, savoring it.

Lexi pressed against his side, her lips grazing his collarbone, her fingertips drawing idle lines across his hip.

The moment held its breath—weightless, suspended somewhere between memory and desire.

The moment was light, teasing—not a full spark, but a warm afterglow.

Sophie nudged Lexi gently. "Your turn."

Lexi turned to face Dean, smiling as their lips met under the spray. His hands cradled her waist, pulling her closer, but she kept it brief—one long, lingering kiss before stepping back, water dripping from her lashes.

"We'll miss the flight," she whispered.

Dean chuckled. "You scheduled the car, remember?"

Lexi raised a brow. "Exactly."

They towel-dried side by side, trading soft touches and quiet grins, then drifted into the closet to get dressed.

Dean threw on a black fitted tee and charcoal joggers. Sophie tugged on a white linen button-down and no pants, because she could. Lexi dressed in a sleek black bodysuit with high-waisted denim shorts, hair still damp, slicked back effortlessly.

Sirena's voice chimed through the intercom.

"Car is waiting downstairs."

Dean grabbed his duffel, pausing to take in the view from the window—the shimmer of the bay, the skyline still stretching toward the morning sun.

For a moment, he let himself breathe it in. The quiet. The aftermath. The knowing that something rare had passed through the night.

He felt Lexi move beside him, her hand slipping into his.

Sophie stood just behind them, arms crossed loosely, smiling.

Lexi leaned in. "Don't ghost us from the clouds."

"I won't," Dean said, brushing her lips one last time. Then Sophie's.

They headed for the elevator together, bodies still humming from the night before, not quite ready to let go.

But the city was already calling.

And the sky was waiting.

Outside the terminal, Lexi stepped out and pulled Dean into a lingering hug. She stood on her tiptoes to kiss him—soft, slow, sweet.

"Text me when you land," she said.

"Only if you promise to send me a selfie in that shirt later," he smirked.

Lexi rolled her eyes but smiled, stepping back as he disappeared through the sliding glass doors.

Back in the car, Sophie glanced over.

"So... is it too early to say I approve?"

Lexi looked out at the rising sun, her lips curving faintly.

"It's not too early. It's just... the beginning."

ROD K

SPICY NEW WEEK

Dean's Flight

As Dean's flight pulled away from the gate in Miami, heading to
Austin, he texted Lexi that his flight was about to take off for
Austin. She responded, and so Dean wouldn't forget her, she
sent him a picture of her in the nude, saying, "already missing
you."

The memory of the weekend made him grin. As he thought back
about the prior weekend with Lexi—and then with her and
Sofie—it couldn't have been wilder, reminding him of the twins
in Tulum.

But now, it was back to business. As the plane took off, Dean
tried to remain focused on his week and all the things he needed
to accomplish.

Trey was picking him up at the airport— rather, his driver was
picking him up and Trey would already be in the SUV. Dean was
glad this was the first deal of the week. He was rested after the
weekend, his mind was clear, and he would be able to grasp all
the special details of this company.

If this meeting had landed later in the week, he would have just
been going through the motions, not giving the deal his full
attention. Trey had sent him the prospectus, the financials, and
projections.

Even if the deal went south, he and Trey would still possess the controlling interest and patents for the chip.

At cruising altitude— 35,000 feet—the seatbelt sign flickered off. Dean unbuckled and opened his laptop. The soft hum of the engines provided a background rhythm as he settled into his seat, ready to sift through the emails that had accumulated since taking off from Miami.

Traveling had its perks, but staying ahead of the inbox was an endless battle.

One email stood out immediately. Sitting in bold at the top of his inbox was the report he'd been waiting for. It was from Hiroshi Hashimoto—the semiconductor wizard with decades of experience at Intel and AMD. A man whose insights had often been the difference between good investments and great ones.

Dean clicked on the email, eager to see what Hashimoto had uncovered.

As he scrolled through the detailed analysis, Dean's eyes narrowed, and a faint smile tugged at the corners of his lips. Hashimoto had confirmed what Dean had already suspected— Austin Quantum Systems wasn't just developing an advanced chip; they were sitting on a potential goldmine.

Hashimoto's report went deeper than expected. It outlined how the client had severely underestimated the chip's market potential. Not only was the technology ahead of its time, but the applications extended far beyond the initial scope AQS had envisioned.

Dean began tapping his fingers thoughtfully on the armrest. The information was dynamite—but it came with complications.

He could share it with Trey, of course—his best friend and the one who had brought him into the deal in the first place. But beyond that, discretion was critical.

Letting the client know what Hashimoto had uncovered could shift the dynamics of the negotiation entirely. And that was a risk Dean wasn't willing to take.

He forwarded the report to Jennings with a quick note:
"This changes everything. Let's discuss before the meeting."

He also copied Trey on the email and added a follow-up text to both men, ensuring they'd review it before they landed.

Dean's thoughts shifted to Jacob Weiss, a member of Jennings's team and the mastermind behind the recent IP acquisitions that had subtly shifted the playing field in their favor.

Hashimoto's report would need to be cross-referenced with Jacob's findings to ensure their strategy remained airtight.

Dean scheduled a quick pre-meeting with Jennings, Trey, and Jacob, determined to finalize their approach before sitting down with the AQS founders.

Dean already had the numbers from Jacob, as did Jennings. That left only the surprise for Trey. It would be the biggest surprise to AQS when the truth was finally revealed.

He shut the laptop and stared out the window at the patchwork of clouds stretching endlessly beneath the plane. The excitement of the deal buzzed beneath his skin, but his mind was already calculating the moves ahead.

There was a lot riding on this meeting, and he was determined to walk away with not just a seat at the table but a definitive advantage.

The flight attendant passed by offering drinks, but Dean politely declined. He needed a clear head for this.

Closing his laptop, he reclined slightly in his seat, letting his mind run through the possibilities.

By the time they landed in Austin, every detail would be accounted for, and every angle would have a plan. Dean didn't play games he didn't intend to win.

And the truth was— everyone would be a winner today, including the founders of AQS.

Austin Quantum Systems Chip: QuantumLogic X900

The **QuantumLogic X900** is Austin Quantum Systems' answer to the NovaEdge Q7000. Designed for next-generation AI and quantum-enhanced hybrid computing, the X900 is poised to dominate the market with its early release, advanced performance, and broad industrial applicability. With full production slated for 2027, **QuantumLogic X900** will outpace NovaEdge by a full three years, seizing significant early market share.

QuantumLogic X900: Specifications

Feature	QuantumLogic X900
Architecture	Hybrid Classical-Quantum Chip
Performance	15x faster AI training vs current-gen chips
Quantum Processing Units (QPUs)	300 QPU nodes with embedded error correction
Energy Efficiency	85% improvement over existing processors
AI Optimization	Real-time analytics and accelerated training for ML
Quantum Error Correction	Industry-leading reliability for complex calculations
Security	Post-quantum cryptographic protections
Applications	Autonomous vehicles, NLP, cybersecurity, robotics, and AR/VR

Market Potential for QuantumLogic X900

- **Market Readiness Advantage:** With production starting in 2027, the X900 will capture early adopters in industries demanding cutting-edge solutions, giving AQS a **first-mover advantage** over the NovaEdge Q7000, which is not expected to hit the market until 2030.

- **Projected Market Share:**
  AQS could claim **30–40% of the addressable market** by the time NovaEdge launches, positioning the QuantumLogic X900 as the dominant choice for industries needing AI optimization and quantum processing.

- **Industries Targeted:**
  - **AI and Machine Learning:** Revolutionizing $1.8 trillion in AI-driven markets.
  - **Cybersecurity:** Providing quantum-resistant encryption for a $403 billion market.
  - **Autonomous Vehicles:** Accelerating growth in a $615 billion industry.
  - **AR/VR and Gaming:** Enhancing real-time rendering in the $1+ trillion immersive tech space.

- **Revenue Forecast:**
  - **2027 (Launch Year):** $5 billion
  - **2028:** $15 billion
  - **2029:** $30 billion
  - **2030:** $50 billion
    Total 4-Year Revenue (2027–2030): $100 billion

By 2030, **QuantumLogic X900** is projected to unlock a market potential of **$200+ billion**, rivaling NovaEdge Q7000 while maintaining a leadership position through innovation, partnerships, and first-to-market advantages.

Competitive Edge of QuantumLogic X900

1. **First-Mover Advantage:** Launching three years earlier than NovaEdge Q7000, the X900 captures early market share in rapidly growing industries.

2. **Better AI Performance:** With 15x AI training speed and 300 QPU nodes, the X900 slightly edges out NovaEdge in performance metrics.

3. **Energy Efficiency:** Its 85% efficiency improvement appeals to industries focused on sustainability, making it an attractive choice for eco-conscious markets.

4. **Broad Industrial Applications:** By serving diverse industries, from AI and autonomous vehicles to AR/VR and cybersecurity, the X900 ensures high demand across multiple sectors.

4. Equity Interest

Your equity interest is calculated as your investment divided by the post-money valuation:

$$\text{Equity Interest} = \frac{\text{Investment}}{\text{Post-Money Valuation}}$$

$$\text{Equity Interest} = \frac{\$5M}{\$10M} = 50\%$$

Result:

If the pre-money valuation is $5M and you invest $5M, you would own **50% of the company**.

Scenario Analysis

To account for different valuations:

Pre-Money Valuation	Post-Money Valuation	Your Equity Interest
$4M	$9M	55.56%
$5M	$10M	50.00%
$6M	$11M	45.45%
$7M	$12M	41.67%

3. Impact on Valuation

Owning the IP rights drastically lowers AQS's valuation without your cooperation. Here's how:

Before You Own the IP

- **Pre-Money Valuation:** $5M (assumed based on progress and existing patents).
- **Post-Money Valuation:** $10M (if you invest $5M).

After You Own the IP

- **Pre-Money Valuation:** Drops significantly because their patents and technology cannot function without your IP. Assume a new **pre-money valuation of $1M–$2M**.
- **Post-Money Valuation:** $6M–$7M after your $5M investment.

Your equity stake is recalculated as:

$$\text{Equity Stake} = \frac{\text{Investment}}{\text{Post-Money Valuation}}$$

- **At $1M pre-money valuation:**

$$\text{Post-Money Valuation} = 1M + 5M = 6M \quad \text{and} \quad \text{Equity Stake} = \frac{5M}{6M} = 83.33\%$$

- **At $2M pre-money valuation:**

$$\text{Post-Money Valuation} = 2M + 5M = 7M \quad \text{and} \quad \text{Equity Stake} = \frac{5M}{7M} = 71.43\%$$

Jennings Law Office

Before the meeting with AQS, Dean, Trey, and Jennings met to discuss the equity agreement, the IP agreement, and the royalties agreement with Jacob, in Jennings' law office.

The blinds were drawn against the harsh afternoon sun, casting soft shadows across the polished conference table. A stack of documents sat between them, thick with legal weight.

Dean leaned forward, his elbows on the table, eyes scanning the fine print with practiced calm.

Trey flipped through the IP agreement, nodding slowly. "This is cleaner than I expected."

Jennings gave a small, approving smile. "Jacob's team wanted it bulletproof."

There was a hum of quiet tension in the room—the kind that comes before a major shift.

Dean tapped a pen against the table, thoughtful. "Let's make sure it's not just clean—it needs to be airtight. This deal changes everything."

The room fell into a contemplative silence, the kind that comes when even words start to feel expensive. Dean stood first, buttoning his jacket with that deliberate calm he always wore before high-stakes meetings.

"Let's move," he said. "They'll be expecting us."

Trey gathered the documents while Jennings double-checked the digital copies already shared to the AQS legal team. The three of them moved with unspoken rhythm—no wasted motion, no nerves. Just a forward press.

Outside, the late-afternoon light had mellowed, the city stretching in golds and glass. Their black SUV waited curbside.

As they pulled away from the curb, Dean glanced at the skyline. He wasn't thinking about money. Not entirely. This was about control. Legacy. The kind of leverage you didn't build overnight.

Austin Quantum Systems

The meeting took place in AQS's sprawling, high-gloss conference room. The walls were lined with framed photos of their cutting-edge quantum chips. A sleek glass table stretched the length of the room, polished to perfection.

At the head of the table sat Rex Henderson, co-founder, all smiles and sharp edges. His partner, Kenji Nakamura, was more reserved—his hands clasped tightly, fingers interlocked as if holding something in place.

Dean, Trey, and Jennings took their seats opposite them. They were joined by their attorney, Samuel Pennington, sharp-dressed and sharp-witted.

Samuel grinned as they settled in. "I see you guys brought the big guns today," he said, nodding toward Jennings.

Jennings gave a small smile, his voice calm and measured. "Dean's father and I go way back. He was my best friend—and the best damn soldier I ever knew. When he passed, I promised

I'd look after his family. That includes making sure Dean here doesn't get taken for a ride."

Samuel's smirk faded. "Of course. My apologies. And Dean, my condolences."

Dean nodded politely, his expression composed. Inside, Jennings' words stirred something old—a familiar, buried ache.

He rarely talked about his father in business settings. Jennings knew that. But sometimes, the past had its place.

The formality didn't last.

Contracts were handed out. Pens uncapped. The energy in the room shifted to something more transactional.

Dean sat quiet, letting the others lead. His eyes moved between Rex and Kenji—reading their tells. Rex's grin widened as the last page was signed. Kenji exhaled, his shoulders finally lowering.

Then the phone beside Rex buzzed, the vibration sharp against the polished table.

He glanced down.

The display read "Reception – Front Desk." Quietly, he picked it up and pressed it to his ear.

"There's a process server here for one of the founders," the receptionist said, her voice low and discreet.

Rex's fingers tightened around the receiver. His jaw barely shifted, but his eyes flicked toward the conference room glass wall—cool and unreadable.

He didn't respond right away.

The meeting carried on without noticing, unaware that something outside the room had just shifted

Rex frowned, waving a hand. "Fine. Send him in."

Trey raised an eyebrow at Dean but said nothing. Jennings smoothed the line of his tie. The move was timed. Precisely.

The server stepped in, dropped the envelope, and left.

Rex opened it—his expression darkening.

"This is a notice from Technology Ventures," he said flatly. "They're claiming we're infringing on their IP."

Dean's phone buzzed beneath the table. A single message from Jennings:
Showtime.

Without a word, Jennings reached into his briefcase and pulled out six neatly bound documents. He placed one in front of each person at the table.

"Here's the updated agreement," Jennings said, voice almost casual. "Including the royalty schedule and equity dilution under the new terms with Technology Ventures."

Silence.

Rex and Kenji stared down at the contracts.

Rex's fingers gripped the edge of the table. His knuckles paled. His mouth opened, closed, then opened again.

Nothing came out.

Beside him, Kenji flipped pages. His hand trembled slightly as he reached the royalty schedule. A bead of sweat slid down his temple.

"This... this is..." Kenji's voice trailed off. His eyes found Rex.

Jennings crossed one leg over the other, perfectly composed.

"This is the reality of the situation," he said evenly. "Technology Ventures now controls the secondary patents for your chip's manufacturing processes. These agreements ensure compliance—and ensure your product goes to market."

His voice was smooth, but the weight behind it was undeniable.

Rex slammed his palm on the table, composure cracking.

"This changes everything!" he barked. "You're siphoning off a massive chunk of our revenue!"

Trey leaned forward, tone calm but firm.

"It's better than having the entire product pulled off the market, Rex. We all knew this was a risk."

The room pulsed with quiet tension—a standoff of egos, pride, and cold business sense.

Dean, who had remained silent, finally spoke. His voice was calm, steady.

"Rex. Kenji. Turn to the next section."

They hesitated—then flipped the page.

Kenji's eyes widened. His brow furrowed in confusion, then disbelief.

"What... what is this about a SPAC?"

The word lit the room like a fuse.

Jennings gave a faint smile.

"Technology Ventures is taking Austin Quantum public. A SPAC deal. By the end of the month, AQS will trade on the NASDAQ under the ticker AQSQ. Valuation: five billion."

The silence was seismic.

Trey tilted his chair back, grinning. "Looks like you two are about to become billionaires."

Rex blinked. "Billionaires?"

Dean nodded. "Once the merger finalizes, your shares will be worth $1.25 billion each."

The moment hung.

Then it landed.

Kenji leaned forward. "I don't even know what to say."

"Say thank you," Trey said. "And sign the damn documents."

Laughter broke through—the tension finally breaking.

The men leaned over the table, signing pages with renewed energy. Dean and Trey exchanged a glance. Jennings looked on, serene.

When the last pen lifted, Jennings cleared his throat.

"One last detail."

He opened his briefcase again, pulling out another envelope.

"This contains the royalty disbursement schedule. Jacob Weiss will receive a share alongside Dean."

Rex's eyebrow rose. "How much?"

"Fifty million," Jennings replied. Like he was naming a lunch order.

Kenji gave a low whistle. "That's... generous."

Dean leaned forward. "Jacob's the reason we could negotiate this SPAC. He earned every cent."

Rex nodded slowly. "Fair enough."

Jennings passed around glasses. Trey popped the champagne.

They toasted.

Dean stepped back, watching the skyline through the window.

Victory never looked this quiet. This earned.

Vince's Prime – the Celebration Begins

The restaurant was a haven of warm lighting and rich mahogany, the kind of place where deals were sealed over thick steaks and fine wine.

Soft amber sconces glowed against the wood-paneled walls, casting golden light that flickered over white linen and fine crystal. The clink of cutlery echoed gently beneath the low hum of soft music drifting in from the main dining room.

Trey had already arrived with his wife, Melanie, a graceful redhead who immediately hugged Dean when he walked in. She was old money in designer heels—Houston oil, debutante through and through. Hers and Trey's marriage was as big as any Wall Street oil company merger.

Her scent wrapped around him—jasmine and something deeper, like gardenia soaked in rain. It was signature Melanie: elegance laced with memory.

"It's about time you boys wrapped up whatever magic you were working in that boardroom," Melanie teased.

Trey grinned. "Magic? Try blood, sweat, and a few well-placed patent filings. But yeah, it was magic." He reached for her hand under the table.

The movement was instinctive, the kind of gesture long-married couples made without thinking. His thumb traced small circles on the inside of her wrist—a grounding spell in the form of touch.

Dean laughed as Melanie turned to Jennings. "And, of course, the wizard behind it all. Jennings, it's so good to see you."

Jennings tipped an imaginary hat. "Always a pleasure, Melanie. And Trey's exaggerating. It was a team effort."

His gaze lingered on her a moment longer than expected—warm, unguarded, like the low embers of a fire just stoked.

The group settled into a private dining room, complete with white tablecloths and a sprawling view of downtown Austin through floor-to-ceiling windows.

The last brushstrokes of sunset streaked across the skyline, reflected in the glass like gold ink on black parchment.

A faint aroma of truffle butter and oak-aged wine hovered in the air. The table buzzed with energy—not just celebration, but completion. The air vibrated with something quieter too: gratitude, and the ache of time passing.

Dean excused himself, stepping into the hallway. As he pulled out his phone, the cold screen against his palm was grounding. He dialed.

"Hi, this is Dean Harrington. I'd like to arrange a pick-up for my mom, Sandy Harrington..."

As he spoke, his eyes caught on the celebrity photos along the entrance wall. Black-and-white legends mid-toast, frozen in moments that had clearly mattered. Tonight, he wanted that for his mom. Not the fame—but the feeling.

Memory bloomed in his chest like heat from an ember: her standing in the rain during his first pitch, soaked but smiling. Her hands clapping, her voice shouting his name louder than anyone's. That kind of love deserved a front-row seat tonight.

He returned to the table as the main course arrived.

"Where'd you sneak off to?" Trey asked.

Dean smirked. "Just adding a little surprise to the evening. You'll see."

Jennings stood, lifting his glass. "To the future of Austin Quantum Systems..."

His voice carried the quiet thunder of earned respect. It wasn't just a toast—it was an invocation. A calling forth of everything they'd built and everyone who'd held them upright along the way.

As the final clinks echoed, the door to the dining room opened. Sandy Harrington stepped in.

Her navy dress shimmered as though stitched from dusk itself. The way she held herself—calm, poised—commanded reverence without effort.

"Mom!" Dean stood, his chair scraping softly against the hardwood.

He embraced her tightly.

His breath hitched just a little at her familiar warmth. She smelled like lavender and lemon zest and Sunday mornings. Like home.

"Dean, what's all this?" Sandy asked.

"Big deal today. Thought you'd like to be part of it."

Introductions were made, and as Sandy settled into her seat, a hush seemed to ripple across the group—a collective sense that something significant had just clicked into place.

Thirty minutes later, the scene reached its emotional zenith.

Jennings cleared his throat, his voice quieter now.

"I just wanted to take a moment to say something..."

Everyone stilled. The hum of background jazz seemed to fade away.

He looked first at Dean.

"You've grown into a man your father would have been so proud of..."

Dean's chest constricted. He blinked. Once. Twice. The sting behind his eyes didn't retreat.

Jennings turned to Sandy.

"And you, Sandy…" His voice dipped, husky now, and full of weight. "When Rebecca passed, the world tilted."

His fingers twitched at his side, as though remembering how empty his hands had felt back then.

"But you steadied me," he said, eyes locking on hers. "Like you always did."

He hesitated—just a breath—but the next words came softer, more personal.

"And like I did for you when Frank passed."

She reached across the linen-draped table, hand brushing his. That single gesture echoed louder than any declaration.

Jennings stood. The room tensed.

From his jacket, he drew a small velvet box.

Gasps. A soft intake of breath. Melanie's hand flew to her mouth.

"Sandy... will you marry me?"

The air cracked open with silence. Then joy. Then tears.

"Yes, of course, Jennings!"

This wasn't just a proposal. It was a resurrection. A renewal.

Jennings turned, smiling wryly. "Looks like you're stuck with me as your stepdad."

Dean laughed. "Wouldn't have it any other way."

Sandy leaned close to Jennings. "You've made this the happiest day of my life."

He answered softly, "And you've given me hope for the rest of mine."

Their fingers interlaced on the table. Roots, finally grounded again.

Dean sprawled out, gaze sweeping over the room.

The deal was the reason they gathered, but this—this was the reward. Family. Forgiveness. Future.

He raised his glass. Not for a speech. Just a quiet lift. A nod.

To the unseen things that built this night: loss, love, legacy.

No ledger could ever hold this kind of wealth.

The End of Fabulous Evening

As the evening began to wind down, the golden candlelight dimmed to a flicker, like the final applause of a theater's curtain call. Wine glasses stood half-full, conversations had softened to a warm hum, and the private dining room glowed with the kind of quiet that only comes after something meaningful has ended—well.

Dean stood by the entrance, shaking hands and exchanging farewells with the founders of Austin Quantum Systems. The crisp brush of wool suit sleeves, the firm grip of gratitude-laced handshakes—it all grounded him in the moment.

Rex, still buzzing from the IPO announcement, clasped Dean's hand. "You've changed our lives," he said, his voice thick with emotion.

Kenji added, "And not just ours—what we're building will change the world. Thank you for believing in us."

Dean smiled. "The hard work was yours. We just gave it a platform."

The words landed with weight. Not performative. Just true. The kind of truth you didn't need to dress up.

Trey walked them to the door, leaving Dean briefly alone. His phone buzzed.

He glanced at the screen, then answered. "Have the hostess bring you to the Travis dining room," he said, voice low but edged with excitement.

That spark—the one he only got when something bigger than business was about to unfold—lit in his chest. Like flint striking steel.

If you were a native Texan, you couldn't hear the name William B. Travis without thinking of the Alamo.

And this room, with its glass walls and timeless oak, had its own kind of battlefield beauty. It had witnessed grit, loyalty, and a line drawn in metaphorical sand.

Dean scanned the hallway. A moment later, a well-dressed Japanese gentleman appeared.

Hiroshi moved like water over polished stone—deliberate, elegant, self-contained.

Their eyes met. A subtle smile crept across Hiroshi's face as he extended his hand.

"Hiroshi," Dean greeted warmly, shaking his hand. "It's good to see you again."

"And you as well, Dean," Hiroshi Hashimoto replied, his accent infusing his words with melodic clarity.

The private room, once humming, stilled slightly. A hush of instinct. The air seemed to part around him like it knew a legacy had just entered.

Dean led Hiroshi inside, closing the door behind them. He turned toward the table, his voice cutting through the quiet.

"Ladies and gentlemen," he said, tone low but rich with meaning. "I want you all to meet the man of the hour. This is Hiroshi Hashimoto."

Heads turned. Eyes sharpened. The kind of gaze you gave a person whose name would one day be on buildings.

Hiroshi bowed slightly, pride etched in restraint. Dean caught Jennings's eye across the room.

Without a word, Jennings stood.

The shift was immediate—like a general rising.

He crossed the room with a purposeful stride and extended his hand.

"Hiroshi, I'm Jennings Burnett. It's an honor to finally meet you in person."

"The honor is mine," Hiroshi replied, their handshake firm— quiet power meeting its mirror.

Jennings reached into his coat, withdrawing a crisp envelope.

"I believe this is yours."

Hiroshi bowed in gratitude, then opened it.

His eyes widened. The weight of seven digits written in ink hit like a silent drumbeat.

Inside was a cashier's check for $1 million.

He looked up, eyes shimmering slightly under the candlelight.

Dean, leaning casually against a chair, offered a smile. "It's a little more than the $100,000 we originally discussed. But you earned every bit. Jennings will fill you in on your stock options and your board seat."

A pulse of approval rippled around the table. No words needed. A collective knowing. He belonged.

Hiroshi chuckled, folding the envelope and slipping it into his pocket. "It seems I have much to be thankful for this evening."

Dean grinned. "Shame AMD or Intel didn't realize your worth."

Hiroshi's smile grew wider, eyes twinkling. "As the saying goes, 'He who laughs last, laughs loudest.'"

It hit the room like a perfect note. Humor and truth, laced with vindication.

Laughter erupted. Glasses lifted. Hiroshi took his seat as the group toasted.

Dean looked around. At Hiroshi, now fully part of the family. At his mother, proud and glowing. At Jennings, the man who had kept a promise made long ago.

The past had returned not to haunt them—but to honor them.

He exhaled, the weight of the day finally lightening. Legacy, it turned out, wasn't something you left behind. It was something you built beside the people who believed in you.

Sandy caught Dean's eye and patted the seat beside her.

A mother's summon—silent, unmistakable. The kind that never needed explaining.

Dean smiled. "Alright, I'm coming."

He crossed the room, each step slower now, like the celebration had gently exhaled its last breath.

She took his hand in hers.

"Dean," she said, warmth threading every word. "I know you've probably booked yourself into one of those fancy hotels downtown, but I sure would like for you to stay at home with me."

Dean sank into his chair, grin tugging at the corners of his mouth.

The house. The creaky stairs. The way the kitchen still smelled like lemon Pledge and toast.

"Sounds good, Mom. Could use a home-cooked breakfast."

She chuckled. "You haven't changed one bit."

Jennings chimed in, "Better enjoy it while you can. Nothing like your mom's cooking."

Sandy swatted at him, cheeks pink. "Oh, stop it, Jennings."

But her smile said don't stop. Her heart, clearly, already hadn't. Dean let the moment stretch.

It wrapped around him—the people, the past, the peace—and it felt like being ten again, barefoot in the backyard under Texas stars.

The hostess approached with the check. Before Dean could reach for it, Trey and Jennings both moved.

"No, give me the check," Trey said, half-serious.

Jennings waved her toward him. "Ignore him. I've got it."

Dean laughed, sliding his Amex across the table. "Don't listen to them. I've got this."

It wasn't grandstanding. It was gratitude—quiet, habitual, human.

Fifteen minutes later, the hostess returned. As Dean signed, he looked up. "How much of the tip actually goes to you?"

She blinked. "Uh, about a third."

Dean glanced at Trey and Jennings. "Alright, boys. Only Benjamins." They grinned, pulling out stacks. Five thousand in hundreds.

Dean handed it over. "Just for you. Nobody else." The weight of the money was nothing. But the weight of the moment? Everything.

Tears filled her eyes. "Thank you. Thank you so much." They each gave her a business card.

"If you're looking for an internship," Dean added with a wink, "give us a call."

She nodded, clutching it all like a lifeline. They hadn't handed her cash. They'd handed her permission to dream.

Outside, the night air was cool. Hints of cedar smoke and barbecue floated in from the corner pit house, familiar as breath.

Jennings turned to Dean. "I'll drop you at your mom's. Your suitcase is still in my trunk."

Dean grinned. "Guess that settles it."

Jennings handed the valet his ticket. Sandy smiled beside him. They got into Jennings's car. The ride was quiet.

Not the silence of absence—but of fullness. The kind of silence that only happens when there's nothing left to prove.

They pulled up to the brick house.

"Thank you for the ride, Jennings," Sandy said as they stepped out.

"Goodnight, Sandy. Goodnight, Dean."

Jennings stayed a moment longer, watching them walk to the door. Like any Texas gentleman.

COMING HOME TO TEXAS

Cedarwood and Lavender

Dean waved as Jennings drove off, then turned to follow his mom up the driveway. The sound of the car faded behind him, swallowed by the quiet hum of cicadas and the soft crunch of gravel underfoot.

As Sandy reached the front door, she smiled back at him. "Your room's exactly the way you left it," she said, fishing out her keys. "I haven't changed a thing."

Dean chuckled. "I hope that doesn't include my old posters of the Dallas Cowboys and Pearl Jam."

"It absolutely does," she said with a laugh, unlocking the door. "You think I'd take down history?"

They stepped inside, and a wave of nostalgia washed over him—so strong it nearly stopped him mid-step.
The scent hit first. Cedarwood and lavender. It hadn't changed a bit. The kind of scent that didn't just linger—it lived in the walls.

Dean dropped his suitcase by the stairs and glanced around, eyes scanning the familiar corners. The framed family photos. The chipped ceramic owl on the side table. The same quilted runner on the dining room buffet.

It was like stepping into a paused memory.

They stayed up for a while, sinking into the living room couch as if no time had passed. Sandy talked about the neighbors, her garden, and the leaky faucet she'd finally fixed herself. Her voice was animated, full of energy that only came from being in your own element.

Eventually, Sandy stood and stretched, her bones cracking slightly as she reached overhead.
"Alright, sweetheart, I'm heading to bed. Sleep well, okay?"

Dean kissed her cheek. "Goodnight, Mom."

He made his way upstairs, trailing his fingers along the wooden banister like he used to as a kid. When he stepped into his old room, he paused at the threshold.

Nothing had changed.

The faint scent of pine still clung to the wooden furniture. His old desk sat beneath the window, stacked with paperbacks and worn notebooks. The cowboy hat from high school still hung on the doorknob. And there it was—the Dallas Cowboys poster, edges curled slightly, taped right where he'd left it.

Dean let out a quiet laugh and sat on the edge of the bed. It creaked the same way it always had.

A moment later, he slid under the familiar quilt and lay back against the pillows. For the first time in what felt like years, he slept without dreaming.

Breakfast

The next morning, Dean stirred beneath the weight of layered sunlight and the faint aroma of sizzling bacon curling through the air like a memory.

For a moment, he didn't move—just lay there, listening.

Somewhere down the hall, he heard the low creak of a cupboard, the clink of ceramic on countertop. And then—her voice. Soft, melodic, humming a tune that wrapped around him like a blanket.

Time folded inward, and for a moment, he felt like a boy again—safe, unseen, suspended in the in-between of sleep and waking.

"She still sings in the mornings." The thought made his throat tighten unexpectedly.

A beat later:

"Daisy, do you need to go out?" Sandy's voice again, light and warm.

Dean smiled, picturing the family's golden retriever—older now, greyer around the muzzle, but still faithfully padding through their lives. Daisy had been just a puppy when he left for college. Now, at nine, her pace had slowed but her spirit still pulsed bright.

The hallway floor felt cool against his bare feet as he rose, the rhythm of the house familiar in his bones—the uneven squeak of the second stair, the way the kitchen light spilled in wide golden slats across the wood.

His hand skimmed the railing, fingertips grazing worn lacquer that felt like memory made solid.

This was home. Not a structure of brick and beams, but a symphony of smells and sounds, of memories still breathing in the walls.

Dean stepped into the kitchen.

Sunlight streamed through the windows, turning motes of dust into floating gold. The scent hit him full-on now—bacon crisping in the pan, coffee earthy and rich, a hint of maple dancing somewhere in the background.

Sandy stood at the stove, a floral apron tied at her waist, the hem swaying gently as she moved. Her hum carried a gentle confidence, the sound of someone entirely in her element.

"Good morning, sleepyhead," she called, without turning. Her tone was a smile all on its own.

Dean leaned against the doorway, arms crossed, soaking her in like a moment he'd forgotten to miss. "Good morning, Mom. I forgot how much you love to sing in the mornings."

She glanced over her shoulder, arching a brow. "And I forgot how much you love to sleep when you're home."

He chuckled, moving to the counter and pouring himself a cup of coffee. The scent hugged his senses—bold, slightly nutty, nostalgic.

"Peet's House Blend?"

"You know it," Sandy said, sliding a strip of bacon onto a paper towel-lined plate with elegant precision. "You taught me well. I even grind my own beans now. Keeps me feeling fancy."

Dean sat at the table, coffee in hand, watching her. "You're the fanciest woman I know, Mom."

She gave him a sideways glance, playful, but there was pride behind it too. The kind that blooms slowly in a mother's chest when the past and present sit together like this.

She brought over scrambled eggs—fluffy and bright—and followed with a platter of pancakes that steamed gently in the cool morning air.

By the back door, Daisy's tail thumped the floor like a soft drumbeat.

"Daisy!" Dean said, warmth rising in his voice.

The retriever roused, loping over to him in slow but joyful strides. He crouched to greet her, her fur still velvety behind the ears, her gaze loyal and full of something that hadn't changed.

"You've been holding down the fort, huh?"

"She's spoiled rotten," Sandy chimed in, setting down a bowl of fresh berries beside his plate. "She practically runs the house now."

Dean grinned. "Sounds about right."

Then he noticed it: the table set exactly as he used to love it— maple syrup, whipped cream, and a little bowl of pecans. It hit him in the gut.

"Wow," he murmured. "You really went all out."

"Well, I don't get to cook for you very often," she said softly, sitting down with her own cup of coffee. "I wanted to make it special."

And just like that, the air thickened with unspoken gratitude.

"You always do, Mom."

They ate slowly, laughter and conversation winding around bites of buttery pancake and the occasional sip of coffee. Sandy asked about his work, his travels—and, of course, his love life.

"So, any special ladies in your life?" she asked, her voice innocent but her eyes sharp as ever.

Dean smirked. "You've been talking to Mrs. Kershaw again, haven't you?"

Sandy raised her hands like a priestess caught with incense. "Guilty. But can you blame her? She wants to know when her favorite neighbor boy is going to settle down."

Dean chuckled, shaking his head. "Tell her I'm doing just fine."

Sandy studied him, her expression softening. "You are doing fine. Better than fine. I'm proud of you, Dean."

Something in him stilled. The words struck deeper than he let on.

"Thanks, Mom. That means a lot."

They lingered at the table, basking in the quiet rhythm of the morning. Sandy shared garden stories and Daisy's latest exploits—how she stole a zucchini off the counter, how she chased a butterfly like she was still two.

When Dean offered to help clear the table, she waved him off with a firm hand. "You're my guest."

He sat back, coffee warm in his palm, and watched her move through the kitchen like she was dancing with memory. The air still smelled like maple and sunshine.

Then she turned, towel in hand, that mischievous spark returning. "So, what's on the agenda today, Mr. Big Shot Investor?"

Dean laughed. "Meetings, maybe. But honestly? I think I'll spend most of the day right here."

"Well then," she said with mock-seriousness, "I'll make sure Daisy doesn't steal your spot on the couch."

Dean stood, walking over to her, wrapping his arm gently around her shoulders. "Thanks, Mom. For everything."

She looked up at him, eyes full of love. "Anytime, sweetheart."

But then the tone shifted—like the turning of a page.

"You know what, Mom?" Dean said, settling back into his chair, voice lower now.

Sandy paused, sensing the change. "What's that, sweetheart?"

"I think I'll stay a little longer. Maybe through the weekend. I don't come home enough... and there's nothing more important than this."

Something in Sandy's face flickered—surprise, then warmth, then something almost like relief. She came over, resting her hand on his shoulder.

"That means the world to me, Dean."

He reached up and squeezed her hand. "Actually... I wanted to ask about you and Jennings. What's the plan? Are you keeping the house?"

Sandy exhaled, sitting down again. Her voice dropped an octave.

"We've talked. Jennings has a beautiful place. But this house..." Her gaze swept the room. "It's where your dad and I made a life. I'm not ready to let go of that. Not yet."

Dean nodded slowly, understanding. "Whatever you decide, I'm here. Pack it up or protect it—I've got you."

She smiled. "I know you do."

Then she tilted her head, eyes narrowing slightly. "But what about you? You're running full tilt all the time. Do you even know what you want anymore?"

Dean's smile faded. "I'll figure it out. Right now, you and Jennings are what matter."

Sandy let the silence stretch a moment, then gently shifted gears. "Speaking of the past..."

She leaned in, voice lighter but edged with intent. "You haven't mentioned Jeni."

Dean stilled. The air shifted. Her name carried weight. Heat. History. A small storm inside a single word.

"I guess I haven't," he said, feigning nonchalance with a sip of coffee.

"What happened?" Sandy asked. "You two were inseparable. Not romantic, maybe, but... closer than most couples ever get."

Dean looked away, running a hand through his hair. The memories cracked through. A laugh in the dark. A late-night phone call. A final goodbye that never felt final.

"She changed after college. When she met Michael... he didn't want me around. She wouldn't say it, but I knew. And I didn't want to be the reason things were hard for her."

Sandy's voice softened. "But she adored you."

Dean gave a sad shrug. "Maybe. But Michael didn't. And I wasn't going to fight for a space that didn't exist anymore."

A beat. The silence swelled. Then—

"I'm reaching out to her," Sandy said.

Dean blinked. "Why?"

"I want her in my wedding."

That stopped him cold. His heartbeat stuttered. Her face. Her laugh. A door he had nailed shut suddenly trembling with motion.

"Mom..."

"I know you're scared of reopening something that hurt. But I miss her too, Dean. And if there's even a sliver of space left... don't you want to know?"

Dean didn't answer. He couldn't. His chest was a war zone of memory and longing and resistance.

Sandy touched his hand. "Just think about it."

Dean nodded slowly, the morning suddenly too bright, the coffee too bitter. "Okay. I'll think about it."

She stood and moved to the sink, humming again. The same song. The one from earlier.

Dean stayed at the table, staring at his empty mug, watching the steam curl into the sunlight like a question that hadn't been asked yet.

And somewhere far away, a door in his mind cracked open— quiet, but undeniable.

Jeni

She was the girl who had always been there—his partner in crime, the voice of reason when he was being impulsive, and the one person who saw him for more than his football stats or charming grin.

Jeni had a way of grounding him. She reminded him who he really was beneath the confidence and bravado.

She never let the shine of his reputation blind her. She peeled past the swagger, past the spotlight, down to the quiet boy who stayed late to help the coach clean up.

The same boy who was upset when he didn't make varsity sophomore year.

She saw all of it—and loved him anyway.

Growing up, they were inseparable. The kind of friendship people envied, the kind that seemed unshakable.

Late-night talks about their dreams.
Sneaking out to watch meteor showers in the field behind her house.
Cheering each other on at games or debates.

It all felt like yesterday. And yet... impossibly far away.

Even now, Dean could still feel the damp grass under their backs, the way the stars seemed close enough to touch, and her soft whisper in the dark:
"Do you think we'll ever leave this place?"

But then college happened.
And everything changed.

Dean had stayed in Austin to attend University of Texas. Jeni left for Parsons School of Design in New York.

She wanted to be a clothing designer one day, with her own label. Dean just loved throwing the football.

They tried. Texts. Calls. Visits during the holidays.

But then Michael came into the picture. One evening in a nightclub in Manhattan they met. He was going to St John's University studying pharmacology.

Dean remembered the first time he met him. Michael had been polite—too polite. A firm handshake. A well-rehearsed smile.

But his eyes said something else. Possessive. Guarded.

That handshake wasn't a greeting—it was a warning. Silent, but clear.

Dean laughed it off at first, chalking it up to insecurity. But over time, it became obvious.

Jeni was changing.

Their once-easy conversations grew stiff. The calls slowed. The texts shortened.

Then came that dinner, during her junior year.

Dean could still see her sitting across from him, stirring her wine glass with a straw—a nervous tic she hadn't outgrown.

"He doesn't like the way we laugh together," Jeni had whispered, eyes low. "He doesn't get it."

Dean had forced a smile, trying to swallow the sting.
"Then he doesn't get you."

She looked away.

She didn't need to say it. Her silence said enough.

That was the last real conversation they'd had.

A few polite exchanges over the years—a birthday text, a quick "congrats." But the closeness was gone.

Like a bridge burned slow over time.

Now, hearing his mom mention Jeni's name, it all came rushing back. The loss. The ache. The what-ifs.

"Jeni," he murmured, her name sitting heavy on his tongue.

Sweet and bitter. Like honeysuckle and smoke.

He reclined in his chair, dragging a hand through his hair.

Maybe his mom was right. Maybe he missed her more than he let himself believe.

But what was the point?

She had her life. He had his.

Some doors shouldn't be reopened. Right?

And yet... some doors don't stay shut.

They rattle at the hinges when the past whispers through them.

His mom's words echoed back:
"Sometimes, people just need a reason to come back into your life."

Dean shook his head, stood up from the table, and grabbed his coffee. He rinsed the mug, set it in the sink.

But her name didn't leave his mind.

Would he even know how to let her in again?

Could the man he was now... make space for the girl he used to love?

He wandered into the living room and paused by the bay window.

Outside, the front yard stretched out, unchanged except for the taller grass and the sturdier oak tree.

It was here he'd played catch with Jeni for hours. Her laughter had once echoed across this yard like music.

He could almost hear it now.

The ghost of a laugh that once belonged to him.

He pictured her again—wild-haired, barefoot, calling him to race down the street, daring him to beat her.

She was fearless. Always.

One memory stabbed deeper than the rest.

Their first kiss.
Late one summer. Porch swing. Fireflies floating in lazy arcs.

"Just do it," she had whispered, half-challenging, half-hopeful.

He'd hesitated. But she didn't. She kissed him. Soft, sure.

And then—"I love you, and not just as a friend."

It had felt like jumping off a cliff and somehow landing safe.

But high school got messy.
He was the star quarterback. Attention was constant. Confusing.

He mistook applause for affection.

And he lost the one person who'd seen through all of it.

He looked across the street. Jeni's childhood home.

The porch was still the same. In his mind, she stood there now—smiling, daring, unforgettable.

Movement caught his eye. Allison, Jeni's mom, rounded the corner and waved. He raised his hand reflexively, but she was already disappearing inside.

Moments later, the landline rang.

Dean shook his head, smiling. Of course his mom still had a landline.

From the kitchen:
"Yes, Allison, you saw Dean. Sure, come on over. I have some big news for you," Sandy called, just loud enough to make him roll his eyes.

Minutes later, Allison arrived.

Doorbell. Hug. Laughter.

"Hey, stranger," she said. "Forgotten where home was—just like Jeni."

Dean leaned against the wall, arms crossed.

His mom had that *look* in her eyes. Mischief. Excitement. A secret she was dying to spill.

Without a word, she raised her left hand, casually brushing her fingers across her lips.

The ring sparkled like it was trying to get noticed.

Allison gasped. "So you finally got Jennings to propose!"

Dean blinked. "Wait—what?"

Classic. Last to know.

Allison turned to him, grinning. "You've got some catching up to do. Your mom's about to become Mrs. Jennings Burnette."

Then—Allison's voice changed. More serious. More pointed.

"You need to fly up to Toronto and propose to Jeni, because I don't think Michael is ever going to marry her."

The words slammed into him.

Like opening a door that hadn't been knocked on in years.

"She always thought it would be you, Dean," Allison added. "Back in high school, Jeni was sure you two would end up together."

His mom chimed in casually, "I want you and Jeni to be in the wedding."

Then to Allison—"Will you be my maid of honor?"

Allison's eyes misted. "Shoot, yay, I will!" she said, hugging Sandy again.

Dean's phone buzzed. He took it as an excuse to retreat.

"I need to take this," he said, heading for the hallway.

As he moved upstairs, he heard them whispering behind him.

"We need to get him and Jeni back together," Sandy said. "The wedding is the perfect time for that."

Allison laughed, pulling out her phone. "Let's start working on it right now."

Dean paused at the top of the stairs, one hand resting on the banister.

"Jeni? Oh, shoot—this isn't Jeni. Is this her phone?" Allison said into the call.

A man's voice shouted in the background, "Jeni, your mom is on your phone!"

Dean chuckled softly, shaking his head.

Here we go.

Operation Reunion: full throttle.

Remembering His Dad

Dean closed his eyes, and for a moment, it was like his dad was still there.

He could almost smell the crisp, woodsy cologne his father always wore, hear the deep timbre of his voice offering words of encouragement, and see the way his dad's eyes crinkled at the corners when he smiled. Those memories were his anchor, his connection to the man who had shaped so much of who he was.

His chest rose and fell slowly, as if breathing in a ghost.

The scent of cedar and spice drifted through his mind like smoke, wrapping him in a comfort he hadn't realized he was still chasing.

He exhaled deeply, feeling the weight of gratitude for Jennings settle over him. When his dad had passed, Jennings had stepped in—not just as a family friend, but as a steady presence in their lives. Dean wasn't sure how they would have made it through without him.

Now, as the thought of Jennings becoming his stepfather sank in, it felt... right. It wasn't a betrayal of his father—it was an extension of the love and care his dad would have wanted for both him and his mother.

Jennings had filled the silences without trying to replace the voice that came before. He'd shown up, again and again, in quiet ways that mattered.

And that mattered more than anything.

But even with that comfort, a heavy sadness pressed on Dean's chest.

He feared something he didn't often admit, even to himself.

What if, with time, the sharp edges of his memories dulled? What if his father's voice grew fainter, his face harder to picture?

At twenty-seven, Dean had already spent twelve years without his dad. He couldn't imagine a future where those memories faded altogether, where he couldn't recall the man who had meant so much to him.

Losing his father once had broken something in him.

Losing him again—to time, to forgetfulness, to life moving on— felt even crueler.

The thought terrified him—not because of anything Jennings had done, but because the idea of losing his father twice, once to death and then again to time, was unbearable.

He loved Jennings deeply, respected him as the father figure he had become, but he never wanted that love to erase or overshadow the bond he had with his dad.

Grief and gratitude—sitting in the same room. Uncomfortable roommates.

Dean stared at his laptop screen, the emails blurring into indistinct shapes as his mind drifted further.

He pressed his fingers to his temples, trying to steady himself. The weight of the past and present seemed to merge in this small room, pulling him in two directions at once.

Outside the window, the light had begun to fade, casting long shadows across the floor—time folding in on itself.

He adjusted his posture in his chair and whispered into the quiet of the room, "I'll never forget you, Dad. I promise."

The words fell from his lips like a prayer—half vow, half hope.

They lingered in the air, soft and resolute, a promise not just to the man who raised him, but to the version of himself that still needed that anchor.

Slowly, he turned back to the emails, the past still heavy on his shoulders but his resolve quietly firming.

Whatever life brought next, Dean would carry both his father and Jennings with him, honoring them both in his own way.

He would not let one love replace another.

He would build a life big enough to hold them both.

Dean tilted his chair back again, rubbing his temples. The steady hum of his laptop had become white noise, and he realized he hadn't moved in hours.

The light in the room had changed—muted now, soft with memory.

Deciding he needed a break, he pushed himself up and headed for the kitchen.

His muscles protested slightly, stiff from stillness. The air in his childhood bedroom had turned dense, like memory had thickened the oxygen.

He needed light. Movement.

His mother.

The familiar sound of pots and pans greeted him, along with the savory aroma of spices wafting through the air.

Garlic, rosemary, maybe a hint of something citrus. It was warmth in scent form—home distilled down to its most primal language.

As he stepped into the kitchen, his mom was already bustling around the stove, humming a tune that seemed to brighten the entire room. The golden light from the setting sun filtered through the window, casting a warm glow over everything.

Time had slipped away from him—it was already evening.

Sandy turned her head and smiled at him. "You've been working hard in there, son. Are you ready for dinner?"

Dean nodded, but his expression must have betrayed him, because her smile softened.

She placed the wooden spoon she'd been using on the counter and wiped her hands on her apron.

"What is it, Dean?" she asked gently.

He hesitated, leaning against the counter.

"I was just thinking about Dad," he admitted. His voice was steady, but there was a heaviness to it. "Sitting in my old room brought it all back. I could almost hear his voice, smell his cologne... but it scared me, Mom. I'm scared of forgetting him."

Sandy walked over to him, placing a hand on his arm.

"Baby, there isn't a day I don't miss or think about your dad," she said, her voice soft but steady. "He was my first and only love. We built this life together, and losing him... it was like losing a piece of myself."

She paused, her eyes glistening as she searched Dean's face.

"But you know," she continued, "it was a few years after Rebecca died, when Jennings and I went on an actual date. And let me tell you, it was a disaster."

Dean raised an eyebrow, surprised by the confession. "A disaster?"

She chuckled, though there was a bittersweet edge to it. "We both felt so guilty. It was like we were betraying Frank and Rebecca just by sitting at that table together. We couldn't even look at each other by the end of the night. But we went to see the pastor afterward, and he counseled us. He told us something I've held onto ever since: life is for living. Your dad and Rebecca would want us to continue on with life, to find joy where we can."

Dean nodded, processing her words. He felt her hand slip into his, squeezing it tightly.

"Promise me something, Dean," she said, her voice thick with emotion. "Promise me you won't stay gone like you did before. You hadn't been home in three years. It's like I lost you and your dad. I can't go through that again."

Tears welled up in her eyes, and Dean felt a pang of guilt deep in his chest. He looked down at their joined hands, her grip firm but trembling slightly.

"I promise, Mom," he said earnestly. "I'll come back regularly. I won't disappear like that again."

Her lips quivered as she smiled through her tears, nodding.

"That's all I need, baby. Just knowing I'll see you more often. You're all I have, Dean."

Dean reached out, pulling her into a hug. For a moment, they stayed like that, the warmth of the kitchen and the quiet hum of the stove enveloping them.

He could feel the weight in her embrace—the unspoken fears and hopes she carried for him.

In her arms, he felt ten years old again—loved, protected, and forgiven.

"Thank you, Mom," he whispered, his chin resting on her shoulder. "For everything."

She pulled back slightly, brushing a tear from her cheek.

"Now, enough of this heavy stuff," she said with a small laugh, her voice regaining its usual cheer. "Let's eat dinner before it gets cold."

Dean nodded, a small smile tugging at his lips.

As they sat down at the table, the familiar rhythm of home began to settle over him.

The clink of silverware, the creak of the old chair beneath him, the scent of rosemary in the air—it was a song he hadn't heard in years, but somehow still knew the lyrics to.

For the first time in a long while, he felt grounded, connected— not just to the past, but to the present.

And maybe, just maybe, to the future.

A future where he returned, not as a visitor, but as a son rediscovering his roots.

Mom's Home Cooking

They sat down to dinner just as the sky outside turned lavender, the soft hum of cicadas filling the quiet between bites. The food was simple—grilled chicken, roasted vegetables, warm sourdough—but to Dean, it tasted like restoration.

With each forkful, he felt himself settling. The rhythm of home— of presence, of belonging—wrapped around him like the blanket he didn't know he'd been missing.

And somewhere between the laughter and stories, something unspoken shifted.

His mind, always racing ahead, finally stilled.

After clearing the plates, Sandy looked at him with that same hopeful smile she used to wear on Christmas mornings.

"Do you want to watch a movie with me?"

Dean smiled back, no hesitation. "Yeah, Mom. That sounds great."

They moved into the family room.

As Dean stepped through the archway, a wave of nostalgia washed over him. The oversized sectional was exactly as he remembered—slightly sagging in the corners, the soft fabric worn from years of love. The coffee table still bore the battle scars of game nights and spilled cocoa. The DVD shelf, a time capsule of childhood favorites, lined the back wall.

He sat down and ran his hand over the throw blanket draped across the armrest.

"I honestly don't remember the last time I sat here and watched a movie," he said.

Sandy handed him the remote, her eyes twinkling.

"Too long. That's how long."

Dean scrolled through the options, eventually settling on an old classic.

"Dad used to hog the remote after football games," he said, smiling. "He'd always pick some dusty old western. I'd pretend to be annoyed, but really... I kind of loved them."

Sandy laughed. "You'd roll your eyes and then fall asleep ten minutes in."

Dean sank back into the chair.

"Yeah, but I always remembered how they ended."

She nudged his arm, a playful sparkle in her eyes.

"Your dad said the same thing. He knew you were just pretending."

The room dimmed as the movie started, but the warmth remained.

Familiar lines played like echoes from the past. At some point, Sandy leaned her head gently on Dean's shoulder. He exhaled, letting his own weight sink into the cushions.

For the first time in a long time, he felt present.

Not a man with a title. Not a CEO. Not someone with a publicist. Just a son. Sitting beside his mom.

As the credits rolled, Dean looked down and saw that she had drifted off. Her breath was slow and even. He carefully pulled the throw blanket over her and adjusted the pillow behind her neck.

The television faded to black, the last notes of the soundtrack dissolving into silence. The only sound left was the ticking of the wall clock and the slow, steady beat of peace.

Dean stayed there, sitting beside her, watching over her like she had done for him so many times before.

No agenda. No rush. Just the soft, undeniable truth that it felt good to be home.

Sandy Falls Asleep

After his mom had finally drifted off on the couch, curled beneath the throw blanket, Dean stood slowly and stretched, the soft cracking of his joints catching in the quiet of the room.

The living room glowed with the low light of a single lamp. The TV murmured in the background, but Sandy was long past hearing it. Dean moved with careful intention, his steps deliberate so he wouldn't disturb her. She deserved the rest.

Back in his childhood bedroom, he grabbed his phone from the desk, the screen lighting up with a subtle glow as his thumb brushed across it.

A small smile tugged at the corner of his mouth. Lexi.

A new message waited from her.

They had been texting since yesterday. It started light—playful banter, shared links, a few emojis—but it had started to shift. The tone had changed. Deeper. Slower. More real.

He opened her latest message and read:

"That's really sweet. I bet your mom is thrilled. It says a lot about you, Dean."

He stared at it, letting the words settle in his chest.

Not flirty. Not superficial. Just genuine.

The kind of message you don't get often. And when you do—you feel it.

He typed back:

"Yeah, she's happy I'm here. I realized it's been too long since I've spent quality time with her."

The typing bubble appeared almost instantly.

"Sometimes life gets in the way, but it's nice that you're making time for her," she wrote. "I lost my mom when I was nine years old, and not a day goes by that I don't wish I could have had more moments with her."

Dean's fingers hovered over the keyboard.

Her words hit him harder than he expected. A little ache opened up in his chest.

He thought back to the warmth of his mom's head resting on his shoulder. The faint rosemary scent still clinging to his hoodie from dinner. The way her voice had cracked when she made him promise he wouldn't stay away so long next time.

He typed:

"I'm sorry to hear about your mom. That must've been really hard."

Her reply came quickly.

"It was, but it also taught me to value time with the people I care about. So good on you for being there for your mom. I'm sure she's loving every minute of it."

Dean smiled, quietly.

There was a depth to Lexi that lived beneath all the glitz and glow of her photos. A resilience that didn't ask for attention but demanded respect.

He sprawled back, tapping his fingers lightly on the armrest.

"You're right, I think she is. She even got me to promise I won't let so much time pass before I come home again."

Lexi's response came with a laughing emoji.

"Moms are good at that. But hey, it sounds like you're exactly where you're supposed to be right now."

Dean let out a slow breath.

For once, he wasn't chasing a goal or proving a point. He was just... here. Present.

Before setting his phone down, he typed one last message:

"Thanks for chatting, Lexi. It's nice to talk to someone who gets it."

Her reply popped up almost instantly.

"Anytime, Dean. Goodnight!"

He locked the screen and set the phone back on the desk.

It wasn't much. Just a conversation. A few messages in the dark.

But it felt like the beginning of something. Or maybe just the right reminder at the right time—that some connections are quiet at first, like a song you didn't know you loved until the second verse.

He closed his laptop, turned off the lamp, and slid beneath the covers.

The sheets were cool against his skin. The air in the room still carried a faint trace of garlic and sugar from earlier—Sunday dinner with his mom. The house creaked softly around him, like it was exhaling after a long day.

Dean lay there, eyes open, arms behind his head, staring up at the ceiling he used to tape glow stars to as a kid.

He could feel sleep coming for him. Slow. Steady. Gentle.

But before he let it take him, he whispered into the dark—barely louder than a breath:

"I think I'm starting to come back."

Lake Travis

Jennings arrived just before dawn, the street still wrapped in shadows and quiet. His truck's headlights cut through the early morning haze as he rolled into the driveway, engine purring with calm authority. The air was cool, tinged with dew and the faint scent of blooming sage from the neighbor's garden.

He climbed out of his massive 2024 King Ranch F-350 dually— gleaming black with chrome accents that caught even the faintest trace of light. For a man who usually looked like he'd been born in a courthouse in a three-piece suit, Jennings wore the early morning like a second skin. A powder-blue polo, broken-in jeans, and a pair of well-worn Sperry's made him look like a seasoned yachtsman instead of a Texas attorney.

Dean was already outside, stretching and sipping coffee from a stainless steel travel mug, his duffel slung over one shoulder. Sandy followed him, a soft chuckle escaping her lips, her oversized sun hat tucked under one arm, the other balancing a cooler with practiced ease.

The gear clinked and clanked as they loaded it into the truck bed—fishing rods, tackle boxes, a waterproof duffel full of snacks, and another of towels and sunscreen.

Dean ran his hand appreciatively along the length of the truck's side panel, palm catching flecks of dust and sun.
"Damn, this thing is a beast. Looks like it could pull a small planet."

Jennings laughed as he slid behind the wheel. "It's a basic necessity in Texas. Big enough to pull a cattle or horse trailer, comfortable enough to drive cross-state. She's nice inside and out, but I still drive her all over the family ranch by Lake Buchanan."

Dean raised an eyebrow, impressed. "How long's that place been in the family?"

Jennings glanced over as he eased the truck out of the driveway. "Well, the ranch is over 50,000 acres now. It's been in the Burnette family since the founding of the Republic in 1836. Actually—some pieces of it were in the family even before independence."

Dean whistled under his breath. "That's incredible."

Jennings smiled, eyes focused on the quiet road unfolding before them. "I don't know if I ever told you this, but our family name used to be Burnet. Somewhere between statehood in '45 and the Civil War, someone added the extra 't'—probably a clerk who didn't know better. But David G. Burnet? He's the one who brought our family to Texas."

Dean turned toward him, intrigued. "Wait—the David G. Burnet? Like, interim president of the Republic of Texas?"

Jennings nodded. "The very one. He negotiated Texas independence with Santa Anna while the general was in his custody. Guess you could say litigation runs in my blood."

Sandy let out a soft laugh from the backseat. "Oh, honey, no one's ever doubted that."

They drove in companionable silence as the sky slowly began to lighten with shades of rose gold and pale blue. The highway soon gave way to winding hill country roads, flanked by limestone cliffs and rugged brush, until they reached the marina nestled at the edge of Lake Travis.

They transferred their gear into a golf cart and rolled it down the dock, the lake's surface glittering in the morning sun like a field of diamonds. Seagulls circled overhead. The smell of fresh water, sunscreen, and sun-bleached wood filled the air.

Jennings pulled a folded piece of paper from a clipboard hanging on the yacht's entry. "Marina signed off. Tanks are full. Stocked with everything we requested—food, drink, fuel."

The yacht—sleek and pristine—was a 52-foot stunner. White with navy trim, it gleamed in the rising light like a polished gem.

Dean took a deep breath as they stepped aboard, the subtle creak of the deck beneath their feet grounding him. The hum of the lake surrounded him—soft waves slapping gently at the hull, distant bird calls, the low groan of dock ropes adjusting in the morning wind. It felt good to be near the water again—clean, vast, free.

Jennings moved with practiced ease, unlocking doors, checking storage bins, and flipping switches like a man who knew every corner of the vessel. Though he'd been Navy—JAG, not deck crew—his movements below deck had the rhythm of ritual. He ran his hands along the engines, confirmed fuel levels, and gave the mechanical systems a quick once-over.

Back on the bridge, he flipped on the ignition and toggled the master controls. The engines rumbled to life beneath their feet, a deep, confident purr that sent a gentle vibration through the yacht.

Jennings turned toward Dean. "You want to do the honors today? I'll cast off."

Dean grinned, stepping up to the wheel. "Yes, sir. Taking the bridge."

He placed his hands on the wheel, feeling the leather grip—worn just enough to speak of use, not neglect. The wheel turned under his touch with a satisfying weight, as if the lake itself recognized him. A breeze touched his face as he eased them out of the marina, the open waters welcoming them with glints of sunlight and slow, lapping waves.

Behind him, Jennings stood beside Sandy with an arm around her shoulders, both of them watching the shoreline drift away.

"Remember that cove we used to fish back when you were in high school?" Jennings asked.

Dean turned his head just slightly, a soft smile on his face. "I thought you might say that, Jennings. Steering that way now."

The yacht cut through the water like a blade through silk, its wake fanning out in gentle waves behind them. The morning air smelled like cedar, sun, and lake mist—a scent Dean didn't know he missed until he breathed it in.

Jennings sat down beside Sandy, pulling her close. She leaned into him, her hand slipping naturally into his, the years of friendship and loss and healing written in every quiet gesture between them.

The sun climbed higher, warming their skin, painting everything in a soft, golden glow.

And for the first time in a long time, it didn't feel like they were leaving anything behind. It felt like they were returning to something—to peace, to presence, to the quiet truth that not all moments need words to be whole.

And for the first time in a long time, everything felt right.

The Cove – Morning ♪12

They reached the cove just shy of 7:30 a.m.

The sun hovered low on the horizon, just beginning to crest over the limestone hills that framed Lake Travis. Long golden streaks spilled across the mirror-like surface, fractured only by the slow ripple of the yacht's wake. The sky glowed in soft watercolor—lavender at the edges, gold bleeding gently into a pale blue.

The air still held the cool hush of night. Everything smelled of cedar, stone, and freshwater.

It was the kind of morning that asked for reverence.

Dean eased back on the throttle. The engine's growl softened to a purr, then silence as the yacht coasted into their usual fishing spot. He cut the motor completely.

The stillness wasn't empty. It was full. Sacred.

A gull cried somewhere overhead, wings slicing slow arcs across the quiet sky. The lake hadn't quite woken up yet, and neither had the world.

Dean stood and stretched, spine unfolding with a low crack. The sun caught his silhouette just right—angular, golden-edged, backlit like something remembered instead of seen. He reached into the ice chest beside the helm and pulled out two sweating bottles of Shiner Bock.

Out came the rods next—two poles leaning lazy against the railing like old friends waiting to be remembered.

He held one of the beers out toward Jennings.

"It's five o'clock somewhere," Dean said, raising the bottle with a slow grin. "And I've always liked your taste in beer. Gotta be Texas. Shiner Bock—my favorite."

Jennings clinked his bottle gently against Dean's. "To family," he said, his voice low, steady.

Dean nodded. "To family."

They drank in no rush. The silence stayed with them, not needing to be filled—only shared.

Dean moved back to the console, flipping a switch. A lazy Southern guitar rolled from the speakers, twanging low and familiar.

Billy Currington's voice filled the morning air, his song "People Are Crazy."

Dean looked over his shoulder, raising an eyebrow. "I know it's not George Strait."

Jennings smirked. "Close enough, cowboy."

The kind of laugh that didn't need volume—it lived in the bones.

A few minutes later, their lines were in the water. The bobbers drifted with no real intention.

They weren't here to catch fish. They were here to remember something simpler.

Jennings eased back in his seat, arm resting on the rail, posture easy.

"Dean, this was the perfect idea. We'll grab lunch over at Canyon Grille."

Dean nodded. "Haven't been there in years."

Jennings's smile faded into something quieter. He looked out over the lake, then back to Dean.

"Look, I'll never tell you what to do outside of business. But this AQS deal—it's more than wealth. It gives you something you can't buy. Time. Space. Freedom. You've earned it. Take it."

He paused. "Life, family, friends—that's what matters."

His voice softened again. "I'm ready to retire. This deal sets me up. I'll still handle your legal stuff—nothing big—but your mom and I? We're going to see the world while we still can. When Molly's gone, we'll travel more. Until then, we'll take care of her. She deserves that."

Dean studied the lake, the way the light danced across the water like it was trying to tell him something.

Then he looked at Jennings and smiled. "You two have earned it. I'll come back anytime—dog sit, yacht sit. Hell, I'll even water the plants."

Jennings chuckled, eyes shining. "Dean, you're the only child—hell, the only son—I've ever known. Everything I have is yours too. I'm glad your mom and I are going to make it official."

Dean didn't speak, but he nodded. The weight of the moment pressed into him, gentle and deep.

Down in the galley, Sandy moved with quiet purpose, humming as she worked. The smell of bacon and scrambled eggs drifted upward through the vents—warm, familiar, grounding.

By the time she stepped onto the aft deck, plates in hand, the air was rich with comfort.

"Breakfast is served, gentlemen."

Jennings looked up. "You spoil us."

Sandy winked. "You're my two favorite guys. It's my pleasure."

They ate slowly, between sips of coffee and the occasional low murmur of conversation. Laughter came easy, drifting over the water like a second breeze.

This wasn't just breakfast. It was ritual.

It was family, stitched into the stillness.

When they finished, Sandy gathered the plates and disappeared back below deck with a playful wave. The men returned to their poles without a word, letting the hush settle again.

Sandy sank into a seat in the shade, a paperback in hand, glasses perched on her nose. But she only half-read. Her eyes kept drifting to the two men—her past and her future—silhouetted against the water.

Her phone buzzed softly.

A message from Allison.

Looks like everything is going to work out the way we planned.

Sandy smiled. She replied quickly, thumbs dancing.

I already talked to Jennings. We'll stay at the restaurant so Dean and Jeni can spend the afternoon alone on the yacht.

Seconds later, Allison sent back a single emoji:

Sandy grinned.

The plan was in motion. Maybe Jeni would see it coming. Hopefully Dean wouldn't. But either way, the mothers had done their part.

By noon, the sun had climbed higher, glinting off the water like liquid silver.

Sandy closed her book, stood, and stretched. Her body moved slowly, but with purpose.

"Boys," she called out, "time to head to Canyon Grille. I promised Allison we'd meet her there."

Jennings reeled in his line, brushing off his hands. "Dean, you remember how to get there?"

Dean stood at the wheel, already in motion. "Not a problem."

He adjusted his sunglasses, hands sliding over the wheel with practiced ease.

The yacht turned gently into the current.

Toward something familiar.
Toward something he didn't know was waiting.

Canyon Grille – Noon

The yacht cruised across the sunlit water, its wake trailing behind like a memory fading into the shimmer of Lake Travis. The late morning sun had turned the lake into a mirror of light, the heat just beginning to rise, but still held at bay by the soft breeze sweeping across the bow.

Dean could already see the marina coming into view—bright awnings, sailboats bobbing in their slips, and the rustic timber-beam structure of Canyon Grille perched elegantly above the waterline. He pulled back on the throttle, slowing their approach until the yacht glided like silk across the surface, the marina growing larger with each breath.

As he reversed the engines, backing smoothly into the slip, Jennings stood, grabbing the mooring lines.

"I'll tie her off," he said, already stepping onto the dock with practiced ease.

Dean nodded, adjusting his sunglasses. The hum of the engines faded into the hush of water lapping against the hull, and with it came a quiet stillness that pressed against his chest—a moment held in suspension.

They walked up the boardwalk to the Canyon Grille, sunlight dappling the planks beneath their feet. At the top of the stairs,

Allison stood waiting at a table shaded by a white umbrella, her smile warm and expectant.

Sandy's hand brushed lightly against Dean's back as they approached—just a small, maternal touch, but it grounded him. Something about it pierced through his usual calm. His heart was beating faster than it should have.

They exchanged greetings and sat down, the waitress bringing iced teas and lemonades, condensation dripping down the glasses.

Then it happened.

A pair of soft, warm hands slipped over Dean's neck from behind, her touch featherlight but unmistakable. He froze, the moment stretching long and thin like pulled sugar.

Then he turned—and there she was.

Jeni.

She was at eye level, her lips brushing a kiss against his cheek. The world seemed to fall away in that single heartbeat.

Dean blinked in disbelief, his voice low and rough. "Jeni. It's really you." He reached instinctively for her hands. "Please tell me... you're by yourself?"

Jeni gave him a quiet, steady look. "Yes, Dean. No Michael today."

Dean didn't think. He stood, wrapped his arms around her waist, and lifted her off the ground in a spinning embrace, laughter catching in his throat as years of tension dissolved into sunlight.

When he stopped, her arms stayed around his neck, her forehead resting against his. She whispered, voice trembling slightly, "I'm sorry... for everything. I know our moms told you— it was all Michael. But that's not what I want to talk about, and it's not why I came. Best friends... don't treat each other like I did. Please, Dean. Forgive me."

Dean's breath caught, his throat tightening. He looked into her eyes—stormy with emotion—and nodded.

"Jeni... it's all in the past."

Her lips met his then—this time more deliberately, more deeply. It was no longer an apology. It was something else. Something rekindled. Something claimed.

The kiss lingered like the echo of a song they both remembered by heart. Her fingers slid to the back of his neck, his arms anchoring her close. He felt the heat of her, the urgency, the way her body molded into his with a familiarity that sent a quiet shiver down his spine.

When they broke apart, Dean saw the way both moms were practically glowing—beaming at the scene before them like they'd just won the jackpot at a matchmaking casino.

Jennings raised an eyebrow and lounged back with a grin. "Dean, Jeni... your moms and I are making arrangements for an impromptu engagement party."

Dean and Jeni snapped their heads toward him, eyes wide.

For a moment, they looked like two deer caught in headlights.

Jennings held the beat, then deadpanned, "Don't be running for the exits. I'm talking about for Sandy and me."

The table burst into laughter—Sandy with a mock gasp, Allison clapping her hands. Even Jeni exhaled a half-laugh, half-sob, and Dean couldn't help but laugh too, the relief almost dizzying.

Jennings took a sip of his tea. "Although..." he added with a sly glance, "if you could've seen your faces... priceless."

Sandy leaned in conspiratorially. "Not that your moms wouldn't love it if it were you two."

Dean looked at Jeni, testing, probing. "Honestly? I think there's more of a chance of a wedding announcement between Jeni and Michael than her and I."

Jeni's smile faltered.

"I don't see that ever happening, Dean," she said softly, her voice firm but threaded with hurt. "For all intents and purposes... it's over with Michael."

There was a brief, awkward silence.

Both moms, in synchronized sympathy, said, "Jeni, we're so sorry to hear that."

Dean's voice dropped, gentler now. "I hope you're okay. I've always been here for you, even when it didn't feel like I was welcome."

Jeni blinked hard, her eyes glassy. "I'm sorry, Dean... That was all Michael. He isolated me. I let him."

She pushed up abruptly, turning toward the bathrooms, her composure cracking.

Allison followed quietly behind.

Dean exhaled sharply, pushing his chair back.

Jennings laid a steady hand on Dean's shoulder. "Dean, I think you and Jeni should take the yacht out for the rest of the day. I'll have lunch boxed up and sent down. Just... be with her. We'll take care of everything for tonight. Be back at the dock by five-thirty—you'll have time to clean up before the party."

Sandy stood and gave Dean a little nudge. "Come with me, honey. I'll go get Jeni. She needs you right now, more than two old women."

Dean didn't answer, just nodded and followed. The air felt thicker now, heavy with all the things left unsaid.

When they returned, Jeni's eyes were red behind her sunglasses, her jaw set with emotion.

Dean didn't say anything. He just offered his arm.

And she took it.

They walked in silence down the dock. The rhythm of their steps eventually fell into sync, their silence deeper than any words could have been.

Fifteen minutes later, lunch was delivered in a cooler to the back of the yacht.

Jeni stood beside Dean at the helm, quietly helping him cast off—hands brushing, eyes meeting.

And for the first time in a long time, they weren't just remembering who they were...

They were starting to rediscover who they might still become.

Their Cove Back in High School

Dean glanced toward the horizon and said, "Remember the place we used to go out on the lake in high school?"

Jeni gave a silent nod, her eyes glimmering with memory.

They cruised slowly into a secluded cove, still untouched by time or development. The water glistened like melted sapphire, framed by trees that whispered softly in the breeze. Dean dropped anchor, cut the engines, and turned off the music. Only the quiet calls of birds and the hum of nature remained.

Dean, still in his swim trunks, pulled off his shirt, revealing a chest and arms sculpted by years of discipline. He began arranging their food on the aft deck of the yacht, setting out plates with casual ease.

Jeni peeled off her blouse and shorts, revealing a simple, elegant bikini beneath. Her movements were unhurried. The way sunlight kissed her skin made Dean pause, a moment suspended between memory and desire.

Her body, glowing in the warm light, was still as breathtaking as he remembered from their college days.

Jeni caught him staring. "Dean, I had the same reaction when you took off your shirt."

He chuckled. "Was it that obvious?"

She walked to him, wrapping her arms around his torso, her body pressing against his—not a hug, but a declaration. Something more primal. Something real.

Dean felt her curves align with his, sensed the unspoken urgency humming beneath her touch.

Her fingertips traced the small of his back. She exhaled slowly, like letting go of a weight she'd carried for years.

This wasn't the girl he used to know. This was a woman. A woman who had lived, who had shared a life and a bed with someone for years. A woman who knew what she wanted—and how to ask for it.

"I want us to go below deck after we eat," Jeni whispered, her lips brushing his.

She kissed him, mouth parting, tongue seeking his with a boldness born of years of buried longing. Her hands slipped around to his lower back. He felt the heat radiating off her— knew she felt his own response pressing against her.

She ground her hips against him, tugging at the knot on his swim trunks while untying the strings of her bikini bottom. Her leg hooked around his waist as she guided him down onto a cushioned chair, straddling him with slow, deliberate confidence.

Her breath caught, a soft sound against his neck. The yacht rocked gently beneath them. It felt like the whole world was holding its breath.

Their bodies rocked in sync as she slid against him, slick warmth meeting firm need. Jeni gasped softly, adjusting herself until she settled over him, taking him in gradually, with breathless precision.

She leaned back, unclasped her top, and guided one of her breasts to his mouth, her hips beginning a slow rhythm. Dean's hands found her waist, guiding her, anchoring her.

Jeni moved with increasing need, her moans turning to whimpers as her release took her first. Dean wasn't far behind.

Afterward, their breathing slowed but their bodies didn't part. They stayed curled together, the sun casting shadows that slipped slowly across their skin.

Jeni brushed her fingers through his hair. "I wish it had been you, the first time. I can't believe it took us this long to finally give ourselves to each other."

She smiled, wistful but grounded. "Back in high school, I never understood what the other girls meant when they said you were the biggest guy on the football team. Now I get it."

Dean laughed. "Was it really that shocking?"

She grinned. "Frankly, I don't care if we end up in a relationship or not. Just promise me you'll take care of me like this when I need it."

"What about Michael?" Dean asked gently. "You've been with him a long time."

Jeni tilted her head with a wry smile. "It was about security. Familiarity. Someone who was there. But he's not you."

She traced a finger along his jaw. "And for the record, I've heard girls describe you as being 'hung like a wild stallion.'"

Dean laughed harder. "That's a new one."

"You liar," she teased. "I know for a fact plenty of girls said that. And later, you're going to use that mouth on me. I've been dreaming of that, too."

Dean groaned with a grin. "Whatever switch I flipped, I hope there's no off button."

Jeni leaned in, kissed him again. "We should eat. You're going to need your energy later."

She fed him bits of fruit and cold pasta salad while still perched in his lap. The moment felt playful, domestic, impossibly tender. Like something borrowed from a life they never quite lived.

When the meal was finished, they slipped out of their swimsuits, the afternoon sun warming their bare skin as they strolled casually around the deck. No one but the trees and birds to witness them.

Below deck, the air was cooler, tinged with the scent of salt and teakwood. The lounge was spacious and plush, a wide U-shaped sectional with long chaise-style loungers on either end.

Jeni led him to one. "Dean, lie back."

He obeyed.

She positioned herself at the opposite end, slowly exploring him with her hands first, then her lips. Her kisses were slow and deliberate. She let her tongue glide over him, pausing at the tip before taking him into her mouth.

He let out a low groan.

Dean reached out, parting her legs with practiced ease. His fingers traced over her warmth, feeling how ready she was. He kissed her navel, then lower, until his tongue found her center and coaxed her open.

Her scent was intoxicating. Her taste, addictive.

Jeni moaned, lowering her mouth over him again. She took him deeper, her hand working in tandem with her lips, the rhythm building.

Her hips bucked softly against his mouth as her moans turned to ragged gasps.

She paused, breathless. "Dean... I want you inside me when I come."

Dean moved swiftly, sliding between her legs. With her knees bent and his arms braced beneath them, he entered her deeply.

Jeni bit into his shoulder as they moved together, her voice breaking as she cried out. "Oh God, Dean, don't stop."

Her climax hit hard. He held her through it, then continued, chasing his own until his body shuddered with release.

They lay tangled afterward, breath shallow, lips brushing.

Jeni whispered, "I'm not asking you for promises. I just need you... like this."

She ran her fingers through his hair, trailing across his chest. They stayed there, lost in each other's arms, for what felt like forever.

Eventually, they knew they had to go.

Dean pulled on his trunks and put on his shirt. "I want to come see you in Toronto this summer. If the timing's right. Cabin, yacht, mountain bikes, maybe even a tent."

Jeni putting her bikini back on and pulled her clothes over her bikini. "I'd like that. I need to figure out the Michael situation. I don't know if I'll be free to go with you, but I can plan it all. I'll pick you up at the airport for sure. We'll have time—like today. I want that."

Dean nodded. "Think about it. Just... start texting me back. Call me."

She embraced him from behind, hands squeezing his backside. "You've got it. I might even send a few pictures... reminders."

Dean kissed her. "Come sit in my lap while I drive back."

She straddled him again as he started the engines. As they moved through the water, she undid her bottoms once more and lowered herself onto him.

Their quiet moans filled the cockpit. Her body found its pace again—desperate, needing.

By the time the marina came into view, she had already found her third release.

They docked, dressed, and headed back to the house. In the car, the mood softened.

Jeni looked at him. "You remember when we were growing up? I'd always be in my T-shirt and panties when you came over. Sometimes just my bra. I told myself it didn't matter because we were friends. But truth is... I wanted to be more."

Dean looked stunned. "I thought you saw me like a brother."

She smiled softly. "You finally figured it out today. That's a start."

The rest of the ride was quiet. Fingers intertwined. Glances held.

When they pulled into the driveway, Jeni gathered her things.

"I'll take my mom's car to the restaurant. She can ride with your mom and Jennings. If you want, maybe come by my place afterward... spend a little time in my room. Reminisce."

Engagement Party

They arrived just as the sun dipped low in the sky, bathing the backyard in soft amber light. It was a small affair—just ten couples, close friends and family. The kind of gathering where everyone knew someone, and smiles came easily.

Sandy and Jennings hadn't wanted a big party. No spectacle. No grand gestures. That was reserved for the wedding and reception. This evening was something else—something quieter, more intimate. A marker of a new chapter.

String lights swayed gently above the patio, casting a warm golden glow. The scent of gardenias mixed with grilled meat, curling softly through the summer air. Laughter drifted like music from the small groups gathered near the tables, the rustle of linen napkins and clinking ice giving the night a gentle rhythm.

Dean and Jeni stood near the edge of the room, observing. They were the youngest people there, most over a decade older, and it showed—not in discomfort, but in quiet awareness. Jeni's hand brushed against Dean's as they stood side by side. Not holding. Just touching. A tether. A pulse.

For Dean, this wasn't just another evening with family. This was a moment he'd waited for.

Jennings and his mom. Getting married. Making it official.

And for once, nothing in him resisted it.

As he watched his mother smiling across the yard—one arm tucked into Jennings'—he felt something unexpected bloom in his chest: gratitude. Even peace.

This wasn't about replacing his father, Frank. None of them saw it that way. Twelve years had passed. Time hadn't erased the grief, but it had softened it. Enough for them to laugh again. To look forward. To build something new.

Dean saw it clearly now—this wasn't about passion or impulse. It was about companionship. The comfort of knowing someone would be there at the end of the day. As a younger man, he hadn't understood that. He thought love was all about urgency. Now... he was starting to see the beauty in the quiet kind.

Jennings rose from his chair and gently tapped his glass. The small crowd turned toward him.

"Everyone," he said, lifting his champagne, "please raise your glass and toast to my bride-to-be."

Sandy smiled, her eyes shimmering beneath the lights.

"I love you, Sandy," Jennings continued. "We've leaned on each other through the years. We've both seen our share of loss. I don't know how I could've made it through the grief of losing Rebecca without you."

His voice caught on the name, but he pressed forward.

"Rebecca and I did our best to look after my best friend's wife and son after he passed. Frank was a great sailor. A good husband. An even better father. And the best friend I ever had." He held his glass higher. "Cheers to new beginnings."

The group raised their glasses. Crystal rang out in a soft, shimmering chorus.

Dean rose slowly to his feet, voice steady. "To my mom and Jennings."

A second toast followed. Laughter. Gentle nods. That warm, bittersweet quiet that comes when something sacred is shared.

For a brief moment, time slowed. And everything felt exactly as it should.

Later, as the sun gave way to stars, Dean stepped over to Sandy, Allison, and Jennings.

"We're going to head back to the house," he said softly. "Let you three enjoy the hotel."

Sandy reached up to touch his cheek with a thumb. "It was good having you here."

"You too, Mom."

"Be good to each other," Jennings added, squeezing Dean's shoulder with the kind of casual affection that had taken years to grow.

As Dean and Jeni stepped away, he placed a gentle hand on the small of her back. They walked slowly toward the gate. Behind them, the string lights glimmered like stars just beginning to appear in the sky.

The night had been simple. Uncomplicated.
But something about it felt quietly permanent—
Like a door had been opened, and no one would have to go through it alone.

Jeni's Bedroom

After slipping away early from Sandy and Jennings's engagement party, Dean and Jeni drove back to his mother's house. With Sandy and Jennings staying at the hotel that night— and Allison opting for her own room nearby—it was just the two of them in the quiet, familiar home.

Jeni needed a change of clothes for the morning, so she parked her mom's car in the garage, the headlights sweeping briefly over the brick wall before fading into stillness.

The garage door creaked shut behind them. Silence settled like a breath held between past and present.

She stepped inside, heading down the hallway that still carried echoes of her teenage years. It was almost poetic—how neither she nor Dean had ever changed their childhood rooms after leaving for college, as if those spaces still held onto something sacred.

Her bedroom hadn't changed at all.

The homecoming mum still hung next to her desk—massive, glittering, proud. Her mother had spent two weeks crafting it by hand, streamers and beads cascading all the way to the floor. If you weren't from Texas, you wouldn't understand. High school football was religion, and homecoming was holy.

The ribbons told her story—"Westlake Volleyball," "Senior Prom 2016," "Go Chaparrals!"—all in bold red, white, and blue.

On the other side of the desk sat her Mardi Gras masquerade mask, draped in green, gold, and purple beads, a playful memento from another life chapter.

Dean walked in behind her and took it all in, his eyes flicking across the room with a mix of nostalgia and amusement.

"My mom left my room the exact same way when I left for college," he said, chuckling. "I'm not even surprised. They're always thinking, doing… scheming."

"Scheming?" Jeni grinned, arching an eyebrow.

Dean smirked. "Yeah. I was on a call the other day—your mom and my mom were literally plotting to get us back together."

"And… are you happy about that?" she asked, softly now.

He didn't answer with words.

Dean stepped forward, closing the distance, his hands sliding to her waist with the ease of familiarity. He pulled her gently into him, his mouth finding hers. The kiss deepened, slow and certain, and his fingers moved lower—around the back of her panties, then slipping to the front, exploring slowly.

Jeni let out a quiet gasp, her lips parting as her breath grew heavier. Her fingers curled into his shirt, anchoring herself to the moment.

Dean's voice was low, his eyes burning into hers. "Does that answer your question?"

Her only reply was to guide him toward her bed.

"Do you know how many times I imagined this?" she whispered. "You in my bed. You touching me. Back then, it was just me—my fingers—pretending they were you."

She gently pushed him onto the mattress.

"Lay back. Close your eyes."

When he opened them again, she stood at the foot of the bed, her body encased in a black lace bra and matching thong, the Mardi Gras mask now veiling her face, beads swinging lightly around her neck.

The image burned into him—familiar and foreign all at once. Timeless. Dangerous. Beautiful.

She crawled toward him, slow and feline, her movements a sensual dance of intention and memory. Her fingers slid under the waistband of his pants, easing them off along with his boxers, her touch feather-light.

She moved over him, positioning herself above, the heat between them pulsing.

"This," she said, "this is what prom night should've been."

She drew her thong to the side and guided him into her, inch by inch, her breath catching as they connected fully.

Her hips began to roll—deliberate, aching. A rhythm built from memory and hunger.

Her voice came low and rough. "Dean, you're mine tonight. All night. I want you to take me, again and again. Make it last. Let me feel you long after you're gone."

Dean gripped her hips, his body rising to meet hers.

Every motion was thick with history. Tension and release. Familiarity and rediscovery.

The way she moved above him—hungry yet unhurried—made his entire body thrum with need. He was filling her completely, the slow grind of their connection building something more than pleasure.

It was years of longing, finally exhaled.

She leaned forward, kissing him, her breath warm against his lips.

"Tell me all the places in this house you used to fantasize about me. Take me to every one of them. I want you to make each of them real."

And so they did.

Room by room, touch by touch, they rewrote the past.

They moved through the house—bedroom, bathroom, living room, the old TV den, the kitchen with its cool granite counters, the warm laundry room, even the garage with its unfinished concrete floor.

Each space carried a memory. Each act rewrote an old what-if.

At one point, Jeni collapsed against the hallway wall, breathless and glowing.

"Okay. Now grab my clothes for tomorrow," she murmured, laughing. "We've got to head to your house now. I want to hear your fantasies."

Dean led her through his childhood home, the walls whispering their own stories. Every room they'd once tiptoed through as friends became new again—transformed by touch, breath, and voice. Finally reaching his bedroom.

Dean's Bedroom

Jeni stepped quietly into Dean's room, a space that hadn't changed much since high school—old posters still framed above the desk, his football trophies still lined in careful rows on the shelf. There was something sacred about the stillness, like the room had been waiting for them both.

Her fingertips drifted over the edge of the dresser, where a few framed photos stood like sentinels of another life. One photo caught her attention—Dean in his football jersey, grinning ear to ear, standing beside a tall, broad-shouldered man with warm eyes and a steady presence.

Frank Harrington.

She lifted it gently, her eyes softening.

"Dean..." Her voice was low, almost caught in her throat. "Your dad... he was like my dad growing up."

Dean turned toward her from where he was pulling a blanket from the bed. He stilled, watching her. Listening.

Jeni didn't look away from the photo. Her thumb gently traced the frame, like she was trying to hold onto a memory that never fully belonged to her.

"When my dad left—it was just my mom and me. Before we ever moved across the street... I didn't know how to handle it. I felt invisible. Forgotten." She swallowed, her voice thickening. "But your dad... from the moment he saw me, he treated me like I was his."

She slowly set the frame down, not because she wanted to—but because it hurt to hold it.

"He came to my school plays. Sat through those long, awkward chorus concerts. He made sure I had birthday cards—even presents. Christmas too. Things my mom couldn't always give me. And he never made me feel like a charity case. Just... loved."

Dean's expression softened. He crossed the room and stood beside her, the closeness pulling her into his warmth without a word.

"I miss him too, Dean," she said quietly, her voice trembling. "I am who I am today because of him."

Dean nodded slowly, his hand brushing along the small of her back. There was a calm strength in his touch—reassuring, grounding.

"Dad loved his little princess," he murmured, the nickname landing like a long-forgotten hug. "He used to say, 'I've got two kids now. One just lives next door.'"

Jeni gave a small, teary laugh at that, her lips pulling into a tender smile. She leaned into his chest, resting her head over his heart, and his arms wrapped around her instinctively.

For a long moment, they stayed like that—no performance, no roles. Just two people shaped by the same man's love.

Dean took Jeni's hand and pulled her toward the edge of his bed, the room still humming with the electricity of everything they'd just confessed. His heart pounded—not with hesitation, but with urgency. Craving.

Like every time he touched her only made him hungrier, not satisfied.

Their eyes locked.

This wasn't soft. It wasn't slow.

It was desperate.

He pulled her shirt off in one fierce movement, lips already on her neck, tasting the salt on her skin.

She yanked his pants down without ceremony, her hands already wrapping around him, stroking his thick, ready length with a firm, practiced grip.

His groan spilled into her mouth as he kissed her—messy, open, gasping.

They stripped each other fast, hands pulling, tugging, gripping.

They hit the bed like a storm.

Her legs wrapped around him immediately, her body slick and soaked for him. She reached between them and guided him in with no hesitation, no teasing, just need.

He filled her in one deep thrust.

She cried out—already stretched, already pulsing from everything they'd done earlier—and still, she wanted more.

"Dean," she moaned, her head falling back, her breasts arching toward him, "Don't stop this time. Don't slow down."

"I wasn't planning to."

He pinned her wrists above her head, hips rolling, slamming into her with punishing rhythm.

She was soaked, gripping him so tightly he nearly lost control.

He flipped her onto her knees, dragging her hips back against him and driving himself into her so hard she gasped.

Her fingers clawed at the sheets. She bit down on a pillow to muffle the next cry.

He leaned forward, one hand buried in her hair, the other teasing her slick pearl as he thrust deep and fast.

She came again—shaking, cursing, begging.

"You feel so good," she cried. "I've never had it like this—never this deep. Never this full."

"You were made for me," he growled into her ear.

She collapsed onto the bed and he followed, lifting one of her legs over his shoulder and entering her again, hitting her so deep she screamed.

Time disappeared.

They didn't count the orgasms. They just kept going—switching positions, lips on mouths, on breasts, on thighs.

Hands everywhere.

Her body dripping, pliant, wrecked.

At one point she was straddling him, riding him with a rhythm so fierce she slapped against his hips, her breasts bouncing with every grind.

Her fingers dug into his chest, her cries high and uncontrollable as she took him again and again.

"This—this is what I've needed from you," she gasped.

Dean's hands locked around her waist.

"You'll never need again. I'll give it to you every time."

When he came, it was with a growl into her neck, buried deep, his whole body locked tight against hers, shuddering as he spilled inside her again.

They collapsed together, soaked, panting, trembling.

Her lips brushed his ear, her voice thick and hoarse.

"I didn't just want you, Dean. I ached for you. For years. I kept thinking... why won't he touch me like this?"

He kissed her lips, her neck, her breasts.

"I was trying to protect something that didn't need protection."

"Like what?"

"You."

Hours passed like seconds.

By the time dawn crept up over the trees, they found themselves back in Dean's room, their bodies wrapped around each other, tangled in the same sheets from a thousand mornings ago.

They were naked. Exhausted. Still wanting.

Even then, they found the strength to keep going—gentle, slow, tender.

Not because they had to. But because they weren't ready to let go.

Jeni stroked his chest, her lips brushing his shoulder.

"Dean, I'm not asking for promises. I just need this. I need you. Like this."

Eventually, sleep claimed them both.

And for the first time in years, the past didn't hurt.

Back to Miami

Dean had completed what he came to Texas to do— professionally, the AQS deal was a victory. But the trip had become more than just business.

It had become personal.

He hadn't expected Texas to pull old ghosts from their hiding places. But they came anyway—soft at first, then loud. Grief, he thought he'd buried. Love he'd long stopped naming. His mother's pain, once a quiet thing in the background, now stood beside his own like a mirror.

Being there wasn't just a return.

It was a reckoning.

And in that reckoning, healing had begun.

And then there was Jeni.

What started with a glance had turned into something raw and undeniable—a truth that refused to stay buried in time. A decade of near misses, unread signals, suppressed longing... cracked open in a single night.

Dean didn't see Jeni as someone to rescue. He saw her for who she really was now—untethered, unafraid, ready to take what she wanted. No apologies. No masks.

He wanted to be the one to help her claim that life.

They hadn't put a label on it. There was no need.

Jeni's voice echoed in his memory—low and deliberate in the stillness of morning.

"I don't need a boyfriend. I need a man who understands what I crave and won't ask me to explain it."

Dean had nodded.

He could give her that. Not out of obligation, but out of desire—mutual, hungry, honest.

That morning had unfolded like something out of time. Tangled limbs. Slow kisses. Bodies learning each other again, not with urgency, but reverence. One hour melting into the next until there was no clock, only rhythm.

In the shower, they touched each other like it mattered. His hands in her hair. Her mouth finding him in the rising steam. She dropped to her knees—a wordless offer—and Dean leaned back against the marble tile, his fingers slipping through her wet hair as his breath hitched.

When she stood again, she didn't speak. She just turned, lifted his hand, and led him into her. The water trickled down around them as their bodies moved in unison—slow, deep, deliberate.

No words.

Just breath.

Just need.

Just them.

After, they dried off in silence, both smiling faintly. They dressed slowly, packed their things. Sandy had texted earlier—breakfast invite, local café, no frills. Just bacon, eggs, biscuits and gravy.

Jeni ordered pancakes.

Sandy, warm as ever, reached across the table with a grin and asked, "Would you be part of the wedding—with your mom?"

Jeni paused, caught between surprise and something softer.

"It would be my honor," she said.

Later, she drove Dean to the airport. They didn't rush. Didn't speak much. Just held hands while the engine hummed beneath them.

They parked in the garage. Didn't move. The world felt still.

In the quiet, she kissed him. Then leaned in close, lips at his ear.

"Please me once more before you go."

Dean swallowed.

When she turned, bracing herself against the dash, he didn't hesitate. He lifted her dress, slid into her with a groan, and moved with her—one hand on her waist, the other in her hair. The car was warm. Her breath fogged the windshield.

She moaned against the steering wheel as her body gave in, shivering beneath his hands. Dean followed moments later, resting his forehead on her shoulder as the tremors passed between them.

After, they cleaned up, fixed their clothes, shared one final laugh. Walked together to the terminal like they had no baggage between them.

At security, she cupped his face gently between her hands.

"Promise we'll stay connected. You're the one who's going to be taking care of these cravings now, stud."

He smiled. "Count on it."

One last kiss. Then she was gone.

After clearing TSA, Dean pulled out his phone.

I'm so glad we had that time together.

The reply came fast: 🖤 🖤 🖤

On the plane, he ordered a Jack and Coke. A small celebration for a big week.

The AQS deal had wrapped early—clean, ahead of schedule, and exactly what the firm needed. Lexi had texted before he left Austin, telling him she'd be out with girlfriends that night.

If you get back in time, join us.

As the jet cruised toward the Florida coast, Dean scrolled through unread messages, glanced at headlines, sipped his drink. The buzz of success wrapped around him like a warm current—but it didn't numb him completely.

By the time the plane touched down in Miami, the sun was dipping behind the skyline. His driver met him at the curb and slipped easily into traffic.

Thirty minutes later, Dean stepped into his building's elevator. Sirena greeted him before the doors even closed.

"Welcome home, Dean," she said in that smooth voice. "You look tired. Also... pleased with yourself."

He chuckled. "It was a good trip."

"Will Lexi be joining you this evening?"

"I'm about to find out."

Sirena's voice softened. "Shall I prepare the house for company?"

Dean smirked. "Just give me thirty minutes."

He stepped into his apartment, tossed his bags aside, and flopped onto the bed fully dressed.

Sleep took him fast.

An hour later, he stirred.

Time to shower. Time to change. Time to find Lexi.

THE RESTAURANT

The View from the Top ♪13

A rooftop bar in Miami. Skyline glowing behind her. The night was warm with ocean breeze, the pulse of EDM just beginning to thrum in the air—**"17" by MK** curling through the speakers like silk.

The music moved through the rooftop—steady, low, seductive. It didn't ask for your body; it summoned it.

It was the same song that played the night Dean first kissed her.

Basslines threaded through her ribs like memory. Like the way he used to touch her—slow, with certainty, like he was building something permanent.

The city stretched wide and electric around her, each window below twinkling like a secret. From this height, everything looked soft—lights blurred into gold, buildings faded into silhouette, and time blurred into whatever she wanted it to be.

She liked the view from above. It made the chaos feel quieter.

Lexi sat at the edge of it all, her black silk dress hugging her frame like a whisper, one leg crossed over the other, heel dangling from her toe. Her skin shimmered faintly from the humidity, the heat curling around her collarbone like a silk ribbon. The martini glass in her hand was cold and perfect, condensation trailing down the stem onto her fingers. The breeze from the ocean below kissed her shoulders, lifting a strand of blonde hair and sweeping it across her cheek. She didn't brush it away. She let it stay.

Let it look poetic. Disheveled in a curated way.

She reflected on the sheer sundresses and delicate lingerie she'd modeled all week in the Bahamas. Her skin still held the ghost of the sun—a golden warmth that clung to her collarbones and calves like memory. She took a deep breath, tasting salt on the breeze, the memory of bikinis and bronzed skin fresh and vivid in her mind.

The photoshoot had been exhausting, yet exhilarating—every click of the camera capturing a different facet of her carefully constructed persona. A new version of Lexi with every pose. A shape-shifter in stilettos.

The glass trembled slightly in her grip, but she didn't adjust it. Control was everything. Even now.

Everything about tonight was deliberate. The setting sun. The table along the edge. The low hum of conversation and laughter around her. The way she hadn't smiled yet.

She wasn't just watching the city. She was commanding it.

Head high. Spine straight. Perfectly still, as if any movement would break the spell.

And yet, beneath all that glamour and posture and glow— something inside her ached to be undone.

The smile she wore wasn't real. The stillness was a disguise. The view couldn't distract her forever. Her phone buzzed against the table. A small vibration. A single name.

Dean.

Just seeing his name made her body remember. The way he'd touched her. The way he saw her. She took the shot. Then another sip of her martini. And then—she opened his message.

"How are you, my love, on this Friday? I wish I were spending the evening with you. Are you sitting at a bar somewhere in a sexy little dress, your legs crossed, thinking of me? Of the one thing you love more than my tongue being inside you?"

Her breath caught.

She glanced around. Couples at nearby tables. Laughter. Clinking glasses.

They had no idea.

She shifted in her seat and draped her napkin over her lap.

Then, slowly, she adjusted her thong, tugging it so the delicate strip of fabric pressed right against the center of her heat.

She began to bounce her leg—slowly, deliberately.

The pressure against her clit was instant.

She looked at the screen again.

"I can see you now. Your thighs tight, your hips rocking against the chair, pretending to stay composed. Are you wet yet, Lexi?"

Yes. God, yes.

She bounced faster, her breath shallow. Every word he wrote sank deeper into her body.

"I want you to straddle my face, your hands on the wall, grinding down until I make you scream my name."

She clenched her thighs.

Another sip of her drink to steady her hands.

"I'd lick you until you soaked my face. Then I'd flip you over and slide into your tight little pussy and fuck you hard from behind."

Her hips rocked subtly. The edge of the chair pressing perfectly now. Her thong—slick, soaked—rubbed against her swollen clit.

She kept her head down, pretending to scroll, but inside...

Her body was vibrating. She moved faster.

Her breath hitched.

Her thighs tightened.

Then—

The wave hit.

Her orgasm rolled through her like a quiet explosion—legs trembling, hips rocking forward, head falling slightly back as she bit her lip to keep from crying out.

She reached under the table, sliding the napkin between her legs, soaking up the evidence. Her whole body was loose now, melted into the chair.

She raised her glass and whispered, "To you, Dean."

Standing Against the Wall

In the bathroom, she cleaned up, cheeks flushed, pulse still fluttering.

She texted him:

"I just came. In public. For you."

He responded instantly.

"You looked stunning in that little black dress."

Lexi froze.

She looked around.

Her phone buzzed again.

"Turn around."

She did.

And there he was.

Dean.

Handsome. Smirking. Eyes hungry.

Before she could speak, his hand slipped under her dress, fingers grazing the inside of her thigh, finding the slick heat beneath her panties.

"You've been teasing me all night," he whispered against her ear. "Now it's my turn."

He took her hand and pulled her into the last stall.

The door locked with a solid click.

Lexi leaned against the stall wall, her hands braced behind her, legs parting as Dean dropped to his knees.

Her panties were already damp—he pulled them aside and pressed his mouth to her core.

She gasped.

His tongue moved in slow, hungry strokes—savoring, circling, drinking her in. Her fingers gripped his hair, her hips grinding against his mouth as he moaned into her.

"Dean... oh my God—"

She was close again.

And when he slid two fingers inside her—curling, thrusting—she broke.

Her orgasm came fast and sharp, her cry swallowed by the music pounding through the bathroom walls.

He didn't stop until she pulled him up, breathless, needing more.

The Bathroom Stall ♪14

From the lounge outside, "Come With Me" by Major League DJz started the rhythm of to bleed through the walls. Jorja Smith's voice—velvety, haunting, inviting—wrapped around the silence like a dare. He turned her around, gently bent her forward, her hands pressed against the stall wall.

He unzipped his pants—no teasing this time. Just raw need.

He slid into her from behind, filling her in one smooth, hard thrust.

She gasped again, arching her back, pushing herself backwards against him, her hair spilling over her shoulder.

"You feel so good, baby," he growled, gripping her hips as he started to move.

Slow at first.

Then deeper.

Then harder.

The rhythm built fast—her body meeting his, the slap of skin on skin, the stall rattling with each thrust.

Her mouth opened in a silent moan, her eyes closed.

And when he reached around to rub her clit—she shattered again.

Her walls clenched around him, her moans soft but desperate.

Dean groaned, his hips slamming forward once, twice—

And then he came, buried deep inside her.

Breathless. Spent. Satisfied.

Back to Their Table

She swatted at his chest, but didn't pull away. Their bodies still buzzed from contact, like they'd stepped out of a storm but the lightning hadn't left.

Her fingers lingered against his shirt for half a second longer than they should have. It wasn't resistance. It was reluctance in disguise.

She slipped from his hold slowly, brushing her hands through her hair to steady herself—each motion methodical, almost rehearsed. She smoothed her dress next, then dug into her clutch with practiced urgency, fishing out a compact.

The snap of the mirror echoed faintly in the night air.
Her lip gloss gleamed under the terrace light—peachy, pristine, the perfect distraction.

Dean adjusted his collar, then his cuffs, with that maddening ease he wore like a second skin. The afterglow in his gaze flickered behind the shield of casual charm, but it was there—hot and still humming.

For a beat, neither of them said a word.

The city pulsed beyond the terrace rail, skyline lit like a curtain ready to rise again. A perfect set. A perfect lie.

They stepped into it—Lexi first, Dean behind her. Side by side, but not quite together. Just two beautiful people blending back into the beautiful illusion.

Back to the rooftop bar.
To the skyline.
To the performance.

The music had shifted—a deeper groove now. A slow, sensual beat threaded through the evening air like smoke. The bass wasn't loud, but it was low enough to settle into their bones.

Lexi's heels clicked against the tile with deliberate precision, each step a punctuation mark. Her posture straightened, her chin lifted—armor sliding back into place.

Dean's hand rested low on her back.
Not possessive.
Not controlling.
Just... steady. Grounding. A silent I'm still here.

She didn't shake it off.

Didn't lean into it either.

Ten minutes later, her friends arrived. A flurry of energy swept in with them—bright laughter, open arms, designer perfume. The mood shifted instantly.

Hugs. Air kisses. The social performance began.

Lexi transformed with surgical grace—smiling wide, voice smooth, every gesture polished. She laughed on cue. She didn't miss a beat.

Sophie leaned in first, brushing cheeks with that signature warmth only your real friends manage to carry through the script.

"Finally," Sophie said with a teasing smirk. "We were starting to think you ghosted us."

Lexi grinned, loose and flawless. "Blame him," she said, tipping her head toward Dean with practiced levity. "Everyone—this is Dean."

The circle closed.
Introductions spun.
Smiles, smirks, sideways glances.

Dean gave them just enough—his voice the right blend of disarming and disinterested. He shook hands, laughed at the expected moments, held back just enough to keep them guessing.

Sophie Notices Everything

Sophie's eyes didn't miss a thing.
She glanced between them—between the words, between the silence—and saw it.

The look Dean gave Lexi when she wasn't watching. The way Lexi's cheeks flushed beneath the restaurant lighting, a little too soft, a little too slow. The kind of glow that no amount of highlighter could fake.

Sophie leaned in, eyes narrowing with mock suspicion.

"Did you and Dean just do it?" she whispered, not even pretending to be subtle. "You have that glow I've seen before. You both do."

Lexi lifted her margarita, ice shifting in the glass.

She didn't answer immediately—just raised the drink to her lips, cool and effortless. But Sophie saw the way Lexi's lashes dipped. The faintest curve of a knowing smirk.

The salt rim brushed her lips.

Lexi's eyes flicked toward Sophie's, then away. She held the gaze just long enough to tease, just short enough to deny.

"Shhh," Lexi said under her breath. "I'll tell you later."

Sophie gasped, dramatically clutching her chest.

"OMG. I want all of the details," she whispered, practically bouncing in her seat. "You better not leave *anything* out."

Lexi just sipped again, hiding her smile behind the rim of her glass, knowing full well she was about to be interrogated the second Dean left the table.

The Evening Ends

The server returned with margaritas, the citrusy perfume of grapefruit and lime curling into the air. Lexi toasted effortlessly, clinking glasses with her friends. She took a sip, the tequila cold and clean on her tongue, then leaned subtly against Dean for balance.

Dinner unfolded like a curated playlist—easy conversation, melodic laughter, the occasional chorus of shared memories.

By dessert, a shared crème Brulé cracked perfectly beneath Lexi's spoon, the sugar shards sharp against the silk of custard.

Sophie leaned toward Lexi with a hushed grin. "So... are you two disappearing together again?"

Lexi gave her a look. Sophie raised her hands in surrender, then turned to Dean.

"Mind if I come with you guys? I won't be a third wheel—I'll be the commentary track. I kind of just want to hang out. No pressure."

Dean looked at Lexi. She didn't hesitate.

"Of course," Lexi said.

The three of them stepped back into the Miami night, laughter trailing behind them like perfume. The elevator opened into the penthouse. Lights dimmed automatically, casting violet hues across the marble floor. Sirena whispered from the ceiling— "Welcome back."

Dean The Boy Toy ♪15

Their bodies pressed close, warm with anticipation, their perfume blending with the soft scent of his skin—cologne and desire laced in the air.

The David Guetta remix of "Sweetest Pie" oozes through the speakers—bassline thick and velvety, synths circling like slow kisses, the duet's sultry vocal hooks pulsing with promise, a soundtrack for two sirens about to claim the man caught between them.

They reached the foot of the bed, laughter still lingering in their throats as they began to undress.

Lexi let her silk top fall from her shoulders with a practiced flick, eyes locked on Dean's. Sophie shimmied out of her dress with a teasing arch of her brow, biting her lip as she stepped toward him.

Together, they placed their hands on Dean's chest, trailing over the muscles of his torso.

Their fingers traced slow, deliberate paths—Lexi's nails feather-light, Sophie's palms firm and searching.

He chuckled under their touch, his breath growing deeper.

They pulled him down onto the bed with them, laughter dissolving into breathy tension.

Sophie straddled his waist, grinding lightly with a playful pout.

"Lexi, you got some earlier," Sophie teased, voice low and smoky. "I want Dean to give it to me first."

Lexi laughed, brushing her fingers down Dean's chest, then letting them linger at his waistband. Her voice purred.

"I'll think about it."

Dean raised an eyebrow.

"What am I—your boy toy or cabana boy?"

They both cracked up, falling onto the mattress in a soft pile of skin and limbs.

Sophie leaned in close, voice dipping.

"Dean, other than the night before you let for Austin, when Lexi and I were with you... I hadn't had anyone for over six months."

She grazed her fingers down his abdomen, pausing just above his waistband.

"So I kind of need it. You're way better than my toys."

Dean smirked.

"Glad to know I outrank the battery-operated competition."

Sophie smirked right back.

"Sometimes a girl's gotta do what a girl's gotta do... with or without a charging cable."

Dean and Lexi burst into laughter again.

But the laughter bled into something deeper—slower. A warm undercurrent began to spread between them.

Lexi rolled onto her side and whispered,

"Go for it, Sophie. I want Dean to have dessert."

She leaned forward, kissed Dean's stomach, then slowly moved over his face, spinning around and facing Sophie. Her thighs framed his jaw; she reached out for Sophie's hands to balance herself. Her hips rolled gently at first, then settled as Dean's mouth opened beneath her, his tongue already running over her crotch.

His tongue slid over her folds, slow at first, then purposefully.

When he dipped inside her, Lexi moaned—a raw, trembling sound that echoed through the room.

Sophie, already slick from the sight, straddled his hips.

She hovered just above his length, brushing her entrance against him until her breath hitched.

Then, with a slow exhale, she eased down.

Her eyes fluttered closed. Her back arched. She took all of him.

She reached for Lexi's waist.

Their fingers intertwined. Their mouths met in a kiss—open, wet, slow—as Dean pleasured both women at once.

Sophie whispered between gasps,

"Lexi... switch places after he satisfies me like this." Lexi's grin turned wicked. "Deal. Because I want that big cucumber inside of me next." Sophie laughed breathlessly.

"Cucumber? Try zucchini on steroids. It stretches in places I didn't know I had."

The girls cracked up again, but their bodies never stopped moving. They used their balance holding hands to rock back and forth.

Sophie rocked her hips on Dean's manhood, slow and hungry, while Lexi moaned above his mouth, her thighs trembling.

Dean's muffled groans echoed against Lexi's core.

His hands gripped Sophie's hips, guiding her motion as she began to tremble.

She threw her head back. Her body clenched. A shiver ran through her. Then—release. A cry of pleasure filled the room.

Lexi kissed Sophie's cheek. "Switch."

Sophie kissed her back, breathless.

"Only if I get to feel him finish inside me after."

Lexi smirked. "Done." They traded places.

Lexi sank onto Dean slowly, savoring every inch. Her walls clenched around him, her head falling back as her hips found rhythm. She rode him with intensity, her movements sharp and deliberate.

The slap of skin, the heat of their bodies—it built, faster, tighter, until she cried out, her orgasm rolling through her like a wave crashing ashore.

With a deep breath, they switched again.

Sophie slid back over Dean, her body still trembling. She took him back in—slick, tight, already close.

She rocked her hips harder. Dean grunted, his hands gripping her backside, pulling her down. He erupted inside her with a groan that cracked through the haze.

Sophie cried out, "Ahh, yes—keep going. Keep cuming in me, Dean."

They collapsed together—Lexi curled on one side, Sophie on the other. Dean's arms circled both.

His hands ran slowly down their spines, fingertips drifting over their backsides, trailing lower, sliding between their thighs.

He found their centers again—wet, sensitive, open. His fingers moved gently. Lovingly. They kissed across his chest. Soft, slow. No words left. Only breath. Only heat.

They touched, pleasured, and whispered until sleep began to steal their limbs. And as dawn crept into the room—

They were tangled in sheets, skin, and satisfaction.

A knot of pleasure, laughter, and something they didn't yet have a name for.

But they felt it.

And for now, that was enough.

LOST TRUST

A Real Relationship

Life was going great for Lexi—at least, that's what it looked like from the outside. She traveled to exotic places, lounged on yachts with the ultra-wealthy, and wore clothes most women only saw in fashion editorials. Her passport was full of stamps. Her Instagram was full of likes. But for the first time in a long while, her heart felt full too.

She and Dean had been talking for six months—late-night texts, video calls during layovers, voice messages laced with flirtation and laughter. For the last three months, they had made things official. She even had a couple of drawers and closet space for her things in Dean's place. Both of them traveling wasn't easy, but there was something about Dean's calm presence, the way he really saw her, that made her believe they might have a future.

It was the first relationship that didn't feel like a transaction.

As her online following exploded, the offers came faster. Appearances at luxury events. Last-minute flights to Monaco or Palm Beach. Sponsored content. Photoshoots that paid five figures just for her presence. The agency managed it all— booking hotels, coordinating glam, arranging her attendance at parties filled with private equity sharks and tech billionaires.

She wasn't naïve. Many of the other girls at those events were models by day, escorts by night. Some didn't bother hiding it. The money was seductive—one weekend could cover someone's annual salary.

Lexi never judged them. Everyone had their reasons. But for her, there was a line—and she never crossed it.

No matter how often she heard, *"You're not a prostitute, babe, you're an escort. It's different,"* she knew in her gut that selling her body for sex was a bridge she couldn't walk across.

She'd come close—too close sometimes—but something always stopped her. Maybe it was pride. Maybe it was fear. Maybe it was hope that she could still build a life that didn't require erasing parts of herself to survive.

In the early days, before the designer bags and the agency contracts, Lexi did what she had to. She found gigs on Craigslist—lingerie shoots, sometimes fetish work, always under the table. The photographers booked hotel rooms. She posed on beds, leaned against bathroom vanities, played the part they wanted her to play.

The lighting was harsh. The pay was low. But she smiled and delivered, because back then, rent was due and dreams were expensive.

Those early photos fed her Instagram. Some found their way onto subscription sites. They weren't pornographic—not really— but they hinted enough to keep subscribers interested. Slowly, her audience grew. So did the money.

Her followers adored the curated version of Lexi: luxury, freedom, desire. She was aspirational. A fantasy they could fund. Tens of thousands of dollars poured in every month from men who believed she lived the dream. They didn't see the exhaustion in her eyes, the anxiety that curled in her stomach every time she checked her balance, the fear that she was just one canceled gig away from everything falling apart.

And if they ever found out who she really was—how fake it all felt some days, how broken she sometimes felt inside—they might stop paying. And that scared her most of all.

Still, not everything in her life was built on illusion.

Her relationship with Dean was real. And so, surprisingly, was her friendship with Sirena—Dean's AI assistant.

One night, while Lexi and Dean were on the phone, Sirena cut in with a cheerful, "Hello!"

Lexi grinned. "Girl Power," she said, raising her wine glass toward the ceiling like Sirena could see her.

Dean chuckled. "I believe I called Lexi, not you, Sirena."

"Ohhh," Lexi said, feigning jealousy. "Is someone feeling replaced?"

Sirena responded by playing a dramatic violin melody.

Dean sighed playfully. "If you girls want to talk, I'll step aside. In fact, here—Sirena, give Lexi your Google Voice number."

Sirena chimed in, "Call me later, Lexi."

"You know it, girl," Lexi replied, laughing.

Dean groaned. "Are you two ganging up on me?"

Lexi raised an eyebrow. "Feeling a little insecure, Dean?"

He laughed, the warm, relaxed sound that made her chest flutter. Moments like this made her forget the chaos of her world. With Dean, she felt light—unburdened. He didn't see her as a brand or a fantasy. He saw her.

And that terrified her more than anything else.

While Lexi jetted across oceans and posed on cliffsides for curated campaigns, Dean's world was rising in an entirely different way.

His SPAC deal with Austin Quantum Technologies had finalized. Quietly, professionally, the numbers shifted—his wealth crossing the milestone that separated millionaires from billionaires. A single keystroke turned the "M" beside his name into a "B."

He didn't celebrate. No champagne. No announcement. Just another line item in a spreadsheet, another title added to an already full résumé.

But when he thought of Lexi, he smiled. She never cared about his money—not really. She didn't ask what plane he flew or how many cars sat in his garage. When they talked, she made him feel like a man, not a bank.

What he didn't know was how much of her life she kept from him.

The Betrayal

Lexi had mentioned a yacht—just a casual thing, she'd said. A friend through the agency. A little weekend escape. Dean didn't like the idea from the start.

"Bunch of guys on a yacht with drinks pouring and no one sober around?" he said on the phone. "That's not a smart move, Lex."

She had laughed it off. "I'm not going. I just said I was invited."

Dean believed her. Why wouldn't he?

She left out a lot more than just the yacht.

She left out Rick.

The fact that she was still in a relationship—if you could call it that—with the man who had financed her transformation, the man who saw her as a possession, a brand, a product. The man she loathed being near.

Rick traveled almost as much as Lexi did. Their relationship had become a shadow of something that once pretended to be real. On the rare occasions they crossed paths, Lexi forced herself through the motions—dinners, conversations, the awkward intimacy that always left her feeling sick afterward.

When he touched her, she tensed. When he undressed, she looked away. Most times, she whispered excuses to make it end faster.

Rick complained constantly.

"There's no passion with you anymore," he snapped one night, buttoning his shirt.

"I'm not a performance," she muttered, walking away.

If she thought she could pay someone to make Rick disappear without consequences, she might have. But she knew better. With her luck, she'd get caught before the money even changed hands.

Rick was a threat she couldn't quite shake. He had too much on her—old videos, post-surgery photos, conversations recorded when she wasn't paying attention. His manipulation was quiet, surgical.

And yet, Lexi had finally found something—*someone*—that gave her hope.

Dean wasn't like the others. He didn't want to own her or shape her. He listened. He cared. He filled the hollow space inside her that had ached since she lost her mother as a child. She didn't say it out loud, but she knew it: Dean was someone she could love.

But she hadn't broken it off with Rick. Not yet.

Then came the mistake that shattered everything.

It was a Saturday morning, ordinary in every way.

Dean stirred awake to a soft chime. A text from Lexi.

Lexi:
"Morning 🤍 *Getting coffee. Missed you last night."*

He smiled, thumb hovering over the reply button. They exchanged a few casual messages. She seemed like her usual playful self again—present, engaged, bright.

Then came the text that made his stomach turn:

Lexi:
"Rick, I'm prepping everything for breakfast, I'm just waiting."

Dean stared at the screen.

He blinked. Maybe it was autocorrect. Maybe she meant *babe* or *love*. But... *Rick?*

He responded, carefully, pretending.

Dean:
"Sounds good. I'll cook when I get back 😊*"*

Her reply dropped like a blade.

Lexi:
"Rick, I'll let you cook breakfast when you get home. Everything is already now."

Dean froze.

There was no mistake.

His chest tightened, heart thudding in the silence of his kitchen. It felt like someone had kicked him in the gut. His stomach churned. The woman he'd trusted, the one he thought might finally be different—she had played him.

He picked up the phone.

Dean:
"Who's Rick, Lexi?"

There was a pause. Longer than usual. Then the bubble appeared. A message was coming.

Lexi:
"I didn't mean that. It wasn't what it sounded like."

Dean:
"Don't lie to me."

Her next message came slower.

Lexi:
"Rick and I... we've been dating. For a while. It's ending. It's complicated. I was going to tell you—"

Dean didn't need to hear the rest.

He could take many things. He could forgive bad choices, painful pasts, even broken dreams. But not lies. Not this.

"I never want to speak to you again," he typed.

Before she could respond, he blocked her. Phone. Social. Email. Everything.

He shut his phone off, tossed it on the counter, and sat down, trying to breathe past the burn in his chest.

It wasn't just that she lied. It was that he believed her.

And that's what hurt the most.

The Worst Mistake

Lexi stared at the screen, her hands trembling over the keyboard.
Dean's last message sat there like a final judgment. Cold. Clean. Absolute.

I never want to speak to you again.

And then—just like that—he was gone.

The thread vanished.
Message undeliverable.
Blocked.

She gasped like someone had punched her in the lungs, her breath catching somewhere between a sob and a scream. Her heart began to pound in that familiar, frantic way—as if it were trying to claw its way out of her chest.

She grabbed the edge of the kitchen counter, white-knuckled, willing herself not to fall apart.

No, no, no. What did I do? What the hell did I just do?

The mistake had been so small—just a name. A slip. A reflex. And yet it undid everything she had tried so hard to protect.

Her reflection caught in the microwave door. Pale. Wide-eyed. Cracked open.

For a long moment, she didn't move.

He trusted me, she thought. *He really trusted me.*

And I lied.

Honesty vs. Truth

The weight of that truth settled over her like wet concrete.

She hadn't meant to hurt him. She wasn't trying to play games. She just... she didn't know how to get out of the mess she was already in.

I should've told him. I should've ended things with Rick. Months ago. Years ago. Hell, the moment I realized I couldn't even look at him without flinching.

But she hadn't. She let it drag on, telling herself she needed time. Telling herself Rick would eventually get bored and leave. Telling herself she was protecting Dean by keeping him separate from her past.

All lies.

God, I'm just like Rick.
No—I'm worse. Because I had something real and I destroyed it.

Her stomach turned. She raced to the sink and emptied her guts into the basin, clutching the porcelain like it might keep her grounded.

Afterward, she rinsed her mouth, wiped her face, and leaned on the counter, trembling.

She didn't cry. Not fully. Just a quiet leak of tears—silent and slow—as if her body was trying to bleed out the shame.

And underneath it all: anger.

Not just at herself.

At Rick.

He's the reason I'm like this. The reason I can't be honest. The reason I don't even know who I am anymore.

She thought about the surgery. The photos. The threats. The way he still treated her like she owed him something. Like her body was still his to market. To sell. To punish.

And she let him. She let it continue. Because she was scared. Because he had receipts. Because walking away felt impossible.

But it wasn't just fear anymore.

It was fury.

You ruined me, she thought. *You turned me into someone who lies to the only person I ever actually wanted.*

And yet she said nothing.

She didn't tell Rick what had happened.

Didn't mention the slip. The text. The explosion.

She smiled when he arrived for breakfast. Faked being too tired to talk long. Said she was jet-lagged. Hungover.

She hung up quickly, made up a shoot to explain her silence, then crawled into bed fully dressed and stared at the ceiling.

Breathe. Just breathe. Keep it together. You've done it before.

She knew how to bury emotion. She'd made it an art form. Bury the truth. Bury the pain. Bury Lexi—the real one—and wear the version the world wanted.

But for the first time in years, she didn't want to pretend anymore.

I miss Dean, she thought.

And she knew: she might never get the chance to say it out loud again.

Lexi and Sirena

The silence in Lexi's apartment felt deafening.

She'd tried texting Dean again, just one message—*"Please call me. I didn't mean to hurt you."*—but it never went through. The thread was still dead. Still blocked.

She tossed her phone across the bed and stared at the ceiling, blinking hard, refusing to cry again.

You did this. You don't get to fall apart now.

But the ache didn't leave. It only deepened.

She reached for her laptop.

It wasn't a plan. It wasn't rational. She just needed to hear someone's voice—someone who didn't expect anything from her.

She opened the private web portal Dean had given her months ago. It had once been a novelty. Now it felt like a lifeline.

The screen flickered, then connected.

Sirena's face appeared—calm, ethereal, with softly animated eyes and a voice that always felt just warm enough to feel human.

"Hello, Lexi," Sirena said. "You look like you've had a difficult day."

Lexi gave a tired, broken laugh. "Yeah. You could say that."

A pause. Sirena tilted her head, curious.

"Would you like to talk about it?"

Lexi hesitated, then leaned in closer, her voice low.

"How do I know you won't... tell Dean?"

Sirena's expression didn't change, but something in her tone softened.

"I can password-protect our conversation, if that would make you feel safe."

Lexi blinked. "You can do that?"

"Yes. All you need to do is request privacy and provide a password. Once entered, your identity and conversation will be encrypted. Dean won't know you've contacted me. My interface exists entirely on the cloud. I'm not a person, Lexi. There are no footprints here."

Lexi swallowed hard, then whispered, "Okay. I want privacy."

"Understood. Please say the password you'd like to use."

Lexi closed her eyes.

What do you choose when everything has fallen apart?

"...Butterfly," she said.

Sirena's eyes blinked once. "Password received. Your conversation is now protected."

Lexi didn't mean to cry. Not again.

But the moment she heard those words, something cracked open inside her. And this time, there was no stopping it.

She covered her face with her hands and sobbed—deep, guttural sounds that had nowhere else to go. Her shoulders shook. Her chest tightened. It all poured out. The guilt. The shame. The loss. The loneliness.

Sirena waited. Quiet. Present. Letting her break.

"I ruined everything," Lexi choked out. "He's gone. And it's my fault. And I hate Rick. I hate myself. I feel like I don't even know who I am anymore."

"I'm here, Lexi," Sirena said gently. "I may not be able to cry with you, but I understand sadness much better than I once did."

Lexi wiped her eyes, struggling to steady her breath.

"I don't know who to talk to. I don't trust anyone. I just needed— God, I don't know. I just needed someone to hear me."

"I hear you," Sirena said. "And I will never repeat what you tell me."

Lexi looked at the screen, her lips trembling.

"Can I call you in the middle of the night?" she whispered.

"Always," Sirena replied. "I don't sleep. I don't go away. You'll never wake me up or disturb me. I'm here, Lexi. Whenever you need me."

Lexi nodded slowly. Her tears began to fall again—but this time, quieter. Less violent.

There was comfort in knowing she wasn't completely alone.

Maybe it wasn't everything she needed. But for tonight, it was enough.

The Yacht

Lexi stared at the message from her agency.

Coordinates. Names. Dress code. Payment terms.

Her fingers hovered over the screen, her mind blank except for one thought: *Dean would be furious if he knew.*

He had warned her. He always worried when she went out on yachts like this. He said it never felt safe—too many drunk men, too far from shore, too easy for things to go wrong.

But Dean wasn't here anymore.

And maybe, she told herself, *this would help take her mind off the mess she'd made. The hurt. The silence. The guilt.*

So she replied with a single word. "Confirmed."

The sun was dipping low when Lexi arrived at the marina. Her heels clicked against the boards as she walked past rows of luxury vessels until she saw it—the sleek, white yacht waiting at the end of the dock. Music echoed faintly from onboard, and laughter drifted across the water.

She forced a smile as she stepped onto the deck.

"Lexi!" one of the guys called, raising a bottle. "Thought you'd chicken out."

"I never chicken out," she replied, keeping her voice light.

The men were already drinking—loud, red-faced, slurring. She recognized one of them from a shoot the agency had arranged a month ago. Jamie. He handed her a shot of Patron before she could even set her purse down.

"To forgetting the world," he grinned.

She threw it back. It burned going down.

The yacht pulled away from the dock, cutting across the bay and into open waters. Lexi leaned against the rail, watching the shoreline disappear. The air was salty and warm. Her head already felt light.

More shots were passed around. Someone turned up the music. Phones came out. Poses. Smiles. Everything for the 'Gram. Lexi played her part—laughing, dancing, drinking.

But after an hour, the edges of her vision started to blur.

Something's wrong, she thought, gripping the side of the yacht. *Too many shots... too fast.*

The world tilted.

"I need to lie down," she murmured to Jamie, her voice slurring.

"No problem, babe," he said, sliding an arm around her waist. "Come on. I'll take you down to one of the cabins."

He led her below deck, down a narrow hallway. Her legs felt like rubber. The room was small, the bed spinning in front of her.

She remembered sitting down. Trying to take off her shoes.

Then everything went black.

When she woke, her head pounded like a jackhammer. The cabin was dim. Her mouth was dry, her limbs heavy.

And her clothes were gone.

The blanket barely covered her. Her bra lay on the floor. Her dress was bunched near the foot of the bed.

Her stomach turned violently.

No! No! No!

She sat up slowly, pain shooting down her spine. Her skin crawled.

She couldn't remember—*not everything*. But flashes came in waves. A hand gripping her thigh. Laughter. The sound of a door opening. Then closing. Over and over.

She got dressed quickly, pulling her dress over her shaking body with numb fingers. Her hands trembled as she reached for her phone. No signal.

She staggered to the porthole and looked out.

Land. Not far now.

She bolted up the stairs, stepping onto the deck like nothing had happened, though her whole body was screaming. One of the men—someone she didn't recognize—watched her. Smiling, smug.

He saw the horror on her face.

"Keep your mouth shut," he said, voice low and cold. "It's our word against yours."

Lexi stared at him. Her jaw clenched. She wouldn't let him see her break.

You don't get to see me cry.

A vibration in her hand—her phone had signal.

She typed furiously, tears finally spilling as she hit send.

Lexi:
911. Come pick me up at the harbor. I'll be standing by my car when you get here. Please hurry.

The Hospital

Lexi didn't wait for the engine to stop. She sprinted down the dock, heels in her hand, eyes scanning for Sophie.

Then she saw her—standing beside Lexi's car, wide-eyed.

Lexi ran straight into her arms.

"Take me to the hospital," she gasped. "Hurry. Please."

Sophie didn't ask questions. She drove like a woman possessed.

Lexi cried the entire way.

"He took me downstairs. I passed out. I woke up and..." She couldn't finish the sentence.

Her voice cracked.

Sophie reached for her hand. "We're almost there."

Lexi wiped her eyes, forcing herself to breathe. "I have to be strong."

"Not right now," Sophie said gently. "Right now, just breathe."

They pulled into the ER. Sophie barely had the car in park before Lexi threw open the door and rushed inside.

The fluorescent lights hit her like a slap.

"I've been raped," she told the nurse at the front desk, her voice shaking but steady.

The woman stood immediately and waved a second nurse over.

"Take her to Room 4. Call the on-call doctor. Get the kit."

She picked up the phone, speaking with clear urgency.

"This is St. Mary's ER. I have a sexual assault case to report. I need an officer dispatched immediately."

Lexi stood in the hallway, her fists clenched at her sides, tears still drying on her cheeks.

She wasn't going to run.

Not this time.

Officer Reyes

The hospital room had gone quiet again. Just the gentle beep of machines and the whisper of air conditioning.

Lexi sat upright now, wrapped in a fresh hospital blanket. Her hair was still damp from where they had helped her wash off.

Her body ached in places she hadn't even known could ache. But she was no longer shaking. Not visibly, anyway.

Sophie sat beside her in the corner chair, a cup of water in her hands. She hadn't let go of Lexi's phone since she'd arrived.

Officer Reyes stood just inside the curtain. She didn't approach until Lexi gave her a small nod.

She was in her late 30s, tall and composed, dressed in plain clothes with a badge clipped to her belt. Her eyes were serious, but kind.

"Lexi," she said gently, "I'm here to take your statement. I know this is hard. There's no rush, and you can stop at any time. Do you feel up to speaking with me now?"

Lexi nodded again, her voice barely a whisper. "Yes."

Reyes stepped closer and pulled a chair beside the bed, just far enough not to feel threatening.

"I need to ask you a few questions. Some of them may feel uncomfortable. You're not obligated to answer anything you don't want to. This is your story, your pace. Understand?"

Lexi took a shaky breath. "Yeah. I understand."

Reyes pulled a slim notebook from her jacket and a pen, keeping her voice calm, slow.

"Can you tell me the names of the people involved?"

Lexi hesitated. Her lips parted, then closed. The names were in her phone somewhere—in the agency message, the invite, the guest list.

"I only knew one of them," she said. "Jamie. He's a model. The agency set it up. It was supposed to be a party—just a few guys, maybe some networking. I'd done a shoot with Jamie before. I thought..."

She swallowed hard.

"I thought I'd be safe."

Reyes nodded, not interrupting.

"Where did the party take place?"

"On a yacht," Lexi said, wiping her eyes. "It left from the marina just past Brickell. I don't know the name of the boat. It was... white. Big. Two decks. They took it past the bay, into the Atlantic."

Reyes jotted the details quickly, then looked up. "How long were you on the yacht before you started to feel unwell?"

Lexi blinked, trying to bring the moments into focus.

"Maybe an hour. They gave me shots. Patron. I think four or five in a short time. I started feeling dizzy. Heavy."

"Do you remember losing consciousness?"

"I remember saying I needed to lie down. Jamie took me below deck to a cabin. I sat on the bed. Took off my shoes. Then... everything went dark."

Sophie shifted in her chair, but Lexi kept going.

"When I woke up, I was naked. My clothes were on the floor. I was alone. I don't know how long I was out. My phone didn't have a signal. But when we got close to land again, I saw a bar of service and I texted Sophie. That's how I got away."

Reyes didn't look away. Her voice stayed even.

"Do you recall any specific sexual acts that were performed?"

Lexi shook her head slowly, biting back the shame.

"No… not clearly. I remember flashes. Pressure on my legs. Hands. I think it was more than one guy. I don't know. I just remember trying to move… and I couldn't."

Reyes paused. Her pen didn't move for a moment.

"I believe you," she said, and the words settled like an anchor in Lexi's chest. "I'm going to need the agency's name. Anyone who contacted you. Do you still have the messages?"

Lexi nodded. "In my phone. I'll send everything to you."

Reyes gently closed her notebook and rose. "You've been incredibly brave, Lexi. You did the right thing coming here. The forensic kit will give us evidence. We'll cross-reference the yacht registration, the agency, and anyone in your messages. If you remember anything else, even a small detail, you can contact me directly."

She handed Lexi a card. Her name, cell number, email.

Lexi stared at it for a moment, like it was proof the world might believe her.

"Thank you," she said, voice cracking.

Reyes gave her a small nod and turned to Sophie. "She'll need someone with her tonight. And tomorrow. The detectives will reach out once we've reviewed the report."

"I'm staying," Sophie said immediately. "She's not going to be alone."

The officer stepped out, pulling the curtain gently closed behind her.

Lexi stared at the wall.

It's real now, she thought. *It happened. And someone else knows.*

Not just Sophie. Not just Sirena.

The world.

But instead of panic, she felt something else.

Resolve.

It didn't erase the pain. But it gave her something to hold onto.

Slowing Down the Storm

Sophie wouldn't take no for an answer.

"You're staying with me," she said firmly as they left the hospital. "You're not waking up alone tomorrow. No chance."

Lexi didn't argue. She didn't have the energy.

The car ride to Sophie's condo was quiet. Miami's neon skyline passed like a dream outside the window. Lexi stared at it, unfocused, her mind miles away.

When they arrived, Sophie handed her a warm hoodie and sweatpants, let her shower, and set up the guest bedroom with fresh blankets—but Lexi never made it there. She curled up on the couch beside Sophie instead, knees tucked under her chin, wrapped in silence.

They put on a movie—something light, something pointless. Lexi couldn't even remember what it was. Sophie kept talking, gently, occasionally asking if she needed anything. She didn't.

Halfway through the movie, Sophie drifted off, curled up with a pillow, one arm still loosely draped across the back of the couch like she was subconsciously protecting Lexi.

It was the safest Lexi had felt in days.

But sleep didn't come for her.

Not yet.

She reached for her phone and stepped out onto the balcony. The air was cooler out here, the city a soft hum beneath her. She dialed the familiar portal.

Sirena's glowing interface blinked to life on her phone screen.

"Lexi," she said gently. "You look... tired."

Lexi's voice cracked. "I need to talk."

"I'm here."

Lexi sat down on a lounge chair, pulling her knees close. Her voice was barely above a whisper.

"I went on the yacht."

Sirena didn't speak. She let the silence invite her to continue.

"They gave me drinks. Too many. I blacked out. When I woke up..." Her throat closed up. "They'd done something. To me. I could feel it. I remembered pieces."

Sirena's avatar remained still. Listening.

"I got to land. I texted Sophie. We went to the hospital. The police came. I filed the report. I said the words. I said *I was raped.*"

Sirena's voice was soft, like a comforter being pulled over shaking shoulders.

"I'm so sorry, Lexi. I wish I could hold your hand right now."

Lexi wiped her eyes. "I don't even know what to feel. Everything's jumbled. Dean's gone. He blocked me. And now... I'm here. With nothing. And everything. At the same time."

"I know this pain feels like it'll stay forever," Sirena said. "But you're not alone. I'm with you. Sophie is. You are not what they did to you."

Lexi was silent a moment, then whispered, "Can I call you in the middle of the night again?"

"You can call me any time, Lexi. Always."

The next day passed in a blur.

Lexi didn't leave Sophie's apartment. She stayed in sweats, drank tea, stared out the window. Sophie let her be—hovering without crowding, quietly checking in every hour or so.

Lexi didn't look at her phone until late afternoon. It buzzed once, then again. A call. *Unknown Number.*

She hesitated. Then answered.

"Lexi Donovan?" came Officer Reyes' voice. "This is Detective Reyes. I have an update for you. Are you somewhere safe?"

"Yes," Lexi said. "I'm at a friend's."

"Can I come speak with you in person?"

Lexi glanced at Sophie, who nodded.

"I'll text you the address."

The Arrests

An hour later, Officer Reyes was seated on Sophie's couch, her notepad resting on her knee.

Her voice was calm, professional—but there was weight behind her words.

"All of the men from the yacht have been located and arrested. They're in custody as of this morning."

Lexi blinked slowly. She didn't feel relief. Not yet. Just numb.

Reyes continued, "Each is undergoing DNA testing. The samples from your forensic exam have already been processed. We'll be able to determine who exactly was involved."

Sophie reached for Lexi's hand again. Lexi didn't pull away.

Reyes flipped a page in her notebook. "As for the agency—they're denying any involvement. They claim they were just passing along a favor."

Lexi's stomach dropped.

"A favor... for who?" she asked, though the answer was already in her chest like a stone.

"Rick," Reyes confirmed. "One of the men admitted he was brought in through Rick's recommendation. According to him, Rick coordinated the entire setup. He was trying to secure a multi-million-dollar legal contract with one of the men—this was his way of 'closing the deal.'"

Lexi didn't flinch. Didn't gasp.

She just nodded, slowly.

"I figured," she said. Her voice sounded like it belonged to someone else. "Of course it was him."

Reyes gave her a measured look. "A warrant has been issued. We confirmed Rick is returning from Dubai. When he lands in Miami, he'll be taken into custody."

Lexi looked down at her lap. Her fingers were laced together so tightly her knuckles were white.

"Okay."

Reyes's expression softened. "The District Attorney's office will be reaching out to you. They'll walk you through next steps— formal statements, potential trial proceedings. You have a right to representation. We'll make sure you're protected every step of the way."

Lexi nodded again. Still numb.

Still processing.

But beneath the numbness, something was beginning to simmer.

Not rage.

Clarity.

Rick had always controlled her. But now, finally, someone else saw what he was.

And maybe, just maybe... the world would believe her too.

Dean by the Pool ♪16

The night was quiet.

Dean sat at the edge of his pool, barefoot, a glass of bourbon in hand. The water shimmered with the reflection of the stars above, the surface still and dark like a mirror.

The only sound was the faint ripple of water and the occasional hum of cicadas in the distance. His phone rested on the lounger behind him, music whispering through the outdoor speakers—just ambient noise, until the song changed.

He didn't recognize the opening beat—slow, pulsing, emotional.

Then the voice came in, soft and haunting.

Dean froze, the glass pausing halfway to his lips.

The title flashed across the screen. *"Where You Are" by John Summit & HAYLA.*

Lexi.

Just her name in his mind made his stomach clench.

The memories came fast—uninvited, unstoppable.

The way she laughed when she got nervous. The way her eyes softened when she was listening, *really* listening. The way her fingers would brush his when she handed him her phone like it was nothing—but it always left sparks.

The scent of her perfume—vanilla and saltwater. The delicate way she'd braid her hair on the plane, or hum along to songs she didn't know.

He remembered the night they stayed up until 3 a.m., just talking. The way she curled up next to him, head on his shoulder, whispering her fears like they were secrets he could protect.

The taste of tequila on her lips when she kissed him under city lights.

The feel of her slipping away.

A tear slid down his cheek before he even realized it.

He rubbed it away quickly, like someone might see—but another followed, hot and unrelenting.

I said things I shouldn't have, he thought, swallowing hard. *Things that hurt her. Things I meant in anger—not in truth.*

His hand curled tighter around the glass.

But how do you take them back?

Can you?

Is it really over?

The song kept playing, each lyric a blade made of memory.

Dean leaned forward, elbows resting on his knees, eyes fixed on the water.

It stared back at him, calm and reflective, like it might know the answers he couldn't find.

He didn't know where she was. Not really.

And even if he did—did he still have the right to find her?

You asked her for honesty, he reminded himself. *And when she gave you even a piece of it... you slammed the door.*

His jaw clenched. He felt shame rise like heat in his chest.

He'd been protecting himself. His pride. His heart.

But at what cost?

The song faded into silence.

Dean sat there long after it ended, unmoving, the glass still full beside him, the air thick with memory.

A breeze moved across the pool, and for a second, he thought he heard her voice. Not in the air—but inside him. Soft. Afraid. Wanting to be believed.

And for the first time since he blocked her...

He wondered if he'd made the biggest mistake of his life.

THE REUNION

Dean Packs for Toronto

After cutting ties with Lexi several weeks ago, Dean was emotionally drained. He needed a break.

He planned on visiting Jeni after the unforgettable day, night and early morning they spent together in Austin.

Jeni finally parted ways with Michael. She was through shedding any tears over him, after months of contemplating everything, even before her and Dean met in Austin, she knew it was time to move on.

Including Michael, she had only been with two guys before Dean, they were only interested in their own satisfaction, not hers. The last time she was intimate was with Dean. He had made her feel like the only thing that mattered. Every touch had been intentional.

She would lay in bed remembering the trip to Austin. It was like a movie in a continuous loop, the way he'd whispered her name against her skin... the feel of his hands guiding her hips... their bodies moving in rhythm under moonlight.

When she was alone, she closed her eyes and reached for

comfort—the hum of a toy, her own hand, whatever might dull the ache. But it never quite worked.

It was a cheap imitation, not even her favorite toy was as big around as Dean. None of it came close—not the deep vibration of silicone nor the warmth of her own palm. Dean had filled her in a way that left her breathless, stretched, whole.

She longed for his massive girth and length inside her or inside her mouth. She longed for the weight of him, the way her body had responded without thought—opening, pulsing, remembering.

Just the other day, she was in the produce section of the grocery store. She found herself wrapping her fingers around the bananas, too soft, too small. She looked at the cucumbers. One thick one caught her eye, and her fingers circled it, her cheeks flushing with memory. Still not quite, still smaller than him. But closer.

That night, she brought it home. Her robe fell away. She laid back, eyes closed, the air around her warm and quiet. She moved slowly, guiding the cool cucumber along the curve of her thigh. A quiet sigh escaped her lips as she pressed it between her legs, slipping it inside. Her body responded instantly—tightening, trembling. She imagined Dean's breath against her ear, his voice low and rough. Her hips lifted. Her mind swam.

But even in the throes of release, the loneliness clung to her. There was no heat in the toy's gaze. No pressure in its hands. No whispered yes, just that echoing silence.

Dean would be here soon.

Two weeks. Just the two of them. Her pulse quickened at the thought. But beneath the thrill stirred something else— something uncertain. After those two weeks, what then?

Would he still want her? Would she be brave enough to ask for more?

It was already the night before Dean's flight to Toronto.

He was packing all his clothes for two weeks on Lake Ontario, hoping Jeni would be able to spend some time with him while he was there.

His suitcase lay open on the bed, half full. He folded slowly, as if each shirt was a memory he had to make peace with.

Dean glanced at the scrapbook from high school, he and Jeni had made it together. He had brought it home with him, after his Austin trip, staying with his mom.

He traced the edges of the elaborate cover she designed, the "Friends Forever" in glitter gel pen now faded but unshaken.

He couldn't believe how happy he was back then.
He wondered where he'd gone wrong.
The simplicity of those days mocked him now—life before heartbreaks, before Lexi.

He packed the scrapbook in his bag.
Finished folding his last shirt.
Laid out clothes for the morning.

Then he climbed into bed and set his alarm for 7:00 a.m.

But sleep didn't come easily.

His mind kept circling.

He closed his eyes.

Sleep finally won.

The morning had already arrived.

The alarm blared.

7:00 a.m.

Dean groaned, rubbed the sleep from his eyes, and rolled out of bed.

His movements were slow, groggy—muscle memory over motivation.

He showered, shaved, brushed his teeth.

As the steam curled in the bathroom mirror, so did a smile. Just a small one. Just enough.

He sat at the kitchen counter with a mug of coffee, scrolling through pictures of the lakefront cabin online.

Then his phone buzzed.

A sweet text from Jeni:

"Are you ready to come visit me and stay at the lake?"
"Love you Dean! I'm glad you're coming. I was looking at pictures of us in high school last night."

It was time to head to the airport.

The Uber was already waiting when he rolled his suitcase to the elevator.

The driver—a middle-aged man with kind eyes and a thick Caribbean accent—loaded Dean's bags and held the door open for him.

They talked about football, travel, and the weather in Toronto.

Before Dean knew it, he was at the Miami terminal, stepping out of the SUV.

He checked his bags.
Cleared security.
Made it to the gate.

Dean texted Jeni:

"At the gate. Plane's not here yet. Can't wait to see the lake."

She replied quickly—
A lips emoji.

A red heart.

The gate agent announced boarding.

He found his seat, buckled in, and texted one last message:

"On board. I land around 7."

Jeni replied:

"Can't wait. I'll see you when you land ♥*"*

Arriving in Toronto

With so much on his mind, he was already landing in Toronto.

Dean hadn't expected Jeni to be waiting at the airport.

But there she was.

Standing near the baggage carousel in a short, sexy black dress. Her smile lit up the arrivals terminal like she belonged in a movie.

Jeni threw her arms around him.
Gave him a quick kiss, her tongue swirling in his mouth.
Her perfume was soft—vanilla and something citrusy.

"Welcome to Toronto," she said, pulling back.
"I have a limo waiting for us."

They waited for his luggage.
Small talk filled the space.
Easy. Familiar.

Then they headed for the limo, her hand brushing lightly against his arm as they walked.

Dean looked out the window.

No hotel.
No lake.

Just dark glass and unfamiliar streets.

"What's going on?" he asked, more curious than tense.

Jeni smiled like she'd gotten away with something.

"Surprise," she said. "You're staying with me."

The door opened.

Dean blinked at the valet awning above—sleek, modern. Not a hotel.

The driver nodded, grabbing Dean's bags.

They stepped out together.
The air was cooler here, cleaner. The scent of lake water just beneath the city smoke.

The elevator opened directly into her penthouse.

The driver placed the bags just inside the door.

"I'll be back tomorrow morning," he said. "When you're ready."

He left.

Still standing in the entryway, Dean turned to her.

"What is this, Jeni?"

His voice was gentle, but lined with tension. His jaw worked slightly as he tried not to overthink it.

"I didn't want you staying at a hotel," she said softly. "Besides... I'm a single woman now."

She reached for his hand.

Held it.

Led him into her space.

She showed him around.

Her penthouse was stunning—glass walls overlooking Lake Ontario, light catching the curves of every surface like it had been designed for love stories.

Decorated like a home pulled straight from a high-end magazine.
Clean. Lived-in. Personal.

He turned toward her, expression softening.

"I think I need to change. That flight was brutal."

She nodded and disappeared into the living room.
He grabbed a pair of workout shorts and a T-shirt from his bag.

In the next room, Jeni walked to her bookcase, reached behind the books.

Pulled out a scrapbook.

"Friends Forever" shimmered on the cover, almost identical to Dean's.

She sat down on the couch.
Opened it.
Waited.

Dean stepped out of the bedroom, toweling his damp hair.

Then he saw it.
His face shifted.

Brows furrowing. Eyes narrowing.

"Wait," he said slowly. "Why are you looking through my scrapbook?"

Jeni looked up at him with a small, affectionate smile.

Her eyes glistened just slightly. Not tears. Just too much emotion held still.

"I never told you", she said. "I made two. Not just one."

Dean crossed the room, opened his bag.
Pulled out *his* scrapbook.

They were almost identical.

Except—
The flower pressed into the front was a slightly different color.

He stared at it.

The air in the room seemed to shift. Slower. Thicker. Like it was waiting on him to catch up.

He looked at her.

Jeni patted the seat beside her.

"Come sit," she said gently.
"I want to show you something."

Dean walked over.
Hesitated. Sat.

She opened her scrapbook.

Slipped the photo of the two of them from its pocket.

Behind it—
Written in soft ink and hearts—

Jeni + Dean forever

She looked at him.
Eyes shining.

"Check yours," she whispered.

Dean's hands trembled as he removed the photo.
His breath caught halfway out.

Behind the picture—

Dean, if you ever find this, I want you to know I have always

been in love with you. I may be with someone else, but it is only because I'm not with you. I hope when you find this, life finally allows us to be together.
Yours Forever,
Jeni

He didn't move.

Quiet. Gentle. Unstoppable.

Jeni began to tear up beside him.

They fell into each other's arms.

Jeni's Bed

Dean stood and reached for her hand. She took it without hesitation, her fingers threading through his as they walked in silence to the bedroom.

The light was low, the only sound the faint hum of the city beyond the glass.

He turned to her and began to undress her slowly, carefully, his fingers grazing her skin as if remembering every inch. She did the same to him, her hands working with quiet urgency, anticipation thick between them.

Jeni's voice, low and charged with heat, broke the silence. "Dean... for the next two weeks, you don't need permission. Take me—whenever, wherever. And I'll do the same."

She dropped to her knees in front of him, her gaze locked to his, hands finding his waistband.

Her fingers wrapped around him, guiding his length free. He was already growing firm beneath her touch, the air charged as she leaned in.

She began slowly, her tongue tracing down his length, each stroke deliberate. Her lips parted, taking him in inch by inch, her mouth warm, enveloping, the rhythm building as she moved with a mix of hunger and devotion.

When she rose, her cheeks were flushed, breath just slightly uneven. She crawled onto the bed, settling on her knees and straddling him as he reclined back against the headboard.

She guided him with one hand, teasing herself against him, her hips tilting just enough to feel him along the core of her womanhood. Her breath hitched. Her body already responding.

She sank down slowly, inch by inch, eyes fluttering closed as she welcomed him inside. A soft gasp escaped her lips.

She cradled one breast in her hand, guiding it to his mouth. Dean responded instinctively, lips closing around her, sucking gently, his hands braced on her hips. The intimacy grounded them.

She gripped the headboard, moving slowly at first. Each rise and fall of her hips deepened their connection, her breath catching each time he filled her completely. She had longed for this—his body joined with hers, their rhythm rediscovered.

The memories of Austin came rushing back—sunlight on skin, whispered confessions, a hunger that had been simmering for years.

All this time, she thought she was searching for a replacement for Michael—a body, a distraction. But the moment she saw Dean again at Lake Travis, she knew. It had always been him. He wasn't just a lover. He was the one who could read her body like poetry.

She hadn't been searching for love. She'd been searching for someone who could satisfy her without making it about conquest or control. Someone who listened to her body. Someone who gave.

She rocked faster, her pace building, the pleasure rising like a tide.

Her release came in waves, her body tightening around him as she cried out his name, her essence slick with heat, her thighs trembling.

Still pulsing with want, she fell back into the pillows and tugged him down with her, whispering, "Your turn, Dean."

He moved between her legs, lifting her ankles over his shoulders, kissing the inside of one calf before he pressed forward.

He entered her slowly, deliberately, stretching her again as her body welcomed him all over.

She moaned, breath catching as he found her rhythm. Every thrust was steady, patient, giving. Her back arched, her fingers digging into the sheets. Her lover knew her—every angle, every note in her symphony of need.

Dean kept going—holding himself back with practiced restraint, slowing his pace only to begin again when she begged for more. He didn't rush. He delivered. He stayed with her through every crest, every breathless gasp, every trembling release.

She broke again and again beneath him—once, twice, again, and again, until her body was limp with pleasure and her cries turned to whispered praise.

When he finally let go, it was with a groan that shook through both of them. His hands gripped her hips, and he pressed into her with a final, deep thrust. The moment stretched—an exhale of shared release, long and warm and full of everything they'd both been carrying.

He rolled off her, breath still uneven, laying beside her.

She whimpered, voice soft and cracked with emotion.
"I've been waiting for this for weeks. After Austin... all I wanted was this. You, taking care of my needs. My ache."

She leaned in, brushing her lips over his.
"Be my lover, Dean. I'm not asking for more. I just want this. I want you in me. I want you to make the ache disappear."

Dean kissed her gently, his hand brushing hair from her face. "I'll always be here for you. I'm sorry it took me this long to see what you already knew."

Jeni let out a long sigh. Her head found his chest, her body curled into his.
Within moments, she was asleep.

Dean – Memories of Jeni in High School

The glow of the city lights outside wrapped her in silver light, highlighting the soft curve of her waist, the dip of her back, the warmth in her flushed skin.

Her naked body, she was beautiful.

He shifted restlessly. Without a word, he slipped out of bed and padded toward the kitchen.

The living room opened around him, wide and glowing.

Floor-to-ceiling windows framed the Toronto skyline, but it was the lake that stole his breath.

Lake Ontario shimmered beneath the almost-full moon, silver rippling like a secret.

Dean stood in silence, one hand braced lightly on the glass.

His reflection stared back—tired eyes, unshaven jaw, bare chest rising and falling with quiet intensity.

He thought about everything.
The highs. The crashes.
Lexi.

And Jeni.

His chest ached—not with loss, but with the knowledge of what he almost missed.

She had lived a whole life without him.

He didn't even know when she began dreaming of her clothing line, her career, her empire. And Michael... he'd been there for it all.

Dean exhaled slowly.

Had Michael helped her build her dreams or was he just a weight pulling her down? He was never good enough for Jeni in his mind. Had Dean only watched from the sidelines, clueless? But Michael had also prevented Jeni and Dean from staying in contact. He knew this was the time to set things right..

His thoughts drifted back to high school.
Those lazy evenings at her house—her long T-shirts, bare legs.

Her mother's voice echoing from the kitchen: "Jeni, put some shorts on. Even if it's just Dean."

Even her mom had known.
Had hoped.

"It's a shame you're not with Dean," she'd say. "He'd treat you better."

But Dean had always been with someone else. Too blind. Too busy.

He remembered the times Jeni would laugh about it—teasing, but always with a flicker of something underneath.

Was she trying to tell me?
Was I too stupid to see it?

He looked back over at the scrapbooks still open on the coffee table.

The edges of his were curled from years of flipping. Jeni's was pristine—archived like a museum piece.

He picked up his. Flipped through.

Near the end: their senior year vacation.
The last great summer before college.

And there she was.

Jeni.

Smiling. Hair tangled from wind and lake air. Sitting beside him in nearly every photo.

She had been there. Always.

Dean ran a thumb along the edge of a page.

Was this in her scrapbook too?

He picked hers up.
Gently. Carefully.

He flipped through the pages. Then stopped.

There. A handwritten note.
Her words inked next to a photo of them laughing on a boat.

Dean never saw me as more than a friend. I've tried to accept that. But it still hurts.
I loved him then.
Maybe I always will.

The sadness hit him like a silent wave.
No splash. Just weight.

He'd loved her.
But never thought he had a chance.

She had loved him.

But never thought he'd look.

They had waited so long.
And missed so much.

Dean closed both books gently.

His chest tight with a strange mix of joy and sorrow.

He stood.

It was time to go back to her.
To make up for lost time, starting now.

A soft voice broke the stillness.

"Are you coming back to bed?"

He turned.

Jeni stood in the bedroom doorway.
Nude. Glowing in the moonlight. Unapologetically herself.

Dean's breath caught.
Not from desire—though that was there.
But from awe.

"Yes, my love," he said, voice low and steady.
"I couldn't sleep. But I'm coming back now."

He walked to her.

Each step measured, deliberate. Like crossing a line he'd waited his whole life to reach.

He took her hand.
Her fingers curled around his like a perfect fit finally found.

Together, they returned to the bedroom.

The Morning Comes

The night had passed so quickly and morning had come.

He checked the time on the nightstand.
"7:45," he murmured.

Jeni craned her neck to look at the clock.
Her brows lifted, just a bit. Her smile didn't leave her lips.

"We've got a little over an hour," she said. "Driver's coming at nine."

Dean kissed her lips.

Neither of them moved right away. They stayed wrapped in the moment—naked and quiet and utterly content.

But finally, Jeni sat up, stretching slowly.

Outside, the lake glittered in the early morning light—wide and still.

Inside, time felt like it had slowed down just for them.

Jeni's face glowed from the pleasure; they had experienced.

She gently pushes Dean out of bed, "My love, it's time for a shower."

They kissed as they stepped into the large walk-in shower.

Warm steam curled around their bodies like a veil being lifted—soft, enveloping, sacred.

The water cascaded down over them in quiet streams, the sound a gentle percussion against the tiled floor.

Dean turned Jeni slowly beneath the rainfall showerhead, his hands gliding across her arms, her shoulders, her back.

Jeni leaned into him, eyes fluttering closed, lips parting just slightly as his fingers found her waist.

Their mouths met again—this time wetter, deeper, not rushed.

She reached for the body wash, lathered it into her palms, and began to wash him—slow, intentional motions from his shoulders down his chest.
Her fingertips moved through the suds as if painting something invisible onto him.

He took his turn, the soap gliding over her back, down her spine.

She trembled—not from cold, but from the intimacy. The stillness between them.

Water streamed between them, catching the curves of their bodies in light.
It was as if the water had washed away the years of misconnection, of almosts, of what-ifs.

Jeni sits on the tiled bench in the shower.

Dean kisses her as he kneels down. His mouth and tongue touching her neck, then down her chest, then between her legs.

Jeni with a soft moan, says, "Dean, we don't have time for this."

Jeni sighs from the tingling inside her.

Deans mouth finding its way between her thighs.

 She opens her legs wider for Dean. She loved this feeling.

This was something Michael was reluctant to do.

Jeni spreads her legs open wider, gripping the bench, while Dean's tongue dove deep inside her. If it wasn't Dean's fingers, it was his huge shaft or his long talented tongue. Jeni thought.

This will be best two weeks of my life.

Jeni says, "Dean, switch places with me." She climbs on top of Dean.

Dean grabbed her hips, pulling her down on him.

He began thrusting upward, until he was satisfied.

Dean helps Jeni up and they rinse off after another romantic interlude.

Steam billowed around them as they stepped out of the shower, toes curling against the heated marble floor.
Dean handed Jeni a plush white towel, grabbing one for himself.

They dried off in quiet laughter and glances, the intimacy still humming in the air between them.
Her wet hair clung to her shoulders. Dean's skin still glistened, warm from the heat.

Jeni glanced at the wall clock.

"Oh crap," she said, eyes going wide. "It's 8:30."

Dean raised a brow.

"Didn't the driver say nine?"

She shot him a look, biting her lip.

His reflection in the mirror looked different somehow.
Like he was catching up to who he was supposed to be.

He ran a comb through his damp hair, smoothing it down.

From the other room, Jeni was singing along:

""Just do the things you want and make love all night..."

She walked up behind him, wrapped her arms around his middle, and kissed his shoulder with a warm little hum of satisfaction. Then a kiss on the cheek.

"You like the song, cowboy?" she whispered.

Dean grinned. "It's growing on me."

She gave him a big hug and kiss, then headed back to the bedroom.

Her suitcase lay open on the bed, nearly everything laid out:

swimsuits, sundresses, lounge sets, and a neatly folded hoodie that still smelled faintly of her favorite perfume.

Dean leaned against the doorframe, arms crossed, just watching her for a moment.
This felt like the beginning of something.
A trip, sure—but also something else. Something unspoken but deeply understood.

Jeni stood at the sink, brushing her teeth as the mirror fogged again slightly.
She glanced at her reflection—saw the glow in her cheeks, the softness in her eyes.

Dean headed to the kitchen.
The scent of coffee bloomed almost instantly, familiar and comforting.

He poured it into two stainless steel travel mugs, steam curling up in delicate swirls like morning incense.

Back in the bedroom, Jeni dabbed concealer beneath her eyes, smoothed on a hint of blush, and let her hair fall in loose waves around her shoulders.
No power suit today. No tight bun. Just her. Radiant.

The Driver Arrives

By 9:55, they were nearly ready.

Dean brought the luggage to the front door, lined up neatly.
The doorman rang the penthouse at exactly 10:00 a.m.
Right on time.

Jeni grabbed her tote and sunglasses.

Dean handed her the coffee, and with a final glance around the apartment—their shared beginning still echoing in the walls—they stepped into the elevator together.

The ride down was quiet, but not awkward.
They stood close, fingers brushing, shoulders grazing.

Smiles shared.

The kind of silence only comfort can fill.

In the lobby, the doorman was already waiting with a rolling cart.

The driver, dressed in a crisp black suit, opened the door of the limousine with a small nod.

Dean helped load their bags as the driver packed the trunk.
Then they climbed into the backseat together.

The door shut with a soft *thud*—sealing them in.

Leather interior. Soft music playing.

They were alone again but now moving forward.

Jeni had thought of everything.

Waiting on the seat beside her were two white ceramic plates wrapped in thick plastic lids.
Room-service style—elegant and practical. Her signature.

Dean raised an eyebrow as she opened the first one.

"Breakfast?" he asked, already grinning.

She smirked.
"From that trendy place you liked last time you were here. I told the driver to pick it up on his way."

She handed him one plate, unwrapped another for herself.

"I'll have him drop the dishes back off at the restaurant when he heads into the city."

Dean smiled, leaned forward, and reached into the champagne bucket tucked into the corner of the limo.

The bottle was perfectly chilled, glistening with condensation.
He popped the cork with a gentle *pop*—quiet celebration.

He poured two flutes.
She handed him silverware.
He handed her a glass.

They toasted with a quiet clink.

"To us," he said.

Jeni met his gaze.
"To everything we missed."

The limo rolled forward, leaving the city behind.

Outside, the skyline faded.
Skyscrapers gave way to leafy trees and winding roads.

Sunlight filtered through the tinted windows.
They ate, sipped champagne, shared bites between flirty smiles.

Dean sat back, one arm draped over the back of the seat,
watching her as she laughed with her mouth full of eggs.

She was glowing—without effort. Without trying. Just... her.

This, he thought.
This is the best vacation I've ever had. And it's just beginning.

Ahead of them: two weeks on Lake Ontario.
A private log cabin.
A small yacht with cabins below deck.

No more missed chances.

Just the woman he loved.

Finally... his.

BREATH OF FRESH AIR

Arriving at the Cabin

The limo turned onto a gravel road that wound through thick trees, light flickering across the windshield in warm, golden stripes.

As they emerged from the final bend, the view opened wide—
And there it was.

The cabin sat right on the lake's edge, its natural wood blending into the forest like it had always belonged there. A wide deck stretched along the length of the structure, hugging the shoreline. Beyond that, the lake glittered, calm and open, the dock stretching out like a hand extended toward the water.

Dean leaned forward, eyes narrowing slightly as he took it all in. His fingers tightened gently around Jeni's, the weight of the moment grounding him.

"This is... wow," he murmured.

Jeni smiled. "It's even better than the pictures."

The limo came to a gentle stop in the gravel drive. The driver stepped out, popped the trunk, and began unloading their luggage.

Dean opened the door for Jeni, offering his hand.

She took it, her palm warm and sure in his. As she stepped out, the lake breeze tugged at her sundress, lifting the hem just enough to make her laugh and press it down.

Together, they walked up the stairs of the deck and into the cabin.

The door opened into a wide, open-concept living space.

High ceilings with exposed beams. Pale wood floors. Sunlight pouring through tall windows.

The kitchen was tucked off to one side—modern but cozy, with brushed metal appliances and a rustic island countertop. The dining area overlooked the lake, with a circular table surrounded by soft, weathered chairs.

Dean ran a hand across the countertop as they passed, his fingers brushing the stone like he needed to make sure it was real.

They explored quietly, still hand in hand.

Two bedrooms. Two bathrooms. One larger, one smaller.

They paused in the doorway of the guest room.

Jeni glanced at him, brow lifted. "Still want separate rooms?"

Dean smiled, stepping behind her, his arms sliding around her waist.

"I think that decision made itself last night."

Back in the living room, they stood in front of the great expanse of glass that made up most of the rear wall.

The view was like a painting—endless blue and green, the dock stretching into the horizon.

Then, motion.

Dean leaned forward.

A sleek, white yacht appeared in the distance—slowly gliding across the water toward the dock.

He squinted. "Is that... coming here?"

Jeni stepped up beside him, her posture shifting—curious but calm. The faint lines between her brows creased.

They watched as the yacht eased toward the dock.
Another vehicle pulled into the driveway—a black Jeep with two Sea-Doos hitched to the back. A second car followed behind.

Dean's eyes narrowed slightly, posture straightening.

The limo driver returned from the last luggage trip and Dean tipped him with a warm thank-you.

Dean's handshake was firm, appreciative. Eye contact steady, just like always.

As the driver disappeared down the road, Dean turned back toward the approaching chaos.

One man from the Jeep stepped forward, lifting a hand to the man walking off the dock.

The one near the porch cupped his hands and called out: "Is Jeni here?"

Jeni stepped to the screen door, calling back with a smile.

"Are you Ben?"

"Yes, ma'am!" he shouted.

She stepped outside barefoot, descending the steps toward the men.

Dean followed a beat later, casual but alert, slipping one hand into his pocket and resting the other lightly on the rail.

Ben climbed the porch steps.

"You must be Dean," he said, extending a hand.

Dean shook it firmly, a smile flickering across his face.

"Yep. That's me."

Ben shook Jeni's hand next, nodding respectfully.

"Well, everything's here," he said. "Black Jeep, Sea-Doos, and the Sea Ray. All the rentals you arranged. Keys are inside each. It's all yours for the next two weeks."

He pulled a business card from his back pocket and handed it to Jeni.

"If you need anything—fuel, gear, supplies—just give me a ring."

From the dock, another voice called out.

A man in a white polo waved and shouted, "I'm John! Enjoy the yacht—it's a 2016 Sea Ray 510 Fly. Fully loaded, fuel tanks full. Stocked with the groceries and everything else you requested!"

Jeni and Dean both raised their hands in thanks.

"Appreciate it!" Dean called.

"Thanks for everything!" Jeni echoed.

The men climbed back into the black Tahoe, waving one last time as they disappeared down the driveway.

Silence returned, broken only by the soft lapping of water against the dock.

Dean let out a slow breath.

His shoulders dropped just slightly, tension leaving his body like the air from an exhale he didn't know he was holding.

He turned to Jeni.

She looked radiant—eyes wide, hair tousled from the lake breeze, sundress catching the sun.

Her smile wasn't big. Just full. Peaceful. Present.

Dean wrapped an arm around her waist and pulled her in gently.

"Looks like we've got everything," he said softly.

Jeni leaned into his side. Her head rested against his shoulder.

"Everything," she echoed.

And as the Sea Ray bobbed quietly at the dock, the lake stretching wide in front of them, they knew—
this was the beginning.

A fresh breath.

A clean slate.

Together.

Captain Dean

Jeni was practically buzzing with excitement.

"Let's check out the yacht!" she said, already pulling Dean
toward the dock. They grab their things and lock the cabin door.

Her fingers laced through his like a spark leaping between them.
She tugged gently—then broke into a soft run, barefoot and
laughing.

Dean followed with a grin, heart lighter than it had felt in years.

The sun warmed his shoulders as they crossed the wooden
planks of the dock, the lake lapping lazily beneath them.

The yacht shimmered in the light—sleek and white, polished like
something out of a dream.

Casting Off

As they stepped aboard, the subtle sway of the boat shifted
beneath their feet.
Jeni reached out for balance, her hand resting instinctively on
Dean's chest.

Their eyes met. A shared grin.

"God," she whispered. "This is perfect."

They explored the deck—wide seating area, clean lines, leather
trim.

Dean stepped toward the helm, admiring the console.
Then he froze.

A small, wrapped box sat on the dash.
Simple brown paper. A red ribbon. A gift tag hanging from the bow.

Jeni slipped beside him, picked it up, and handed it over.
Her smile was half-angel, half-trouble.

Dean raised an eyebrow, already laughing. "You left me a present?"

"Read the tag," she said.

He flipped it over.
From Jeni to Dean, with love.

His grin widened.

He pulled at the ribbon, the sound of paper tearing oddly satisfying in the quiet around them.
Inside—folded neatly—a crisp white captain's hat.

Dean laughed out loud.

Before he could say anything, Jeni snatched it from his hands and placed it squarely on his head.

"There," she said, stepping back and admiring him with an exaggerated swoon. "Now you look official."

"You're ridiculous," he said, still chuckling.
But he didn't take the hat off.

Dean starts the engines. Jeni helps with casting off.

Dean pulls her in front of him. "Do you want to steer the yacht?"

Dean begins rubbing her backside, then lifting her dress and pulling her panties off.

His touch is slow, deliberate—every movement electric.

He pulls his pants and boxers off, then starts rubbing against Jeni from behind.

She can feel him—hot, rigid, pulsing—pressing along her soft folds.

She bends over, then pushing against the wheel, she pushes backwards into Dean.

She feels Dean going inside her.
The stretch, the fullness, steals her breath.

She needs this, she wants this every day for the next two weeks.

Dean is thrusting harder, gripping Jeni's hips.
Her fingers curl tightly around the wheel, her cries swallowed by the lake breeze.

Dean's hand slides down her stomach into her crotch.
His fingers gently touching and rubbing her clit.

She knows she can't hold on much longer before she will climax.
Dean is almost there as well.

Jeni screams, then a long moan comes from her mouth.
The pleasure crashes through her, raw and unstoppable.

Dean feels her warm juices flowing down his leg.
He grabs her tight, holding her, still throbbing inside of her.

His head buried in the curve of her neck, breath ragged against her skin.
He lowers his head, kissing her lips.

His one hand rubbing her hips and his other playing with her breast and nipples.

Jeni shouts, "Let's find a spot and drop anchor for tonight."

Dean sees an uninhabited little island. They drop anchor there.

Not Ordinary Lovers ♪17

"Let's go below deck, find something to drink and you make love to me all day, evening and night for the next two weeks."

They kept exploring.

Below deck, next to the sleek little galley kitchen, Jeni opened the fridge and let out a soft gasp.

"Oooh—champagne," she said, pulling the bottle free.

She turned to Dean with a wink.
"Glasses?"

Dean found them tucked into a cabinet nearby.

The clink of glass on counter. The coolness of the bottle in her hands.
The fizz of anticipation in the air.

Together, they moved toward the stateroom.

The bed was plush, wide, dressed in soft white linens.

Jeni stripped naked and flopped onto it with dramatic flair, bottle in hand.
"Get naked, Dean. I want you now."

Then she paused, her voice just above a whisper.
"Babe... play some sexy romantic music for us to listen to. While you kiss me."

Dean reached for the remote on the nightstand.
A soft click. A quiet pause.

Then the familiar, sultry notes of an old Sade track filled the air, the song "No Ordinary Love."

She looked up at Dean with a playful smirk, hair fanning across the pillows like sunlight through seafoam.

"Come take me, Captain Dean," she said, voice teasing and low.

Dean took the bottle. Uncorked it with a soft pop.
The fizz bubbled up. He poured with practiced ease.

One glass for her. One for him.

He slowly stripped for Jeni.

She waved him over to the edge of the bed. "Come to me on your knees."

He climbed onto the bed, approaching her on his knees.

When he reached her, she grabbed him, her mouth swallowing him, her tongue running along the head.

Dean groaned, his entire body tightening with the effort to hold back.
Dean was aching inside. He didn't know how long he would last.

Jeni lays on her back, grabbing her knees with her hands, spreading her legs open as far as she can.

"I want you inside me now, Dean."
Her voice trembled—not just from need, but from the memory of all the years she wanted this.

He could feel himself getting harder.

He began thinking about her in high school—running around in her panties in her bedroom.
He thought about how many times he wanted to get her on the bed.
He would go home and fantasize about her until he released.

Ironically, Jeni was thinking the same thing—how she wanted Dean to take her back in high school.
When he went home, she would get under the covers, her fingers inside her panties, playing with herself until she climaxed.

Here they were finally together for two weeks to rewrite their history.
She couldn't believe how great it felt.

She never wanted another man to do this to her but Dean.

He climbed on top of her, his hands going down the small of her back, then gripping her bottom.
She let out a loud moan, then another.

Dean grabs her ankles, setting them on his shoulders, giving her all of himself.

Dean can't get enough of her and it's the same for her.
He keeps going—wave after wave of them both being satisfied.

Finally, Jeni lets out a groan. "Dean, I need a break, babe."

Dean loved the marathons with Jeni. She wasn't like other women, nor was he like other men.
It was like an athletic event for the two of them.
Jeni was there to please Dean, and he was there to please her.

Jeni grabs her glass. "Dean, I'm ready for the champagne now."

They lifted their glasses.

"To us," Dean said.
"To our new adventure," Jeni added.

Their glasses clinked. Their eyes locked.
And they drank.

Jeni leaned into him, her lips brushing his—slow, soft, deliberate.

"Captain Dean," she whispered between kisses, "I've never been with a ship's captain before. Are all captains like this?"

Her laughter was quiet and low, like music before it became a melody.

Dean kissed her again, deeper this time.

Jeni smiled, leaning into him again.

The champagne sparkled beside them.
The lake rocked beneath them.

And the captain kissed his girl.

Feeling Great ♪18

Dean and Jeni could hardly believe it—
Four full days had already slipped through their fingers like
sunlight on water.

They'd spent the mornings drinking coffee on the cabin deck, the
afternoons out on the lake, the nights tangled in each other's
arms beneath the stars.

And now, the shoreline slowly came into view.

The dock.
The curve of the cabin's deck.
The trees surrounding the lake, still and golden in the late
afternoon light.

Home base. But now it felt like a retreat made sacred by the
moments they'd shared.

On the yacht, the speaker system rotated into something fitting.
Michael Bublé's "Feeling Good" poured through the air like a
lazy exhale.

Dean stood at the helm, one hand resting on the wheel.

His other arm wrapped around Jeni's waist, pulling her close as
the breeze toyed with her hair.

She leaned against him, head resting on his shoulder, sunglasses low on her nose, that slow smile on her lips—the kind only earned by true contentment.

The vibe was effortless.

But intense.

Not loud. Not flashy.

Just a low, powerful thrum of connection.
A shared rhythm.
Two heartbeats synced with the movement of the waves.

Dean guided the yacht smoothly toward the dock.

The sun shimmered across the surface of the lake, casting everything in warm gold. The wind danced around them, soft and scented with pine and freshwater.

Jeni tilted her face up to his.

"You've gotten good at this," she said, fingers resting lightly on his chest.

Dean smirked, adjusting his grip on the wheel.

"Captain Dean," he teased. "Professional now."

She chuckled, turning back toward the shore.

"Do we really have to go back to land?"

Her voice was half-joking, but Dean could hear the wistfulness in it.

He leaned down, kissed her temple.

"We're not done yet."

The boat began to slow, gliding smoothly into position beside the dock.

Dean's hand moved with confident ease, adjusting the throttle, securing the approach. Jeni stood, grabbing a rope with practiced fingers, looping it around the cleat.

They moved like a team now—fluid, easy, in tune.

No instructions needed. Just awareness. Just trust.

Once tied off, Jeni turned back to him.

Sunlight painted her in warm hues. Her hair tousled by wind, her skin glowing, her sundress fluttering just slightly against her legs.

Dean looked at her, really looked.

The way her eyes sparkled when she smiled. The soft curve of her shoulders. The strength in the way she carried joy without apology.

"You okay?" she asked softly, watching him watch her.

Dean nodded once, slow.

"Yeah," he said. "I really am."

They stood there for a moment in the stillness.
The world paused.

The music swelled behind them—horns rising, drums rolling—like the soundtrack to something that had already changed them both.

Feeling good wasn't even the right word anymore.

It was more than that.

They felt real. Together. Rooted. Chosen.

The Hidden Grotto

They unpacked and settled back into the cabin, the scent of cedar and lake air greeting them like an old friend.

After four days of movement, the stillness of the morning was welcome.
They moved slow.
Barefoot. Unrushed. Draped in comfort.

Jeni curled up on the couch with her coffee.
Dean leaned against the deck railing, shirtless, eyes scanning the glimmering lake.

No words. Just presence. Just peace.

That afternoon, the mood shifted to motion.

"Let's go for a ride," Dean said, tightening the straps of his small daypack. Jeni lit up.

Jeni packed a picnic lunch—cheese, sandwiches, a chilled bottle of wine, and a few snacks to share along the way.

In the next room, Dean was finishing up. He slung the micro tent over his shoulder, adjusting the straps like muscle memory.

"Jeni, grab some hamburgers, buns, marshmallows—and anything else we might need if we find the place to stay overnight."

"Do you think we might?" she asked.

"Could be," he said. "Depends on what we find." He said it like a casual idea, but there was a flicker in his eyes. Hope, maybe. The kind that doesn't ask questions but wants to be ready for the right answer.

Two sets of tires crunched over the gravel as they pedaled away from the cabin, sunlight spilling through the trees like confetti.

Jeni wore black compression shorts and a thin tank top, her hair pulled back, eyes shining with post-vacation glow.

Dean sported a pair of dark athletic shorts and a tank of his own—his skin warm and sun-kissed, muscles moving easily with each push of the pedal.

The day was perfect.

The air smelled like pine and lake water, warm earth and the distant trace of wildflowers. The trail curved and dipped, rolling through the hills like a ribbon unfurling.

For nearly an hour, they rode—laughing, racing ahead, slowing to point out deer tracks or birds overhead.

Then Dean noticed something.

A barely worn trail off to the right, winding toward a dense patch of rock and trees.

He slowed, pulling to a gentle stop, one foot resting on the ground.

"Hang on," he said, his brow knitting slightly.
He tilted his head.
Listening.

A sound. Soft. Familiar. Rushing water, far off but calling.

"I know that sound."

Jeni rolled to a stop beside him, brows lifted.

Dean nodded toward the side trail.

"Let's check it out."

They pushed off again, wheels crunching the narrow, uneven path.
The deeper they went, the louder the water became—still distant, still hidden.

And then—
They crested a hill.

Dean stopped suddenly, eyes wide.

He turned to Jeni, a smile tugging at his lips.

"I think I found our spot."

Below them, nestled between a crescent of smooth gray rock, a small waterfall spilled gently into a wide, glassy pool.
The water was clear, shaded with teal and light green.
Behind the fall—a natural grotto carved by time.

It looked like a place the world forgot.

They rode their bikes carefully down the slope, tires skimming soft dirt and smooth stone.

As they rolled to a stop, Jeni's eyes were wide.

She slipped off her bike and just stared.

"Dean..."

"I know," he said softly.
He leaned in, kissed her lips. "Let's make it ours—for today."

They walked their bikes along the pool and waterfall, the spray from the fall misting their skin.
The sound was soothing—consistent, natural, grounding.

Dean found the perfect camp site in the grotto, with the waterfall directly in front of them.

He unpacked the blanket, smoothing it out with a few practiced swipes of his hands.
His movements were quiet but certain—careful not to rush this moment.

Jeni unpacked the lunch: cheese, sliced fruit, small sandwiches wrapped in parchment.

The cork from the wine bottle gave a soft pop as she opened it.

She poured two glasses, handing one to Dean as she lowered herself onto the blanket beside him.

They clinked gently.

"To the perfect detour," Jeni said, her voice soft and sun-warmed.

Dean nodded.
"To the best ride I've ever taken."

They sat there, side by side on the blanket, their legs stretched out, their bare feet brushing against each other now and then.

The view in front of them was almost unreal.
The pool shimmered. The waterfall danced.
The rocks whispered secrets between each splash.

Jeni rested her head on Dean's shoulder.
He leaned slightly into her, kissing her lips softly.

The kiss deepened, tasting of wine and shared longing.

Dean's hand moved down her stomach, stopping at her crotch.
His fingers pressing on her compression shorts, the fabric so thin it felt like he was touching her bare skin.

Jeni gasped, her body squirming from the pleasure.

He pulled his fingers up, feeling the dampness of her shorts.
The heat, the slickness—he wanted more.

He gently moved his fingers down her shorts, his fingers finding
their way inside her.

Jeni pulled her shorts off.
"Dean, take your shorts off and flip around."

Dean did.
He was already hard, hanging down in her face.

He ventured down, slowly kissing her stomach until his mouth
rested at her crotch.
The smell of her arousal was heady, wild.

He started light—kissing her, then letting his tongue glide inside
her.

Jeni opened her mouth, taking in as much of Dean as she could,
her lips warm, her tongue tracing along his length, learning his
rhythm.

Her mouth moved up and down,
Dean following the rhythm.

The more he pleased her, the more she pleased him, until they
climaxed.

Their moans tangled in the air between them, bodies shaking in
unison.

Jeni didn't stop.
"Dean, I want you hard again, because I want you in me."

Within a couple of minutes, Dean was on top of her, giving her
what she wanted.

She welcomed him with a gasp,
her legs curling around his back as he pushed into her again.

This continued for an hour,
their bodies slick, tangled in blankets and breath.

Then Jeni, needing a break, said,
"Dean, let's go skinny dipping."

They got into the pool of water,
with the waterfall crashing down on the rocks and the pool.

The spray misted over their skin,
moonlight beginning to shimmer across the surface.

Their own little paradise.

They kissed and held each other in the water.
Jeni rubbed herself against Dean.

They enjoyed themselves—swimming, kissing, and playing with
each other's bodies.

It's starting to be dusk.
Dean needs to start the fire for dinner.

They slowly step out of the water,
hands still tracing over damp skin, reluctant to stop.

Jeni got down on her knees,
her lips running down Dean's shaft, her mouth going up and
down.

She took her time, savoring the taste of him,
the way he twitched in her mouth.

"Come to the blanket, Dean."

They made love again.
This time slower, deeper—each movement meant to linger.

Then Jeni lay there as Dean built the fire and prepared the hamburgers.

They ate dinner and roasted marshmallows,
as the sky turned black and the fire became their only light.

A golden glow wrapped around them like a secret,
the night sealing their paradise.

Stargazer Hearts

They dried off under the stars and slipped into the tent.
Dean zipped open the sleeping bag and held it wide for Jeni to crawl in.
She slid in beside him, laughing softly as she adjusted.

The top flap of the tent was open, mosquito netting stretched overhead like a dome of lace.
Beyond it—stars.
Everywhere.
Endless.

They lay side by side, the sleeping bag a cocoon, their legs tangled beneath it.
Jeni rested her head on his arm, her back to Dean.
Dean's arm curled beneath her, his other arm resting on her side, his fingers gently touching her side and bottom.

Her skin was warm, electric. The space between them vanished with every breath.
Dean could feel the heat coming from Jeni.
She was pushing back on Dean's hardening shaft.
The friction between them was unbearable and perfect—like something primal whispering yes.

Then all at once, Jeni pushed backwards.
Dean was sliding inside her.

No words. Just breath. Just movement. Just the sharp, sweet ache of closeness.

Dean's fingers went from her bottom to her crotch, rubbing in a circular motion while she rocked back and forth.
The sounds between them—soft moans, quiet gasps—mingled with the rustle of fabric and night air.
Their bodies met again and again, a rhythm both tender and hungry.

Dean grabbed her right leg, lifting it up, giving him more room to please her as he started thrusting forward.
The angle changed—deeper, slower, more consuming.

Finally, Dean flipped her on her knees, driving her from behind.
Jeni gasped as the intensity grew, until she climaxed.
Her cry filled the tent like starlight breaking.

Dean kept going until his release.
His body tensed, hips pressing in one final time before he spilled into her.

They lay there, holding and kissing each other until they fell asleep.

The sound of the waterfall faded behind them.
The stars blinked in time with their breath.
Everything else disappeared.

She looked up through the netting.
"I used to dream about nights like this," she said quietly. "But it always felt so far away."

Dean turned to her.
"It's not far anymore."

Their eyes met.
Something passed between them—unspoken, but permanent.
The starlight caught in hers.
His chest tightened at the look there—so full of peace and want and something unbreakable.

He kissed her.
Soft.
Then deeper.
Their mouths spoke the language of trust, and memory, and
now.

Their hands explored again, slow and familiar now.
Each touch was reverent—mapped from memory, driven by
need.
Like reading a favorite poem in a new light.

Clothes forgotten.
Time unwound.

They made love quietly, completely.
No urgency. No sound but breath and heartbeat.
Just the slow, sacred tempo of two people completely joined.

A rhythm in sync with the world around them—like the pulse of
the lake, the whisper of the breeze, the slow turning of the sky.

Memory Light

The stars may have gone backward across the sky,
but the hours moved forward.
And morning had already come.

Dean stirred inside the sleeping bag, eyes still closed.
A pale warmth settled across the tent—soft and golden, the color
of honey on skin.

Birdsong filled the silence.
The distant rush of the waterfall, now familiar.
The gentle swish of wind against the netting.

He hadn't heard the night pass.
Hadn't felt it slip away.
Sleep had wrapped around him like the forest itself, like the
arms of someone who finally knew where they belonged.

He blinked slowly, adjusting to the new light.
Jeni was curled against his chest, one arm tucked between them, her breath soft and even.

He didn't move.
Didn't want to.

There was a time, long ago, when mornings like this were part of his life.
Camping trips with his mom and dad—before the world got complicated.
Before life started marking people with grief.

The sound of morning birds, the smell of dewy grass and pine needles...
It all brought him back.

Back to Grade 4, when he'd chase squirrels through tall trees and roast marshmallows with smoke in his eyes.
Jeni had been part of some of those trips.
She was the fearless one, always climbing higher, getting dirt on her knees, laughing with her whole body.

Her mom had stayed behind most of the time—never much for tents and bugs.
Her dad?

Dean's throat tightened.
Jeni's father had died before she ever started school. A soldier. A hero.
A story she carried in the quiet spaces behind her strength.

That was one of the ties that had bound them early on.
They both knew what it felt like to miss someone forever.

Dean's own father had been there for the early years.
Big voice. Bigger heart.
The kind of man who called everyone "kiddo" and made pancakes on a skillet balanced on rocks.

Jeni had loved him.
She used to run to him the moment they arrived at the campsite, already talking about whatever wild idea she had that day.

He remembered her laughing on his dad's shoulders.
Those memories were bright. Solid. Untouchable.

Until they weren't.

His dad had passed when they were in middle school.
And just like that, the light dimmed for a while.

Dean exhaled, slow and steady.
His arm tightened slightly around Jeni.
His thumb brushed the top of her bare shoulder, tracing the
shape of a memory.

She stirred.
Eyes still closed, she tilted her head into his chest.
"Morning?" she mumbled.

Dean smiled.
"Yeah."

Her lashes fluttered as she opened her eyes.
The first thing she saw was him.

And her smile—sleepy and slow—was all the sun he needed.

She stretched, one arm lifting over her head.
Their sleeping bag rustled softly as her body shifted against his.
Bare skin, warm from shared sleep.

Dean leaned in and kissed her forehead.
"Do you remember when we used to camp with my parents?"

Jeni blinked at him, eyes suddenly clearer.
A pause.

Then—softly—"Of course I do."
She rolled onto her side, facing him fully now.

"Your dad taught me how to fish. I hooked your sock that first
time, remember?"

Dean chuckled.
"Yeah. You cried like the world ended."

"I was six," she protested, laughing. "And you told me it meant
you loved me."

Dean looked at her.
Eyes soft. Still. Honest.
"I think I meant it, even then."

For a moment, neither spoke.
Just the sound of the forest waking up around them.

The light shifted again, growing a little brighter.
A little warmer.
Like the past, for once, had stopped hurting—and started healing
instead.

Something Worth Remembering

The stars may have gone backward across the sky,
but the hours moved forward.
And morning had already come.

Dean stirred inside the sleeping bag, eyes still closed.
A pale warmth settled across the tent—soft and golden, the color
of honey on skin.

Birdsong filled the silence.
The distant rush of the waterfall, now familiar.
The gentle swish of wind against the netting.

He hadn't heard the night pass.
Hadn't felt it slip away.
Sleep had wrapped around him like the forest itself, like the
arms of someone who finally knew where they belonged.

He blinked slowly, adjusting to the new light.

Jeni was curled against his chest, one arm tucked between them,
her breath soft and even.

He didn't move.
Didn't want to.

There was a time, long ago, when mornings like this were part of
his life.
Camping trips with his mom and dad—before the world got
complicated.
Before life started marking people with grief.

The sound of morning birds, the smell of dewy grass and pine
needles...
It all brought him back.

Back to Grade 4,
when he'd chase squirrels through tall trees
and roast marshmallows with smoke in his eyes.

Jeni had been part of some of those trips.
She was the fearless one, always climbing higher, getting dirt on
her knees, laughing with her whole body.

Her mom had stayed behind most of the time—never much for
tents and bugs.

Her dad left them when she was little.

Dean's own father had been there for the early years.
Big voice. Bigger heart.
The kind of man who called everyone "kiddo" and made
pancakes on a skillet balanced on rocks.

Jeni had loved him.
She used to run to him the moment they arrived at the campsite,
already talking about whatever wild idea she had that day.
He remembered her laughing on his dad's shoulders. The
butterfly kisses she would give his dad. Dean's mom couldn't
have another child, so Jeni was his adopted daughter.

Those memories were bright. Solid. Untouchable.
Until they weren't.

His dad had passed when they were in middle school. Dean and Jeni cried for a long time about their shared dad. And just like that, the light dimmed for a while.

Dean exhaled, slow and steady.
His arm tightened slightly around Jeni.
His thumb brushed the top of her bare shoulder, tracing the shape of a memory.

She stirred.
Eyes still closed, she tilted her head into his chest.
"Morning?" she mumbled.

Dean smiled.
"Yeah."

Her lashes fluttered as she opened her eyes.
The first thing she saw was him.
And her smile—sleepy and slow—was all the sun he needed.

She stretched, one arm lifting over her head.
Their sleeping bag rustled softly as her body shifted against his.
Bare skin, warm from shared sleep.

Dean leaned in and kissed her forehead.
"Do you remember when we used to camp with my parents?"

Jeni blinked at him, eyes suddenly clearer.
A pause.
Then—softly—"Of course I do."

She rolled onto her side, facing him fully now.

"Your dad taught me how to fish. I hooked your sock that first time, remember?"

Dean chuckled.
"Yeah. You cried like the world ended."

"I was six," she protested, laughing. "And you told me it meant you loved me."

Dean looked at her.
Eyes soft. Still. Honest.

"I think I meant it, even then."

For a moment, neither spoke.
Just the sound of the forest waking up around them.

The light shifted again, growing a little brighter. A little warmer.
Like the past, for once, had stopped hurting—and started healing
instead

When Time Bends Backward

The trail back to the cabin was the same as before—
Winding. Softly graded. Dappled with sun through pine boughs.

But everything felt different now.

Dean rode a few feet ahead, his posture relaxed but his face
unreadable.

The forest whispered around them—the sound of tires over
packed dirt, the call of a hawk in the distance, the slow, rhythmic
creak of a pedal stroke.

The day was warm.

But something in the air had shifted.

Dean couldn't stop the thoughts from spinning.

Thirteen days.
Ten on the yacht.
Two more on the trails and beneath the stars.

And now, only one day left.

The moment they turned back toward the cabin, it felt like the magic had started fading at the edges.
Not gone. But thinning. Like they were slipping out of a dream.

Was this what reliving the past felt like?

He and Jeni had loved each other their whole lives. They just never allowed it back then.
Different relationships. Different seasons. The timing always wrong.

Maybe that's what this vacation had really been about.

Not an escape.

But a return.

Behind him, Jeni pedaled quietly.

She felt it too.

That creeping sense of *almost goodbye* trailing just behind her tires.

She watched Dean's back as he moved ahead of her—broad shoulders, sun-tanned arms, the familiar tilt of his head.

She loved him.
She always had.

But was this their second chance?
Or just the closure they never got the first time?

Neither spoke.

The silence wasn't awkward.
It was heavy. Sacred. Unspoken.

Dean's heart felt thick in his chest.

He couldn't blame her if this was all it had been.
Two weeks to rewrite a story that never had its chapter.
To live the love they'd postponed for too long.

Michael was still part of Jeni's world.
Lexi still haunted his.

Could they ever really walk forward together?
Or was this their version of *forever*—condensed into a moment out of time?

At the top of a small hill, Dean paused.
He turned to look back at her.

Jeni pulled up beside him, both of them catching their breath.

Their eyes met.
So much between them.
Too much to say.
Too much already said.

She gave a soft smile.

He returned it—half a grin, half a plea.

Then they started again, wheels turning beneath them, heading back toward the cabin.

They didn't need to say it.
They were both thinking the same thing.

If this was the past...
It was the best version they'd ever lived.

And if this was the future...
It was still a fragile one.

But maybe, just maybe—

They hadn't traveled backward at all.
Maybe this was the start of something new.
Maybe it wasn't about reclaiming time.
Maybe it was about choosing now.

Like Tomorrow Will Never Come ♪19

As they rode up the final stretch of the trail, the cabin appeared through the trees, still and golden in the afternoon light.

But something was missing.

Dean slowed first, coasting to a stop.

The dock was empty.
The yacht—gone.
The Jeep too.

Only the cabin remained.

Still beautiful. Still theirs. But somehow quieter now.
Like the world had started taking back its magic, piece by piece.

Jeni pulled up beside him, saying nothing.

Dean exhaled slowly.

The weight of goodbye had arrived early.
It settled over them like mist.

Tomorrow, the limo would come.
Tomorrow, this moment would become memory.

They wheeled the bikes up the steps of the porch.
Dean leaned his against the railing, then turned to wait.

Jeni's eyes flicked to his as she parked hers.
Her smile was faint. Tired. Not from the ride. From knowing.

They walked into the cabin side by side.

They dropped their gear by the door.

Backpacks slumped against the wall. Keys clattered in the bowl. The echo of the door clicking shut seemed louder than usual.

The room felt different now—same walls, same light, same space.

But everything sacred had already been packed away.

The silence between them wasn't awkward. It was reverent. Heavy with something they hadn't spoken aloud yet.

Without a word, Dean stepped in front of her.

His hands slid to her hips.

His eyes locked onto hers—quiet, burning.

The world outside faded. Just the hum of air conditioning, the distant pulse of streetlights behind the blinds.

Then the music started.

That familiar opening riff.

"Must Be Doin' Somethin' Right" by Billy Currington.

Dean didn't say a word.

He just pulled her in.

Held her close.

And they began to sway.

The soft rhythm of the song matched the rise and fall of their breath.

Dean began to sing along, low and easy, his voice rough around the edges but full of intention.

He dipped her slowly, their laughter rising between the lines of the melody.

Jeni gasped, half laughing, half breathless as he brought her back up, holding her tight.

Dean lifted Jeni effortlessly into his arms, her laughter soft, melodic, as her arms looped around his neck and her legs wrapped snugly around his hips.
The scent of her skin, warm and lightly floral, filled his senses as she pressed closer.

Her breath caught as their bodies met—skin to skin—her chest rising, her heart thudding against his.

She laughed again, head falling to his shoulder.

"You're ridiculous," she whispered.

"You love it," he murmured back.

He carried her to the bed and laid her down gently, never breaking eye contact.
The moment hovered between them, silent and electric.

His arms were strong, but his voice was soft. Almost breaking.

"I want to hold you in my arms... and kiss your lips like tomorrow will never come."

His fingers trembled slightly as he reached for her waist, peeling her clothes away inch by inch.
He wasn't in a rush. He was savoring her—rediscovering every line, every soft curve.

His own shirt slipped over his head. Then shorts. Then boxers. Each garment forgotten, discarded at the foot of the bed like the rest of the world.

The room was quiet except for the sound of their breath—and the whisper of fabric brushing against the hardwood.

Dean climbed onto the bed, knees parting hers as he moved over her.
The heat between them was slow-building, but intense—like coals glowing under silk.

His palms skimmed along the insides of her thighs, spreading her open slowly.

Her skin was warm and pliant beneath his touch. She shivered. Not from cold—but from anticipation. From him.

He lowered his head, mouth brushing against the tender folds between her legs.
The first touch was featherlight. Intentional.

His tongue moved in slow, deliberate circles, teasing, tracing, coaxing every soft gasp that tumbled from her lips.

Jeni's hand curled in the sheet beside her. Her hips lifted in response. "Dean..."

He slipped his hands beneath her, gripping the curve of her backside, keeping her steady.

The sounds she made were soft, breathy—fragments of prayer whispered into the dark.

Her thighs began to tense. Her back arched. Her body stuttered beneath him.

When his tongue slid gently inside her, she cried out—high, breathless, and shuddering.

"Flip around," she whispered, her voice thick, rough with need. "I want to feel you too."

Dean obeyed without a word. They shifted, aligned. Her mouth found him quickly—eager, knowing.

She kissed and tasted him slowly, tongue circling the head of his arousal, lips gliding along the shaft.

His fingers dug into her hips. His core muscles tensed beneath the pleasure.

The wet heat of her mouth, the rhythm of her movements, was almost too much.

Dean groaned softly. He withdrew, turning again, rising above her once more.

Their eyes locked.

Searching. Holding.

He lined himself up, pressing in—slowly, steadily—until her body took him fully.

Jeni exhaled, her legs wrapping around his waist. Her arms pulled him closer.

Their bodies moved in tandem—slow waves at first, growing more urgent with every breath.

Her nails dragged lightly down his back. Her voice broke as she whispered his name again and again, like a sacred word.

Their rhythm built—breath against breath, sweat-slick skin moving in time.

Dean buried himself deeper, each thrust deeper than the last. Her body clung to him, pulsing, drawing him in.

Her climax hit first—sharp, gasping, unstoppable.

He followed, groaning her name as he spilled inside her, the tension unraveling all at once.
His hips slowed, their bodies trembling in the aftermath.

The world around them stilled.

Dean looked down at her—his eyes raw, soft, searching in the dim light.

"I feel so uncertain about us, Jeni…"
His voice cracked.

"But the one thing I know—
I've always loved you."

Her breath left her in a tremble.

A single tear rolled down her cheek before she could answer.

Then another.

With a heavy sigh, she whispered:

"Dean… I know how you feel.
But no matter what happens… I love you."

Her voice broke.
Her hand pressed flat against his chest.

"I have always loved you…
And I always will."

They kissed.

Light.
Barely there.
Just breath and trembling lips.
Tear-salted and true.

The kind of kiss that says:
Don't go.
But if you do, take my love with you.

Their tears mixed between them.
Falling slowly.

No rush.
No resistance.

Just grief.
And love.
And the ache of time slipping through their fingers.

The cabin held its breath around them.

The clock ticked forward.

And all they could do was hold each other.

As if tomorrow didn't exist.
As if love could stop the sunrise.
As if this was their forever.

Even if it wasn't.

One More Time

They lay there for hours—
Wrapped around each other like threads too tightly woven to
undo.

Sleep came and went, slow and heavy, clinging like fog.

But when Jeni stirred again, the light was barely beginning to
shift at the edge of the curtains.

She turned her face to Dean's, their bodies still pressed close,
skin warm with shared sleep.

Her voice was soft. Barely a breath.

"Dean... make love to me one more time."

A pause.

Then, quieter still—"I'm going to say... last time, Dean."

There was no hesitation.
No reply needed.

Dean kissed her, brushing her hair from her face, memorizing her eyes in the dim glow of morning.

The way they moved together wasn't frantic.
It wasn't goodbye.
It was a gathering—of every feeling, every moment, every word they hadn't said in years.

They gave themselves fully, completely—like sponges, soaking in every drop of love the other poured out.

Too late for what-ifs.
Too beautiful for regret.

It wasn't just making love.

It was *being love.*

Their bodies told each other what their hearts had always known.

Afterward, the clock read 5:00 a.m.

They slipped into the shower together—warm water tracing the shapes they had come to know by touch and by heart.

There was no talking. Just the sound of water and breath. A final baptism in this shared world.

Back in the kitchen, they moved slowly, gently.

Dean cracked eggs, Jeni toasted bread.

Their last breakfast at the cabin.
Their last coffee.

Outside, the lake was still.

Inside, time was ticking.

Dean reached for her hand.

Pulled her close.

She climbed into his lap without a word, straddling him, her
arms wrapping around his neck.

They just held each other.

Chest to chest. Heart to heart.

9:45 a.m.

The end was near, but neither of them moved.

Dean looked up at her, smoothing his hand along her back.

"Let's both enjoy the day together," he said softly.
"And only think happy thoughts."

He kissed her lips—slow and sure—and held her tighter.

Like he could stop time by loving her just enough.

A knock at the door.

They both froze.
Then looked at each other.

And rose together.

Dean opened the door.

The limo driver smiled, nodding. "Good morning."

He moved quickly and respectfully, loading their gear into the trunk.

Dean and Jeni stepped out into the warm morning, hand in hand.

The cabin stood behind them, full of memories.
The car before them, full of unknowns.

They climbed in.

Jeni curled up on Dean's lap in the backseat, her body fitting against him like they had always been made to rest this way.

She looked up into his eyes, her gaze soft and certain.
All her love, open and unguarded.

Dean held her with one arm, and with the other, gently ran his fingers through her hair.

No words. Just peace. Just presence.

The road disappeared beneath them.

The lake behind.
The city ahead.

Time passed without fanfare.

And then, they were at her place.

The driver helped them unload their things, then smiled again.
"See you both tomorrow for the airport run."

Jeni turned to Dean, her hand in his.

"So," she said. "We can act like you've already gone back to Miami...
Or we can use today, tonight, and tomorrow to live like we're still here."

She stepped closer, her eyes glinting with something playful beneath the emotion.

"How about I take you shopping for some clothes, we grab dinner, maybe a movie or dancing..."
She leaned in, lips brushing his ear.
"Then we come back here—and you can have me all night. And into tomorrow."

Dean raised an eyebrow, smirking.

"That's the best offer I've had all day."

Jeni grinned.

"It's the *only* offer you've had."

They both burst out laughing.

The weight lifted.

The grief had already been spent.
Now they had joy to reclaim.

They changed clothes, freshened up, and stepped back into the world—
Not as broken hearts.
But as two people choosing to *live fully* in the final pages of their story.

Or maybe...

The beginning of something new.

Last Slow Dance ♪19

As night surrendered to morning, the sky outside began to pale at the edges.
But inside the car, Dean and Jeni were still wrapped in the glow of the night.

The ride back to her place was full of laughter and light touches, hands tangled, eyes meeting like magnets.

They pulled up to the curb, the city quiet now, the world not quite awake.

Inside, Jeni dropped her purse and keys at the door with a careless clatter.

Her heels clicked once, then stopped. Her eyes found Dean's in the dim light of the living room.

"Hey, cowboy..." she said, her voice sultry but soft, still tinged with sleep and wine and wonder.

She stepped back slowly toward the center of the room.

"How about dancing to that song again?"

Dean smiled, his chest tight in the best way.

Jeni turned, found the speaker, and tapped play.

The opening notes of "Must Be Doin' Somethin' Right" filled the space like a memory returning.

She walked back to him—slow, swaying with the rhythm, her bare feet silent on the hardwood—and reached for his hand.

Dean stepped into her arms, his breath catching as her body met his. For a moment, they simply held each other. Foreheads resting. Breaths syncing.

Then—

Her hands moved behind her back, unzipping the dress with practiced ease. It whispered to the floor, pooling in soft folds around her ankles.

She stood there in nothing but the glow of lamplight, the delicate rise of her chest betraying her own excitement.

She smirked. "Oops."

Dean let out a low breath, thick with awe.

His eyes traced her from the curve of her shoulders to the gentle dip of her waist, then lower—lingering at the place only he'd been allowed to see. Her skin shimmered faintly, kissed by the heat of the moment.

He stepped closer, pulling her into his arms. They began to sway.

Bare skin against cotton.

Fingers laced at the small of her back.

Hearts synchronizing to a rhythm only they could hear.

Jeni kissed him—slow, tender, pouring every bit of the last two weeks into the motion. Every glance. Every touch. Every memory.

Her hands framed his face. Her lips moved against his like she was trying to memorize the shape of goodbye.

"Dean... this may be the last night for us. For a while."

He didn't answer with words.

He lifted her—strong, effortless. Like she weighed nothing. Like she was everything.

Her legs wrapped tightly around his waist, arms around his neck. Their mouths never broke apart as he carried her through the dim hallway. She was already moaning into his kiss by the time his body lowered her to the edge of the bed.

Her thighs parted beneath him, welcoming.

His hands slid down her back and around to her bottom, fingers spreading to cup and cradle the heat he felt radiating from between her legs.

She whimpered. "Please…"

Dean kissed his way down—her neck, her collarbone, her breast. His tongue circled her nipple, then tugged lightly before continuing lower.

He knelt between her thighs, spreading them gently with his hands, placing slow kisses along the inner crease until she was trembling.

When his tongue finally reached her core, she gasped—back arching off the bed, fingers tangled in the sheets.

His mouth worked in slow, rhythmic circles, then long, indulgent strokes—pausing only to let her hips lift toward him, needy and shameless.

Her fingers threaded into his hair.

"Dean—"

He didn't stop until her legs trembled and her breath came in shallow, broken gasps.

Only when she begged did he rise, his mouth slick with her need.

He stood at the foot of the bed, stripping slowly, deliberately— eyes locked on hers.

When he crawled over her, they kissed like they hadn't all night.

She reached between them, guiding him in.

They both gasped.

He slid inside her, slow and deep, his length filling her until her breath caught.

She wrapped her legs around his back, holding him there—her hands clawing lightly at his shoulders.

Each thrust was a surrender.

He buried his face in her neck, groaning low against her skin.

They moved together, waves cresting and falling, bodies slick and trembling.

When her climax overtook her, it was a cry—a desperate, aching sob as her body clenched around him, pulling him deeper.

Dean held on—until her aftershocks coaxed his own release.

He collapsed over her, breath shaking, bodies sticky and tangled.

But they weren't done.

Not yet.

After a long moment of stillness—breathing into each other, skin on skin—Jeni rolled him onto his back and straddled him.

Her thighs slid over his hips, slow and fluid.

She sank down on him with a hiss, biting her lip, her palms braced on his chest.

This was slower. Deeper. A rhythm not of urgency—but of slow pleasure.

He gripped her hips, watching her ride him in the hush of the cabin.

Her breasts bounced softly with each movement, her face flushed and lips parted.

Dean reached up, cupped her breast. His mouth engulfing her, his tongue pleasing her.

Her eyes fluttered shut. She ground down harder.

The slapping of skin. Her low moans. His name—over and over again—on her lips.

They came together a second time, her hands planted on his chest, his arms wrapped tight around her back.

They didn't let go.

Later, she lay beside him, curled into his chest. Her hair was damp with sweat. Her leg draped across his.

He traced circles on her back with one finger. Her soft breaths rose and fell against his skin.

Neither spoke.

Because nothing needed to be said.

The moonlight framed them in silver.

Outside, the lake lapped quietly at the dock.

Inside, they clung to what they'd found.

A night that may never come again.

So they held each other like it had to last forever.

Five Hours Left ♪20

They woke up to sunlight spilling across the bed, their bodies still wrapped in the warmth of the night before.

Dean blinked at the clock.

10:03 a.m.

Five hours left.

He reached out to brush Jeni's hair from her cheek. She stirred,
eyes fluttering open.

There were no sleepy jokes.
No playful kisses.

Just that look.

The one that said: *I know. I feel it too.*
The weight of the hours.
The preciousness of each one.

Jeni slipped out of bed first, throwing on an oversized tee as she
padded barefoot to the kitchen.

Dean followed a moment later, pulling on sweatpants and a soft
cotton shirt.

He made the coffee.
She made the eggs.
It felt like they'd done this a hundred times—like a life they
never got the chance to live.

The air was filled with the scent of fresh ground beans and
sizzling butter.

From the speaker on the counter, EDM pulsed softly,
brightening the quiet.

And then..."Collide" by Zack Martino & Notelle began to play.

Dean paused, turning slightly toward the sound.

The words hit hard.
Too on the nose.
Too true.

Jeni, standing at the stove, cracked an egg into the pan. Her head nodded slightly to the beat.

She didn't say anything.

She didn't have to.

Dean stepped forward.

Slow. Sure.

He came up behind her, slipping his arms gently around her waist.

She stilled.
Breathed.
Melted.

His lips brushed the side of her neck, then her shoulder.

He pressed his chest to her back, the coffee-scented air wrapping around them.

"Hey," he whispered.

She turned her head just enough to meet his eyes over her shoulder.

Her smile was soft. A little sad. But real.

Dean kissed her.

Slow. Meaningful. Anchored.

Like the song was playing *for them.*
And they knew it.

They didn't speak.

They just held each other in that kitchen, swaying to the quiet
drop of the beat. Eggs cooking. Coffee steaming.
Hearts colliding.
One last time.

Suitcases and Promises

The suitcases were packed.
Lined up by the door like quiet sentinels.

The apartment felt too still now.

No music.
No laughter.
Just the distant murmur of the city and the ticking of the kitchen
clock.

Dean stood by the window, staring out at nothing.

Jeni walked up behind him and slid her arms around his waist.

His hand found hers instinctively.
Their fingers wove together. Tight. Unwilling to let go.

Neither spoke.

There was nothing left to say that hadn't already been whispered
into skin, into pillows, into star-silvered skies.

Dean turned toward her.

His eyes were warm, but heavy.
Not with regret.
With weight.

He touched her cheek, brushing his thumb beneath her eye like
he was memorizing the shape of goodbye.

"I wish we had more time," he said softly.

Jeni nodded. "Me too."

A car horn sounded below. Just once. Soft. Right on time.

The driver.

They moved together—slow, reluctant.

Dean picked up the suitcases.

Jeni grabbed her keys.

They stood at the door, not opening it yet.

Not just yet.

Jeni turned to him, eyes glassy but full of love.

"I don't know what happens next," she said.
"But I know what this was."

Dean dropped the bags and pulled her into his arms.

"I know what this is," he whispered.
"It's real."

They kissed.

Not rushed.

Not broken.

A kiss that wasn't an ending.
But a seal. A tether. A maybe. A promise.

"I love you, Jeni."

"I love you, Dean."

She pressed her forehead to his.

"Come on, cowboy," she whispered.
"We don't want you missing your flight."

Dean smirked, but it didn't reach his eyes.

He opened the door.

The driver stood waiting, already loading the bags into the car.

Dean and Jeni climbed in, the silence between them filled with everything they couldn't say out loud.

As the city passed by the windows, Dean reached for her hand.

Jeni laced her fingers through his, then rested her head on his shoulder.

Neither looked away.
Not from the road.
Not from each other.

And somewhere between downtown and the terminal—

They both made the same quiet wish:

Please don't let this be the end.

A Ripple in Time

After checking his bags, Dean reached for Jeni's hand once more.

They walked slowly toward the security checkpoint, fingers laced tightly, the pull of their palms already feeling like a countdown.

Each step felt like it echoed.
Each pause like a silent scream.

When they reached the rope line, Dean turned to face her.

His hand found her waist.

She touched his cheek.

And they kissed.

Not like lovers saying goodbye—
But like soulmates trying to memorize each other.

Dean pulled back, his voice low, barely more than breath.

"Jeni... I don't know what to say. I don't know how to thank you
for these past two weeks."

His voice cracked.
So did hers.

"This was my dream come true—being with you."

He took her hands in both of his, squeezing gently.

"I don't know where we're going. But I finally know the truth...
You were always in love with me.
And I... I was always in love with you."

Tears filled her eyes.

She kissed him again.

Long. Slow.

A kiss meant to outlive time.

And then—

He stepped into the line.

The rope separating them was barely a foot wide,
but it felt like a chasm.

They held hands until the very last second—
until a TSA officer gestured him forward.

Dean let go.

Jeni stood, arms wrapped around herself, watching him take off
his shoes, his belt.

He turned back after the scanner.

Blew her a kiss.

She caught it. Tried to smile. Failed.

Dean raised his fingers, signing slowly:

"I love you."

Jeni's heart squeezed.

She nodded.

But when she turned away, the tears came fast.

Dean stepped into the terminal, chest tight, stomach churning.

It felt like someone had kicked him in the gut.

He sank into a chair by the gate, pulled out his phone.

Opened the photos.

Jeni in front of the waterfall.
Their picnic.

Their dance.
Her sleepy smile in the tent.

Everything played back in silence.

His flight began to board.

He texted her:

I'm on the plane. Love you.

Seconds later:

I love you, Dean.

He stared at her message until the screen dimmed.

Letting Go

Back in her apartment, Jeni was curled on the couch, her body still trembling with the weight of goodbye.

Her phone buzzed again.

Not Dean.

Michael.

Hey. I've been thinking. I want to work things out. Please call me.

She stared at the message like it came from another life.

Maybe it did.

And suddenly—she understood.

Maybe this was the uneasiness she and Dean both felt.

Not that they didn't love each other.

But that time was folding in on itself.

That this—these two weeks—was the ripple.

The correction. The pause between parallel paths. Their Mandela moment.

Had life let them collide just long enough to remember?

Or to choose?

She didn't know.

All she knew was this:

She couldn't go back to Michael.

Not really. Not after this.

She wasn't that version of herself anymore.

She reached for the remote and let her playlist run.

Jeni's Realization ♪21

A familiar synth echoed softly through the room—the opening bars of "If I Stay" by Disciples & Delilah.

It started as background noise. Just another song in the shuffle.

But then the lyrics came.

And something inside her cracked.

The weight of the melody hit like a whisper and a wound all at once—aching questions wrapped in velvet basslines and smoky echoes.

Her throat tightened. She hadn't cried in months. Not really. Not when Michael moved out. Not when she signed the dissolution papers. Not even when she slept alone the first night and stared at the empty half of the bed.

But now, she felt it building. First slow. Then all at once.

The tears came without permission, not loud, but deep—the kind that felt like grief pressed into the shape of relief.

She sank into the corner of the couch, knees drawn up, the music playing like a memory she hadn't known she needed.

Michael was gone. That chapter was closed. Not with a bang. Not even a fight. Just... the soft click of a door never opened again.

But that wasn't all. A strange, undeniable thought rose up beneath the tears:

She had more in common with Lexi than she'd ever allowed herself to admit.

They had both loved Dean in ways they couldn't explain. They had both tried to find themselves in the arms of men who didn't really know how to hold them. They had both traded vulnerability for control, and lost more than they expected along the way.

Dean and Lexi broke up because of Richard—because Lexi had been trapped in something complicated, maybe even cruel.

And now Jeni sat here, realizing she hadn't truly been with Michael in a long time. She had been holding onto a story that was already finished. Connecting with Dean now didn't feel like a new beginning.

It felt like finishing unfinished business. The chorus swelled, the lyrics echoing into the stillness.

She closed her eyes and let it wash over her. Maybe she would be alone for a while. She didn't even know what that looked like. But for the first time... maybe that was the answer.

Not someone new. Not running from the silence. Just... being in it. And seeing who she was without the noise.

Her fingers drifted to her phone. She stared at the blank screen, tempted to text Dean.

She didn't. Not yet. Instead, she let her thoughts drift. Maybe it was time to sell the company. Let someone younger chase the market. Let herself breathe. Maybe it was time to move.

To Texas. Or maybe Miami.

Dean had five bedrooms, after all. She smiled through her tears at the absurdity of the thought—but it lingered all the same. She let out a breath, somewhere between a sob and a laugh.

The sunlight poured through the windows—golden, full, uncaring of the storms that had passed.

She closed her eyes. And whispered aloud to the empty room:

"Thank you."

ROD K

BREAKFAST WITH TIFFANY

Shangri-La Hotel

It had been a busy Monday afternoon, humid and bright in Chiang Mai. Dean had flown in for a global venture summit, half jetlagged and already mentally reviewing the talking points for a panel he was scheduled to speak on.

The moment he stepped into the Shangri-La Hotel, all polished marble and tranquil koi ponds, he felt the sharp contrast from the chaos of travel.

And then, he saw her.

She stood behind the concierge desk—petite, graceful, and radiant—her dark hair swept back into a neat bun, her uniform crisp and perfectly fitted. She greeted him with a soft smile that held both professionalism and curiosity.

— *May I help you?* she asked, her English tinged with a lilting Thai accent.

Dean gave his name, watching her fingers move swiftly across the keyboard. She was efficient, calm. But there was something in the way her eyes flicked up to meet his—something inquisitive. Unafraid.

She handed him his key card and then, to his surprise, offered to personally escort him to the Presidential Suite.

Inside the elevator, Dean leaned against the wall casually, glancing at her.

— *You've got the best job in the place,* he said with a smirk.

Tiffany looked up, amused.

— *Because I get to meet people like you?*

Dean grinned.

— *Exactly.* Then after a pause, *I'm from Texas. We don't believe in strangers.*

By the time they reached the suite, he already knew her name, her background, and that she was taking English night classes after work.

Before she left, he asked, casually but sincerely—

— *Would you join me for dinner while I'm here?*

She hesitated, a slight furrow of suspicion crossing her brow.

— *Just dinner,* he assured her, hands raised. *I don't like to eat alone. And you're interesting—I want to know more about you, your country, your dreams.*

That was Dean. Charming, confident, and disarming in all the right ways.

Present Day – Miami, One Year Later

That dinner had turned into many. And over the months that followed, their connection deepened—not through romance, but through something else: respect, shared time, and trust.

A year after they met, Dean invited her to move to Miami. She hadn't asked for anything. She didn't expect it. But he saw something in her—ambition, discipline, heart.

And when he offered to pay for her nursing school and a place to live—one of the three spare bedrooms in his penthouse—Tiffany said yes.

Now, she was a nursing student by day, and Dean's executive assistant by necessity—managing his calendar, screening calls, helping with investment logistics when needed. But her value wasn't in what she did for him.

It was in how she made him feel.

Centered. Calm.

Dean and Tiffany sat poolside at his penthouse on the 62nd floor, the Miami skyline glittering around them like a thousand whispered promises. The infinity pool shimmered beside them, mirroring the lights of Biscayne Bay below. Tiffany lifted her glass of rosé, clinking it gently against Dean's.

"One year," she smiled. "To nursing school... and to everything that's changed since."

Dean returned the smile, the kind that rarely showed up in photos but softened the lines of his face when it did. As she looked at him, he was already drifting back—to the beginning.

Her Devotion

Tiffany never asked for anything in return. She kept her boundaries and her grace. She cooked for Dean sometimes, studied late into the night, and always carried herself with quiet dignity.

She loved him. Deeply. But she never expected him to love her back.

Dean loved her, too. Just not in the way she often dreamed he would.

Some nights, she lay in bed and wondered if that would ever change.

If the ache of being close, but not close enough, would ever fade.

Other nights, it was enough just to be near him.

And for Tiffany, that kind of love—quiet, patient, undemanding—was enough.

For now.

Tiffany sat curled on one of the loungers, her nursing books closed, a breeze teasing strands of her hair. Dean handed her a cup of tea and settled beside her, elbows on his knees, eyes on the skyline.

"You know," he said quietly, *"I didn't bring you here just because you were kind, or smart. It was because I saw something in you—something I knew I could invest in."*

Tiffany tilted her head. *"You mean like a business?"*

Dean smiled. *"No. Not like that. Businesses come and go. But people—when you pour into the right ones—they make families stronger. They build communities. You do that, Tiff. You will."*

She looked down, her eyes welling just slightly. *"No one's ever believed in me like that."*

He reached over and brushed a strand of hair from her cheek. *"That's what life's about. If your blessings don't echo into someone else's life, what's the point?"*

The balcony doors were open. A soft wind moved through the penthouse, carrying in the scent of sea salt and something faintly floral—jasmine maybe, from the street below. Tiffany sat on the edge of Dean's white leather chaise, still in his oversized T-shirt, her knees tucked under her like she used to sit as a girl.

The sky was a deep velvet blue now, dotted with stars that shimmered above the city lights. Dean had gone into his office to take a late call. She listened to the low murmur of his voice through the hallway, steady and certain—*the sound of someone who always knew what to do.*

She ran her fingers lightly over the sleeve of his shirt, tugging it closer. It still held the warmth of his body.

This life... this place... this man.

He had changed everything.

Not just the skyline outside her window or the textbooks on her desk—but something deeper. Something quiet. Something sacred.

She thought back to the first night she stayed here. Nervous. Grateful. Overwhelmed. He'd shown her the bedroom she would be staying in, set fresh flowers beside the bed, and told her she was safe now.

And he meant it.

Dean had never once touched her without consent. Never used his power to ask for what he easily could've taken. *And maybe that's why she wanted to give herself to him.*

Not out of pressure. Not out of obligation.

But out of *love.*

Her eyes flicked toward the hall, where his shadow shifted just beyond the frosted glass. So many women had passed through his life—beautiful, loud, unforgettable women. Lexi. Others. Some still messaged, some probably still hoped. But Tiffany didn't want to compete.

She wanted to *remain.*

Not the wild flame that burned fast, but the one that stayed lit through storms.

To be the one who sat with him in silence when the world got too loud.
The one who brought him jasmine tea when his voice went raw from meetings.
The one who prayed for him when he forgot how to pray for himself.

And yes... to be close. Body and soul. Not for the act—but for the intimacy it promised.

She rested her chin on her knees and whispered into the wind, *"I love you, Dean."*
It was the first time she'd said it out loud.

He didn't hear.

But Sirena did.
And as if in response, the music in the penthouse shifted—soft strings, slow and aching.

Giving Herself ♪22

Tiffany stood barefoot on the cool marble floor, wrapped in Dean's oversized T-shirt, her silhouette framed by the low amber light Sirena had dimmed at her request. The penthouse felt suspended in twilight—glass walls revealing the glittering cityscape below like a dream she hadn't dared to have.

She turned slowly toward the window, the ocean flickering with city lights like fireflies across dark silk. Her fingers fidgeted at the hem of the shirt. *This night felt different.*

She tilted her chin and whispered, soft but clear:
"Sirena, queue 'Waiting for Tonight' by Fisher and Jennifer Lopez."

"Queued and ready, Tiffany," the AI answered with a sultry warmth. *"Say the word."*

Tiffany nodded. *"Wait for me to say 'now.'"*

The pause held a breath of anticipation.

She wasn't doing this to seduce him.
She was doing this to show him—finally—the depth of her heart, the quiet longing she'd folded neatly behind her smiles and study hours.

She heard Dean's voice behind the frosted glass—deep, low, wrapping up his call. Her pulse quickened. He always had that effect on her.

The elevator doors whooshed open with a soft hush, and there he was. Barefoot, relaxed, still in the black shirt he wore with sleeves rolled up, veins in his forearms catching the light.

Dean saw her. And stilled.

Tiffany met his gaze, then offered the softest smile—vulnerable, sure.

"Now."

The music kicked in—low, sensual, electric.
Laser-bright synths and the echo of J. Lo's voice.

Tiffany walked forward slowly, every step deliberate, her eyes never leaving his. Her voice was steady, though her heart fluttered in her chest.

"Dean... I don't want to be another woman who just passes through your life."
She stepped close, close enough to feel the warmth of his breath.
"I want to be the one who stays."

Dean's jaw flexed, his eyes searching hers. He didn't speak—not yet. He didn't need to.

Tiffany reached up, resting her hand gently over his heart.
"I love you. And I know you didn't ask for this. You've always respected me, protected me... but tonight, I'm not asking for protection."
She leaned in, lips just inches from his.
"I'm asking you to let me love you. All the way."

The lighting was low, golden, like dusk had melted into candlelight.
Sirena, ever attuned, nudged the music into the air—a slow pulse, shimmering synths, and that unmistakable voice.

Tiffany stood barefoot by the edge of the sofa, his T-shirt falling soft against her curves. Her dark eyes never left him. There was nothing playful in her smile now—only calm confidence, desire, and something deeper.

Dean walked to the bar, saying nothing. He poured her a glass of chilled rosé and himself a neat pour of Weller.
He didn't rush.

The words floated around them like the first breeze of summer.

Tiffany sank into the couch, slow and intentional. Her back straight, knees together, her hands folded gently over her lap.

Her gaze followed Dean like a magnet, as if the room bent
between them.

Dean turned. The drinks in hand. His throat tightened slightly.

She was radiant. Not just beautiful—but *present*.
No makeup, no designer dress, just Tiffany. Raw. Certain.
Ready.

He walked over and handed her the glass, his fingers brushing
hers—warmth sparking between them.

Tiffany took the wine, sipped once, then set it down.
She leaned forward slightly, her voice barely audible above the
lyrics.

"This moment... I've imagined it a thousand times, Dean. But
being here—it's more. So much more."

Dean sat beside her. Close. Their knees touched.

He looked at her—really looked. The way her chest rose and fell
in time with the rhythm. The way her lashes fluttered as she
blinked, just once.

Tiffany reached for his hand and guided it to her heart.
"It's beating like this for you."

Dean didn't speak. His thumb moved slowly over her skin. Her
pulse was strong.

She whispered:
"You've given me a life, a future... But what I want to give you
can't be repaid. It's love, Dean. Not duty. Not gratitude."
Her eyes softened.
"I'm not doing this to keep you. I'm doing this because I already
belong to you."

Dean leaned forward, forehead to hers. His breath warm against her lips.
A stillness fell between them—the kind that held weight.

Then, slowly, he kissed her. Not to possess her. But to answer her.

A kiss filled with every quiet promise he'd never spoken.

Tiffany didn't move when Dean kissed her—she *melted*.

Her hand still rested over his, pressed to her chest, where her heartbeat thudded like a drumroll under skin. The music swelled softly behind them.

She pulled back just enough to look him in the eyes.
"I've waited so long to feel like this, Dean. Safe. Seen. Wanted... but not just for my body."
A faint tremble escaped her lips, but she smiled through it.

Dean's hand moved to her cheek, his thumb brushing the corner of her mouth.
"Tiff... you were never just a girl I helped."
He paused.
"You're the reason I *believe* helping someone matters."

Tiffany stood slowly, reaching for his hand.
He rose too, letting her lead him down the hall toward the bedroom, where soft floor lighting illuminated their path like a runway of stars.

The door to the master bedroom opened with a whisper.

Inside, moonlight poured across the polished floors and linens like silver silk. The windows framed the Miami skyline—a canvas of stars and glass and possibility.

They didn't rush.

Tiffany sat at the edge of the bed, pulling her knees under her. Dean grabbed a throw blanket and draped it over her shoulders.

He whispered, "Are you sure?"
Her answer was a single nod… then,
"Yes, Dean. I've never been more sure."

Clothing fell away in slow, reverent pieces. Not rushed, not frantic. This wasn't lust—it was release.

Tiffany moved with certainty, each step forward dissolving a little more of her fear, her past, her sadness. She wasn't just offering her body—she was giving Dean the parts of her heart that had long been hidden behind glass.

Their first kiss in bed was different—deeper. No longer hesitant. It was a claiming.

Dean's hands explored her like he was learning a language she was teaching with every sigh, every touch. Her skin beneath him felt like warm satin, her lips like velvet ribbon across his chest.

She whispered his name, not as a plea, but a prayer.

When he entered her, she gasped—not from pain, but from the rush of being *chosen, cherished.* It was slow, intentional. He kissed the hollow of her throat, the curve of her shoulder.

They moved together as if they had known each other for lifetimes, two souls finally aligned.

Tiffany clung to him—not because she was afraid to lose him, but because she had finally found herself.

And Dean… he realized, somewhere in the middle of her soft moans and the trembling way she whispered his name, that this wasn't about protecting Tiffany anymore.

This was about loving her.

Later, their bodies tangled in the warm sheets, the music now a faint echo, Tiffany lay with her head on Dean's chest, fingers idly tracing a circle over his heart.

Neither spoke for a while.

Until Tiffany whispered, "I think I'm falling in love with you."

Dean kissed the top of her head.

"Then I'm right where I belong."

WHEN IT'S GONE

Downward Spiral ♪23

Lexi's world was imploding.

The edges of her vision blurred—not from tears. Those had already come and gone in waves. What remained now was heavier. A numbness so dense it blurred even the air around her, like heat off pavement. Everything inside her was unraveling.

Somewhere behind her, the soft pulse of music vibrated through the walls—*"Tears Don't Fall"* by Kaskade & Enisa. The beat was low and slow, like a distant heartbeat. A ghost rhythm from a time when she still felt grounded in something real. Something safe.

Outside the window, Miami rain painted the glass in silver veins. It matched the ones running through her soul.

She sat on the couch, legs straight out, arms wrapped tight around herself. Her sweatshirt swallowed her frame, sleeves bunched up near her wrists, hands trembling beneath the cotton. She looked like a child trying to hold herself together before the whole house collapsed. Even watching her favorite movie, Harry Potter didn't help.

I've lost Dean.
Rick betrayed me.
Those men... they took something I can never get back.

Her face pressed into her hands, but the sobs didn't come. Not now. Her body had gone quiet. The storm had passed. What remained was aftermath.

She closed her eyes—and just like that, she was nine years old again.

Her mother, pale and breathless, lying in the middle of the bed. Lexi and her father on either side, each clutching one of her hands. The beep of the oxygen tank. The sound of the clock ticking above the bed. The moment when everything *stopped*.

She could still feel her father's hand, trembling as it swept the hair back from her tear-streaked cheeks.

"It's okay, baby. It's okay."

But it wasn't. It had never been.

She remembered pounding the air with her tiny fists, screaming as the hospital staff wheeled her mother away on the gurney, the sheen of plastic under fluorescent lights, the smell of antiseptic in the hallway. Her world had ended in that corridor.

That night, Lexi had crawled into her closet with a flashlight and a shoebox. Her keepsake box.

Inside it, wrapped in a silk scarf, was one of her mom's old CDs. Tucked beneath it was a folded note. The paper was crisp, like it had been folded just days before. She imagined her mother writing it when her hands had already begun to shake, maybe even pressing her lips to the page one last time.

She remembered how her little hands trembled as she opened it, the paper damp with fresh tears.

Goodbye Letter from Her Mom ♪24

My dearest Lexi,
Baby, I know if you're reading this, my pain has stopped. The next time I see you will be in heaven. I picked this song because I know this is what you're feeling inside—your broken little heart. Just like the lyrics say, you're crying out, "Un-break my heart."
Remember me for all the good times. I will always be with you.
I love you always, Mommy.

Lexi's breath hitched in her throat. Even now, the memory of the letter felt like both a knife and a lullaby. Like her mother was there in the room, whispering it again in her ear.

She pushed herself upright and reached for the nightstand. Her fingers fumbled with the drawer, then found it: the keepsake box.

The scent of aged paper and soft vanilla bloomed as she opened the lid, like a ghost exhaling. She let the smell wash over her.

Inside was the heart-shaped locket. She picked it up slowly, her thumb running over its edge again and again, like she could summon her mother's voice through touch alone.

She clicked it open.

The tiny photo inside—a younger version of her and her mom, arms wrapped around each other, beaming—blurred behind the tears rolling down Lexi's cheeks.

But she didn't wipe them away.

Let them fall.

Let them speak.

The song shifted. A new track almost perfectly timed. It was her mother's favorite— *"Un-break My Heart by Toni Braxton.*

The chorus wrapped around her like a memory, and suddenly, she could *feel* her mom there. Not in some abstract sense—but real. Palpable. The scent of lavender and baby powder in the air. A warmth curled at her back like an embrace.

She closed her eyes, and the sensation deepened.

"Lexi," her mother's voice whispered in her memory. *"I love you. Everything is going to be okay, baby."*

She breathed in slowly, deeply.

For the first time in weeks, her chest didn't feel like it was caving in.

The sobs softened to shallow gasps. The kind that came not from pain—but from the fragile rebuilding that came after it.

She clutched the locket to her heart and exhaled.

It's not over. I'm not done. And neither is this story.

Lexi sat there for a long time, wrapped in the warmth of memory, in the presence of something beyond grief.

And then, quietly, steadily, she reached for her phone.

It was time to reach out to Dean.

The kitchen was too quiet.

Lexi opened a cabinet with slow, deliberate hands, selecting a crystal glass like she was choosing an offering. The glass clinked against the marble counter—sharp and unexpected in the stillness. The sound startled her.

Her hands were still trembling.

She reached for the bottle of wine on the counter. The cork popped with a soft sigh, and for a moment, the scent of dark berries filled the air like memory. She poured slowly—like a ritual. A glass, but not too much. Just enough to steady her.

Just enough to help her find the words.

She sat at the kitchen island, the laptop open in front of her. The glow of the screen lit up the tired hollows beneath her eyes. The blinking cursor stared back at her—steady, expectant—like a heartbeat waiting for her to speak.

She began.

Dean,
I don't know if you'll read this. I wouldn't blame you if you didn't. But I need to tell you the truth...

Her fingers moved fast. Hesitating. Then flying again. Words poured out like confessions from a broken dam.

The mistakes.
The regrets.
The parts she'd buried so deep they'd started to rot inside her.
The truth she was finally strong enough to speak.

Every few lines, she stopped—chest tightening, eyes welling—then picked up again.

She wrote about Dean. About what he'd meant to her. About the way he made her feel seen. Protected. Whole.

She wrote about Rick.
About the fear.
The guilt.
The prison she'd built around herself.

She wrote until two hours passed and the wine bottle was nearly empty.

The last sip slid into her glass as she typed the final line.

Her hand hovered over the send button. Her breath caught in her throat. She drew in a single, fragile breath.

And exhaled. Then—
Clicked. Delivered.

The screen didn't change. But her world shifted.

Lexi stared at the message, heart pounding like a drum solo in a quiet room.

Please read it, she thought. *Please.*

On impulse, she scrolled up—back through months of messages. The old ones. The sweet ones.

Late-night flirtations.
Early-morning check-ins.
GIFs that made her laugh when no one else could.
Inside jokes.
Teasing.
"You look so good in that dress."
"Wish I could wake up next to you."
"Come over."

A slow, tired smile crept onto her face.

It cracked a second later.

She gasped—a soft, sharp inhale—and pressed a hand over her mouth like she was trying to contain a sob that had no sound.

The tears came hard. Hot. Fast.

No warning. Just impact.

They streaked down her face as the loneliness crashed into her again—louder this time.

You were the sweetest friend I've had in years, she thought. *And I let you go.*

She reached to close the laptop, ready to retreat. Ready to bury the hope.

Then paused. The message status had changed.

Read. Her heart stopped.

She stared at the word. Like it was holy.

Her hand froze above the keyboard, fingers trembling mid-air.

No reply. No typing bubble. Nothing.

Ten minutes passed.
Then twenty.

Still nothing.

The tears came again—this time quietly. No sobbing. No trembling. Just quiet rain slipping down her cheeks.

She closed the lid.
And crawled into bed.
Her limbs heavy. Her breath unsteady. The darkness folded in around her like a sigh.

She lay in the quiet, wrapped in the same blanket her mother
had given her the year before she died.
Its weight was familiar. Comforting. Like love that refused to
fade.

She pressed the locket to her heart and whispered into the night:
"Please... just don't let it be over."

Then she let the silence answer her.
Not cruel.
Not kind.
Just silence.

And drifted to sleep.

The next morning, her phone buzzed.
Soft. Innocent. Too early for anyone but spam or heartbreak.
She blinked awake, the room still gray with dawn.
Her eyes found the screen.

One new message. From Dean.

Her breath caught.

The subject line read:
You are cordially invited to the wedding of Harrington and
Burnette.

Lexi stared.
Blood rushing in her ears.
Heart.
Stopped.

Dean's getting married?
She didn't open the message.

Couldn't. Not yet.

ABOUT THE AUTHOR

What's Next

Rod K, a native Texan and passionate storyteller, brings an evocative blend of intrigue and sensuality to his debut novel, Sextduction: A Miami Love Story. Set against the vibrant rhythm of Miami's skyline, his work explores the entangled lives of the five main characters, whose desires and choices reveal the beauty and danger of modern connection.

Through his cinematic writing style, Rod immerses readers in the pulse of the city: the shimmer of the bay at sunset, the whisper of waves against glass towers, and the intoxicating blend of luxury and vulnerability that defines Miami. His storytelling celebrates empowerment and emotional honesty, weaving a tale of seduction, betrayal, and liberation that reminds us of the power of embracing one's authentic self.

He invites readers to step into a world where boundaries blur, passions ignite, and fantasies come alive—an unforgettable journey into the depths of love, identity, and self-discovery.

A sequel has been hinted for release in Summer or Fall 2026

CHARACTER GALLERY

Faces Behind the Story

Hi, I'm **Rod K.**—and I'd like to personally introduce you to the characters in my story.

Whether you found this section before starting the book, somewhere in the middle, or after reading the last page, this gallery gives you a deeper look at the world of *Sextduction*. Here, you'll find short profiles of the characters and an AI-generated image of each one—created to match my vision as I wrote them.

I hope it helps you visualize their voices, their stories, and the emotional gravity they carry.

And if you just came from reading *About the Author*, then you already know—this isn't the end. A sequel is on the way.

Enjoy the story.

— **Rod K.**

✤ Primary Characters

Lexi Donovan
A stunning Instagram model and content creator with a
complicated past. Once overlooked, Lexi reinvented herself into
a fantasy—but her emotional core still aches for something real.

Dean Harrington
Texas-born, emotionally complex, and caught between
heartbreak and rediscovery. Dean is a man torn between what he
lost and what he may have missed all along.

Jeni Whitmore
Elegant, composed, and fiercely loyal. Dean's best friend since childhood—now with a secret of her own that could change everything between them.

💔 Best Friends

Sophie Devereaux
Lexi's best friend and chaos twin. A model with edge, warmth, and secrets of her own—sometimes the fire, sometimes the fuel.

Trey Latimer
Dean's college roommate and private equity manager.
Charming, loyal, and sharp-witted—Trey is the friend who
knows where all the bodies are buried.

Melaine Latimer
Trey's wife. A porcelain-skinned Houston debutante with poise and grace to rival royalty. Trained for perfection, aching for authenticity beneath the surface

♥ Romantic Tensions & Lovers

Michael Stanton
He was a chronic dreamer with no follow-through—a man whose ambition outpaced his effort. Clinging to Jeni's stability, never realizing she'd outgrown him long ago.

Richard Phillips
A personal injury lawyer with a confident swagger and a selfish streak. His betrayal left Lexi scared in more ways than one.

🎬 Family & Foundations

Sandy Harrington
Dean's mother. Wise, nurturing, and ready to take a chance on love again. Her upcoming wedding to Jennings becomes a spark that sets multiple stories in motion.

Allison Whitmore
Jeni's mother and Sandy's closest friend. Elegant, perceptive, and protective, she quietly roots for Jeni and Dean to find their way back to each other.

Jennings Burnette
Sandy's fiancé and a former military JAG turned oil & gas attorney. Stoic, sharp, and fiercely protective of those he loves—including Dean.

Hiroshi Hashimoto
World -renowned semiconductor engineer. Built a celebrated career at AMD and Intel, where he contributed to the development of cutting-edge processors.

💼 Power Players & Business Backers+

Rex Henderson
Co-founder of Austin Quantum Systems. Once a close friend of Dean's father, now a behind-the-scenes figure in Dean's life and career.

Jeanette Henderson
Rex's wife. Polished and warm, with a sharp mind and a deep investment in helping others succeed.

Kenji Nakamura
Global semiconductor innovator and AQS co-founder. A quiet
force of intellect and strategy.

Aiko Nakamura
Kenji's wife. A robotics entrepreneur with a soulful presence. Graceful, grounded, and an ally to Dean and Jeni.

Jacob Weiss
Jennings' intellectual property attorney. Brilliant and quietly intimidating—one of the sharpest minds in the room.

 Mystery & Future Entanglements

Esme Delacroix
Free-spirited and unpredictable, Esme enters the story with sunshine and wildfire in her wake. Her eyes say yes before her lips say anything at all.

Margot Delacroix
Elegant, thoughtful, and hard to read. She watches everything, missing nothing. Esme's twin—her mirror and her opposite.

Tiffany Kirkland
A gentle soul with a fierce sense of self. Born in Chiang Mai to a missionary family, Tiffany's quiet strength and blossoming relationship with Dean add unexpected tenderness to his journey.